mayhem in the midlands

anthology of mysteries

edited by Robert J. Randisi and
Christine Matthews

HATS
OFF

Mayhem in the Midlands
Copyright © 2001 Omaha Public Library

Published by Hats Off Books™
610 East Delano Street, Suite 104
Tucson, Arizona 85705
www.HatsOffBooks.com
ISBN: 1-58736-091-8
LCCN: 2001119979
Book design by Summer Mullins.
Cover design by Cynthia Vana.
Printed in the United States of America.

EDITOR'S NOTE

The idea of this anthology came to us during our first night in the Convention hotel. Since it was the very first Mayhem in the Midlands, why not commemorate that with an anthology, which could then be sold to benefit the Omaha and Lincoln Libraries? Over the course of the next few days, the attending authors were told about the plan and asked to donate a story. Seventeen authors responded with these 15 stories, a mixture of originals and reprints.

Actually, we should have written a "Collector's" note here. Since these stories were all donated, they are the stories these authors wish to be represented by. For that reason, no editing has been done on them-especially not the reprints. All we did was collect them and send them on to Omaha.

We hope the authors and other attendees at Mayhem In The Midlands II, plus the readers who will find this book in the Omaha and Lincoln Libraries, will enjoy it. Our thanks go out to all the authors who donated their work.

Robert J. Randisi
Christine Matthews

St. Louis, MO, February 13, 2001

INTRODUCTION

In 2000 the City of Omaha, NE, was fortunate to have the opportunity to host the First Annual Mayhem in the Midlands Mystery Convention. This spectacular event brought approximately 200 mystery authors and readers to the Midwest to enjoy a weekend full of mystery. The convention attracted some of the most talented mystery authors in the country. They wanted to commemorate the convention by assembling an anthology that would include stories by contributed by seventeen of the authors who participated in the First Mayhem in the Midlands. This anthology of short stories will be a treat for anyone who appreciates a good mystery.

I want to commend the contributing authors for sharing their talent by donating stories to this anthology. The proceeds from the sale of this collection will benefit the Omaha Public Libraries and the Lincoln City Libraries. I truly hope this event continues in the City of Omaha for many years. We love having you here!

Hal Daub, Mayor
City of Omaha

TABLE OF CONTENTS

FLYOVER COUNTRY

by Barbara and Max Allan Collins

Barbara Collins is an accomplished short story writer whose first collection, *Too Many Tomcats*, was recently published by Five Star. Max Allan Collins is the author of the Nathan Heller series, the most recent of which is *Angel in Black* (NAL). They are both involved in independent filmmaking and their current feature, REAL TIME: SIEGE AT LUCAS STREET MARKET, is available on DVD from Troma.

FLYOVER COUNTRY

by
Barbara Collins
and
Max Allan Collins

Susan Parsus, looking through the pale oval of her own reflection—long dark hair, round silver glasses, still girlishly pretty (she thought) at 34—gazed out the little window of the airplane. Below, the brown and green checkerboard blanket of the Midwest extended endlessly.

Flyover country, she thought, her reflection smirking back at her. How quaint—how picturesque—how boring. Thank God she didn't live down there. She recalled that hokey movie, where the baseball players came out of the Iowa cornfield. "Is this heaven?" "No, it's Iowa." Right.

Not that New York was heaven. Lately, the expense and the hassles and crime and the sheer *smell* of that city had begun to get to her, and started her thinking about moving somewhere, anywhere, else. But that was an impossibility, wasn't it? After all, she was in publishing, and publishing *was* New York.

Even Los Angeles—she was returning from a bookseller's convention there—was a big disappointment: at least as expensive as home, and for all its sprawl *still* over-crowded. Its fabled beautiful weather smothered in a smog blanket. Wasn't there *any* place in this country worth living? Where the quality of living was high, and the cost of living was low?

11

"This is your captain speaking." The male voice crackled urgently over the intercom, interrupting Susan's thoughts. "We're experiencing some technical difficulties. Flight attendants prepare for emergency landing…."

An immediate murmur spread through the cabin, more noticeably on the right side of the plane, where the passengers—Susan among them—could see thick, black smoke streaming from an engine.

The plane fell sharply.

Susan's stomach dropped to the earth, her heart rose to her throat, as a symphony of gasps and screams provided ghastly muzak.

Two flight attendants—managing to hold on to a professional demeanor despite the terror in their eyes—rushed up and down the aisles with a horrible urgency underlying the usual banal instructions to put safety belts on, tray tables away and seats in an upright position.

In the rear of the cabin a mother wailed and clutched her baby tighter to her bosom. Others hugged, some sobbed, while many dug into pockets and purses to scribble a final farewell note to loved ones below.

Fear spread upward from Susan's stomach to her throat like a bad, brackish case of heartburn. She tensed and grabbed onto the armrests. Next to her, an older woman with gray hair and orange lipstick (who hadn't been too much of an annoyance on the trip) turned toward her for consolation, but Susan moved away. If this was going to be her last few moments alive, Susan Parsus wasn't about to share them with some complete stranger.

Dear Lord, she prayed as the airplane shimmied and shook, *if I make it through this, I promise to be a better person.*

Her thoughts shifted to Steven, her fiancé, back in New York. She'd been so awful to him just before she'd left. Arguing about plans for their wedding….

A much better person. I promise, I promise….

As the plane broke through the clouds on its rapid descent, Susan could see they were no longer over farm country, but a city, now. Brilliant morning sun bounced off tall glass buildings, and everywhere, lush green trees lined clean streets where little toy cars moved up and down. If she hadn't been so frightened, she might have appreciated this pristine, modern city.

Susan closed her eyes tight, because the ricocheting silver bullet of a plane seemed much too close to the tops of the trees, and neat little houses. She hoped that beyond them was a runway or highway and not more homes.

A big jolt lifted everyone out of their seats, as wheels touched asphalt—it *was* a runway, she could see out the window—then a smaller jolt followed, and the passengers lurched forward, bracing themselves as the plane braked hard to a stop. A collective sign of relief disseminated throughout the cabin.

Twenty minutes later, Susan walked through the airport terminal on wobbly legs toward a bank of phones, her Louis Vuitton carry-on (a gift from a former fiancé) slung over one shoulder. She sat on one of the little round seats smoothing her black Donna Karan dress (discounted in the District), then dug in her black leather Picasso bag (half-off at Bloomies) for her phone card.

"Steven? It's Susan."

"Where are you?"

"Des Moines fucking Iowa."

"What are you doing there?"

"The plane had engine trouble, and I'm stuck in the God-awful boonies because I can't get another flight to New York until tomorrow. I have to find a room, and..." She moaned. "Oh, *why* did I have to fly on Super Value Jet? This is your fault!"

"My fault? It was *your* idea to cash in the first class ticket on United, so you could use the extra money for shopping!"

"Well, you should've talked me out of it. Every time I do something on the cheap, I get in trouble."

There was silence, then Steven said, "Sometimes trying to save money ends up costing you more."

So they were back to that. The argument before she left.

She said, "I just thought if we got married around Easter, we could use the church's flowers. It's called being economical. What's wrong with that?"

"Why don't we just wait for a funeral?"

"Beat me while I'm down, why don't you, Steven?"

"Maybe it's just an excuse, Susan. Maybe you don't really want to get married at all."

"Of course I do."

There was silence again, and when her fiancé spoke, his voice seemed sad. "Call me when you get in and I'll pick you up."

And he hung up without any further goodbye.

Susan, carry-on in tow, walked away from the phones. With the whole day, and night, in front of her, she might as well rent a car. Bad enough to be stranded in flyover country, let alone not have wheels.

The line at the Hertz counter was short, and Susan started toward it, then stopped. They'd be the most expensive, she thought. Her eyes traveled down the line of the other car rental companies—Avis, National, Alamo, Budget—and landed on the last sign: "U-Save—Iowa's Own Rental Alternative!" That shouldn't cost her an arm and a leg.

A big man in a bright yellow sports coat (why didn't he wear an "I'm a Big Fat Guy" t-shirt, if he wanted to draw attention to himself?) was just stepping away from the counter when Susan came up to it, setting her bag down. Behind the counter, which came almost to Susan's chin, was a forty-ish woman with short, dull brown hair and the sort of plain face that Susan wasn't sure even a full-scale makeover would help. Next to the woman, somewhat incongruously, was a plant with broad thorny cactus-like leaves in a terra-cotta pot; maybe compared to the plant the agent was supposed to look pretty.

"I need a car until tomorrow," Susan told the agent.

The agent smiled. "Will you be bringing it back within twenty-four hours?"

"I should certainly hope so. I intend to get the hell out of here as soon as I can. What's that going to cost me?"

"We have a luxury model for fifty-four dollars, or a mid-size for thirty-four."

"Thirty-four."

"Would you like collision insurance?"

Susan laughed. "Please. I'm fully insured already. What kind of sucker do you take me for?"

"All right, then," the woman said, her brown eyes seeming to study Susan, the pleasant demeanor continuing. "Please sign here, and here..." She put the contract out on the high counter top.

Susan had to reach up to sign, and inadvertently shoved aside the thorny potted plant, tipping it over, spilling rich dark soil onto the counter top.

For a brief second an irritated look flashed over the agent's face, then the professional smile returned, and the woman scooped up the dirt and put it back in the pot, setting the plant upright again.

Susan didn't apologize; the ugly thing shouldn't have been in the way in the first place.

"I'll need to see your driver's license," the woman said.

Susan dug into her purse and handed the agent her card.

The woman studied the license and commented, "New York City. I've always wanted to go there."

"Yeah," Susan snorted, "it's a regular theme park."

The agent finished up the paperwork and handed a copy of the contract to Susan. "Just catch our shuttle bus out front," she instructed. "They'll take care of you." Then she added, "Have a nice stay in Iowa."

Susan mimicked the agent's sweet smile. "You really think that's possible?"

While the smile remained on the agent's face her eyes grew cold; then suddenly they softened, and her voice became soft and sympathetic.

"I know how you feel, stranded in a strange place...wanting to get home," the woman said. "Tell you what, I'm going to upgrade your car...You're obviously having a rough day and I'd like to help you turn it around."

"Oh. Well. Thank you...."

"Are you interested in doing a little sightseeing?"

"I suppose it would beat staring at the television in a motel room, or wandering some excuse for a mall."

The professional smile blossomed into genuine friendliness. "Well, then, let me give you some advice on where you might go. There's a quaint little village..."

The town of Prosperity, the car rental agent had told Susan, was located fifteen miles south of Des Moines. And there, the agent had said, the newly refurbished Grand Hotel would cost her a mere forty dollars (as compared to one hundred in the city). The money she would save, Susan thought, would underwrite the little sightseeing expedition.

Susan drove along the highway in a red Mustang convertible. She could never drive anything like this in New York. With the top down, the wind blowing her long dark hair around, she felt like a teenager again.

The air was so fresh! Like a cool, sweet drink of water, a gentle breeze riffled the slender stalks of green corn growing in the neatly tended fields along the road. She'd never thought of corn as beautiful, but it was: tall and graceful, each stalk topped with yellow tassels that hung like golden strands of hair. Iowa was not at all the flat, boring cow country she'd expected, rather a lovely landscape alive with rolling green hills and brilliant wild flowers, and every mile or so a tidy little farm, with its own little garden, and clean clothes flapping on the line....

Susan closed her eyes, breathing in through her nose, remembering how wonderful clothes that had dried outdoors smelled, back in Poughkeepsie, where she was raised by her mother who had very little money. After high school, a scholarship to NYU brought her into the city, and a part-time job doing clerical work at a now-defunct paperback house gave her some monetary help—that and latching onto some well-heeled friends.

After graduation she landed a job at a prestigious New York publishing house—Bigelow and Brown—working as a copy editor. She had a good eye for detail, and was smart enough to know not to meddle with an author's style and attach herself as an uninvited collaborator, like some frustrated unpublished editors she knew. This was a happy time in her life...except for still not having much money.

Soon she was promoted to senior editor, and put in the uncomfortable position of deciding the fate of the hundreds of manuscripts that crossed her desk every week. She thought she'd been doing a good job selecting the list, but after a while the publisher called her into his office and told her she was within an inch of losing her job.

"Susan," the older man said, tugging at his coarse, gray mustache, "we're in the book turning down business, not the book buying business. Get it? Now reduce your list."

After that, she was afraid to buy anything.

Up ahead, the road narrowed to almost one lane, and the tall cornfields gave way to dense forest. A fresh water stream now appeared on the left of the highway and after a curve in the road a weathered wood-covered bridge led her across the brook, reminding Susan of a certain best selling novel she'd turned down a few years ago.

About a half mile across the bridge, a large painted sign depicting an exotic plant welcomed Susan to Prosperity, population 8,000. As she entered the town on a cobblestone street, she slowed the Mustang. Grand old homes appeared on both sides of the road, and a canopy of ancient maple trees provided shade in the warm summer day.

Here and there, neighbors stood chatting, while young children played—many unattended—in open yards, their bikes and toys scattered along the sidewalk. No one seemed worried here, about theft or kidnapping, much less drive-by-shootings.

At the end of the block Susan saw something that made her laugh out loud as she drove by: a large parcel sat on top of a blue corner mailbox; too big to fit inside, the owner had just left it, without a concern that someone might take it.

The turn-of-the-century downtown buildings of Prosperity were built in a square around a small, immaculate park with a white wooden bandstand in its center. Here and there, wrought-iron park benches sat next to flower gardens of roses, geraniums, petunias and mums. On one of those park benches sat an elderly couple, gray-haired and be-spectacled, enjoying ice cream cones, and each other.

She couldn't remember the last time she saw a happy old couple on the streets of New York; if they weren't scowling, they were in some heated argument.

Susan parked the Mustang in a diagonal spot in front of a hardware store, its ancient façade freshly painted, candy-striped awning flapping gently in the breeze. As she started to get out of the car, her foot kicked something on the floorboard by the brake. She reached down and picked the item up, a tan leather appointment book that must have been under the seat, sliding forward when she stopped.

Susan opened the appointment book to a business card tucked in a plastic see-through pouch on the left; on the right was a calculator with faux-jewel pads, and in the center, in the fold, was a beautiful brown Cross pen. Her first notion was to mail these things to the poor woman—Madeline Winter, the business card said, a vice president with a pharmaceutical company in Dallas—as soon as she could, because Susan knew how upset she herself would be to lose her own appointment book.

But then, Susan thought, as she got out of the car, the woman had probably replaced it by now, and besides, *she* could use a new calculator and pen. Which Susan took and put in her purse, tossing the appointment book in a curbside trash can.

She was digging in her wallet for some change for the meter when a friendly male voice said, "Don't got none of them here."

Susan looked up to see a plump man around the age of sixty, with handlebar mustache, wire-framed glasses and mostly bald head. He was wearing a striped apron (which nearly matched the awning) over a short-sleeved blue shirt and brown pants. The man was sweeping the sidewalk with a big push broom.

"Pardon?" Susan asked.

"Why punish people who come to spend their hard-earned money by puttin' in meters?" he asked with a shrug, and gave the cement walk one last sweep before turning and disappearing into the store.

Susan closed her purse. "No parking meters—maybe this is heaven," she said to herself.

Then something in the window of the hardware store caught her eye, and she moved toward the glass.

The object of her desire in the carefully arranged display window wasn't the blue bottle of perfume called Ode to Venus, or the plant next to it with its large, thorned leaves spread open, nor even the pseudo-gold necklace carefully laid out on a piece of blue velvet... What she was gaping at was an ordinary claw hammer.

"Oh, my god," she whispered, reading the price-tag sticker on its handle, her face nearly pressed up against the glass. "A dollar ninety-nine."

It had been a miserably cold, windy day last February that she had traipsed all over Manhattan to find a claw hammer because she'd loaned *hers* to a neighbor who'd never returned it before he'd left town. And the hammer that she finally did find (a cheaply made foreign one whose plastic handle fell off) cost her eight dollars and ninety-nine cents.

Susan rushed into the hardware store. She crossed the gleaming wooden floor and wound her way through the narrow aisles of neatly arranged items toward a large counter in the back behind which the man in the striped apron stood, filling a glass jar with jelly beans.

"I'd like that hammer in the window." She said.

He looked up from his work. "It's a beauty," he told her. "Made right here in the U.S. of A."

He came around the counter and plucked the same hammer from a pegboard on a display nearby. "And you can't beat the price," he added.

"You won't believe what they cost in Manhattan."

Back behind the counter, the man wrote up a receipt on a little pad. "I bet just about everything's expensive there," he said. He gave her an odd smile, showing white, perfect teeth. "You come a long way to comparison shop for tools, ma'am. Or are you staying in Prosperity a while?"

"Just an overnight trip." Suddenly she was embarrassed, as he handed her the plain brown sack. "I just can't resist a bargain."

"Well, I hope you enjoy our little town while you're here. We do try to make visitors welcome."

"Everyone does seem friendly." She turned to leave, then looked back to ask, "Say, where's the Grand Hotel?"

"Directly across the square. You can't miss it."

"And a good place to grab some lunch?"

"The Venus Diner serves up a great pork tenderloin."

A pork tenderloin! She hadn't had one of those since she was a kid on vacation in Oklahoma.

Susan thanked the man and left the store and stood out on the sidewalk by her car in the warm summer sun, wondering which way to go to the diner, when two teen-aged girls walked by her, whispering, ogling her, giggling.

Susan only made out one word—"Witch"—and guessed she did look a little like that, all in black, while they wore colorful, crisp, cotton clothes: one, a bright yellow dress with pink flowers; the other, sky blue over-alls with a whiter than white blouse underneath. And sandals! Their toes painted lime and orange. Where were the ratty t-shirts and baggy jeans and pierced body parts of a normal teenager?

How she envied them. They didn't know that in New York their bright clothing would make them stand out...ripe for an attack, and flimsy little sandals were exchanged for combat boots in order to maneuver the filthy mean streets.

A mother walked by, holding the hand of a small boy—they were in matching nautical outfits, peculiar attire for a town as landlocked as this one—and when the boy saw Susan he pointed. "Mommy, is that lady going to a funeral?"

The mother seemed embarrassed, smiled apologetically, and pulled her son along.

That did it! If it was one thing she hated, it was feeling out of place. She hurried down the street, entered a woman's clothing store, and emerged a half hour later in a peach rayon dress and brown sandals, her long dark hair braided loosely down her back and held at the end with a peach floral clasp.

She felt euphoric, so feminine, like a college student again. And the best part was she got the whole outfit half-price—and it wasn't even on sale! The owner, a nice woman in her forties, wanted Susan to "have a good time" in Prosperity.

The Venus Diner, two doors down from the clothing store, was a turn-of-the-century ice cream parlor that had stayed in one family for three generations; Susan read this on the back of the menu as she sat on a stool at the counter, hungrily eating a huge breaded tenderloin sandwich with ketchup and pickle, washing it down with a lime phosphate. The owners, Mr. and Mrs. Satariano, a friendly couple in their sixties, ran the establishment together.

The booths were dark mahogany, as were the lower halves of the walls. The upper walls were mirrors on which were written menu items in orange marker. A wooden fan hung from the high tin ceiling, churning slowly, providing a soothing breeze. It was all very quaint and charming.

Right now, Mr. Satariano, a slight man with thinning gray hair and a bulbous nose, was fixing Susan a High School Special: coffee ice cream topped with whipped cream, gooey marshmallow and Spanish peanuts. He set the dessert down in front of her with a wink. "That one's on us." He said.

Susan's mouth dropped open, from both the kind gesture and the sight of the heavenly concoction. "Really?"

"Enjoy yourself."

"How sweet!"

And it was; she eagerly dug into the ice cream. In between delicious bites she asked, "Was this place always called the Venus Diner?"

Mrs. Satariano, a tall handsome woman, washing a glass in a small stainless steel sink behind the counter, answered Susan. "No, the original name was the Candy Kitchen. But we changed it a few years back."

"Why is that?"

The woman and her husband exchanged glances. Mr. Satariano, wiping the counter around Susan, stopped. "Prosperity wasn't always so prosperous," he explained. "As a matter of fact, seven or eight years ago the town went bankrupt along with half its citizens."

Susan set her spoon down. "Oh my. What happened?"

"A couple bad years for the corn crops. First a flood, then a drought. That's all it took to put everybody under."

"But the town seems to be doing fine, now."

Mr. Satariano nodded. "Thanks to our little friends," he said, gesturing to a thorny plant sitting in a terra-cotta pot by the cash register.

"What *is* that?" Susan asked, intrigued. "I've been seeing that plant in all the shop windows. Is it some sort of town mascot?"

Mrs. Satariano smiled proudly, like a pleased grandparent. "It's a Venus flytrap," she pronounced.

Susan leaned forward and had a closer look at the plant. This one was about a foot tall, much bigger than the others she'd seen. Out of its center rose a stalk bearing a cluster of tiny white flowers, and around the stalk were leaves about six inches in length. Each of the kidney-shaped leaves lay like a partially opened book and was fringed with long stiff bristles.

"For heaven's sake," Susan murmured. "I didn't know the Venus flytrap could grow in this part of the world. You mean, that *plant* saved this town?"

Husband and wife nodded together.

"But how?"

The screen door of the shop opened with a creak, then banged shut.

Mrs. Satariano looked toward the door and threw up her hands, "Johnny! How is my boy today?"

Susan swiveled on the stool, also looking toward the door, where a young sandy-haired man stood, wearing jeans and a faded blue short-sleeve work shirt. The sun, shining in behind him, enveloped him in an angelic glow. Then he walked out of the light toward the counter, with a shy little smile, his head tilted slightly.

"'lo, Mom...Pop," he said, taking a seat one away from Susan at the counter.

Susan looked from Mrs. Satariano to Mr. Satariano to the young man, whom she guessed—now that he was closer—to be in his late twenties. She couldn't imagine that they were related, with the Satarianos so dark and the young man so fair.

Mr. Satariano, with the rag still in his hands, must have read Susan's thoughts, because he said, "Johnny's not our son, but you might say we think of him as one...ever since his folks died a few years back."

Susan turned toward Johnny. "Oh, I'm so sorry."

For a moment, sadness flashed over the man's rugged face, then the cheerful but shy manner returned and he said to Susan without looking at her, "That's all right. I'm doing fine...but, of course, Mom and Pop here think I can't tie my own shoes without their help."

Mrs. Satariano set one of the heavy ice cream glasses down on the counter with a loud noise. "Is that so? When have we ever stuck our noses in your business?" She asked with mock anger. "We just give you a little friendly advice on how to run the farm...and other things." She looked at her husband. "Isn't that right, Papa?"

"That's right, Mama," he agreed. "Just a little advice now and then." And he winked at Susan.

"You can see I'm outnumbered," Johnny said, swiveling on his seat so that he faced Susan.

He was handsome—by any woman's standards—but not like some slick male model. While his body was muscular—deltoids and biceps undulated under his chambray shirt—they were muscles obtained from *real* work, not working out. And his bronze tan came from laboring in the sun, not relaxing in a tanning bed. He was the real thing, not contrived, which made him so much more exciting.

And there was something else that aroused Susan: the scent coming off him; a combination of honest sweat and fresh country air, mingled together, an intoxicating olfactory cocktail that made Susan dizzy.

"Be careful," he warned Susan, his brown eyes playful, "or Mom and Pop here'll start running your life."

She looked down at her High School Special and felt herself blush (when had she last done that?). The ice cream was a melted puddle; so was her heart.

"Mom...a cherry Coke, please," Johnny said, and slid off the stool. Then to Susan he asked, "Would you like to join me in a booth?"

Now it was Susan who smiled shyly. "Okay."

"And bring her one, too," he told Mrs. Satariano.

The booth Johnny led her to was against the back wall of the long, narrow room, giving them some privacy.

"You're not from around here, are you?" Johnny asked.

"No. New York. Manhattan."

"I thought as such." He paused. "From your accent, I mean. Anyway, I'd remember you if I'd seen you before."

She studied his face, so open and honest, and thought of all the pick-up lines in sleazy bars from sleazy men she'd ever heard and this approach was so sincere.

Mrs. Satariano appeared with the Cokes and Johnny dug in his front pocket. Susan reached for her purse.

"I'll get mine," she said.

"You will not," Johnny said firmly. "You're my guest here. If I get to Manhattan, you can buy me a Coke."

"Fair enough," she said, then thought wryly, *Johnny in Manhattan...There'd be a fish out of water! Nice kid like this, prey to all kinds of pitfalls and traps.*

The next hour passed quickly for Susan, as she and Johnny talked about this and that, nothing and everything, their conversation punctuated with laughter. She found herself telling him things...personal things...that she'd never told close friends or even her fiancé, Steven.

Reminded of Steven, she suddenly, impulsively, lowered her hands beneath the table, removed the engagement ring and tucked it away in her purse.

She returned her attention to Johnny. What she loved most about him, apart from his good looks, was the way every single thought registered on his face. With a man like this, a woman would always know *exactly* where she stood. No evasive looks or cold silences, no wondering what you'd done, or hadn't done.

Susan looked at her watch. "I'm afraid I'm keeping you from your work."

"Chores, you mean?" Johnny asked, with a hint of a smile. He was leaning back comfortably in the booth, biting on the plastic straw, as if it were a real piece of hay. "I do need to tend to the Venus plants," he said.

Susan leaned forward in the booth, elbows on the table. "Mrs. Satariano said growing them saved the town's economy," she said. "Sounds like a fascinating story."

He straightened, brow furrowed. "Not really...."

"Are they female?" she asked. "Or male?"

Now he leaned forward, his elbows on the table. "You really are interested, aren't you?" His brown eyes were eager, like a cocker spaniel, hopeful for a treat.

"Of course," she said.

He grinned. "Then let's blow this pop stand!" And he edged out of the booth, tossing a crumpled dollar bill on the table.

Behind the wheel of the red Mustang, she followed Johnny in his blue Ford truck; if the town had been like something out of Norman Rockwell, the countryside was pure Grand Wood, with its gently rolling blindingly green hills. About three miles outside of Prosperity, at the bottom of the one of those hills, Johnny turned off the blacktop onto a gravel road.

After another mile or so, Johnny's truck slowed and pulled into a short lane that led to a prosperous-looking, old-fashioned farm. To the right sat a white two-story house with green shutters and a large porch with white pillars. A porch swing hung by chains from the ceiling, rocking gently in the warm summer breeze. The front door to the house was old and beautifully refinished, with an oval window in etched glass.

Behind the house, to the left, was a big red barn that looked freshly painted. A black wrought-iron weather vane of a rooster perched proudly on its roof. The summer sky above was a bright blue, and clouds—like dollops of whipped cream on a High School Special—drifted slowly by. The sun, beginning its descent in the late afternoon, made everything cast long shadows over the farmyard, bringing all its colors to a brilliant hue.

Susan parked her car behind Johnny's truck in the large driveway, which separated the house from a cornfield. Even the grass was picture-postcard perfect: freshly mowed, not an unsightly weed anywhere.

Johnny approached and opened the Mustang door for her. "Well, what d'ya think of the old homestead?"

Smoothing out her summery dress, Susan took a deep breath. "It's so beautiful," she said. "So peaceful." It would be wonderful to live here, she thought.

"The greenhouse is around back," he told her, and led the way.

They stood just inside the screen door of the long, narrow greenhouse. Unlike the other structures on the farm, this one was new, with a curved, Plexiglas roof. Wooden tables ran the length of the building, with narrow paths in-between. And on those tables were hundreds, perhaps thousands, of tiny green plants in black plastic trays.

"You wanted to know about the Dionaea," he said, gesturing to a nearby table.

"I did?"

"That's the scientific name of the Venus flytrap."

"But they're so tiny..." She moved to the table, taking a closer look at the little green sprouts.

"That's because this is a brand new crop," Johnny explained. "I start one each month." He gestured again to the plants. "These will be transplanted to the back field, where we're harvesting the crop planted last month."

Susan shook her head. "How on earth did you get the idea to grow them? I thought the Venus Flytrap was some kind of tropical plant."

"No, they're found in the bogs of North Carolina," he told her. "The soil there lacks certain nitrites." He picked up one of the plastic trays holding about a dozen plants and looked at them.

"Seven or eight years ago," he went on, "you wouldn't have recognized this farm. It looked like something out of the depression: the land fallow, soil robbed of nutrients that would take years to replace." He was staring now, at the tray in his hands, like it was crystal ball into the past.

"At that time," he continued, "I was in agricultural college— I never did graduate, 'cause I had to come home and run the farm—but, anyway, we were studying about these plants...And I thought, hey, that was one thing that might grow in this soil."

"And they are, obviously."

He nodded at Susan. "With the help of some special plant nutriments. And I found there was a demand for 'exotic plants,' particularly in urban areas, and the farm began doing well. I didn't keep my good fortune a secret from my neighbors...that's not how we do things here."

"I've noticed."

"The whole town started to grow the plants, and we sold them all over the world."

Johnny set the tray of little plants down on the table.

"Since then." He continued, "the corn crops have made a comeback, and the other folks 'round here have stopped growing Dionaea—except for me, on the back forty. And everybody helps me out with the harvest and half the proceeds go to better the community."

Susan was touched by his story, and generosity; her eyes were moist.

Johnny's stomach growled. "Sorry," he said. "Except for that Coke, I haven't had anything since early morning." His face brightened. "Would you join me for dinner? I have some left-over fried chicken, and corn from the garden."

She touched his upper arm; his bicep was hard as a rock, "I'd love to," she smiled.

In the cozy kitchen of the farmhouse, they sat at a round oak table. Before them lay a feast of fried chicken, sweet corn, and garden vegetables. The meal was simple, but delicious. Like Johnny.

As they ate, he told her about taking over the farm the summer after his third year of college. After his parents died, his father in a freak combine accident, his mother of a broken heart. And how hard he had worked to keep the place going, fixing it up, little by little, even buying back family heirlooms, piece by piece, that had been sold to an antique dealer when times were hard.

And she told him about growing up poor, and never having any money, and how she hated her job and New York.

"Funny," she said. "I didn't realize I hated the city, and my job, till today."

"Prosperity can do that for a person," he said.

Later, after the dishes were washed and dried, they went out on the front porch, and sat in the swing, eating vanilla ice cream covered with fresh strawberries, watching the purple-pink sunset, saying very little. And still later, when the fireflies came out, and a chill in the air drove them inside, they sat on a couch in the parlor, in front of a fireplace with a walnut mantle, sipping red wine, watching the flames hypnotically.

"Aren't you lonely, Johnny? By yourself here?"

"It's a lot of work, looking after this place."

And now she has the questions she'd been afraid to ask: "You've never been married?"

"No."

"Never serious about anyone?"

"Well...there've been ladies in my life. I wouldn't kid you. But I'm fussy. I guess I'm always thinking about finding the perfect mate."

She slipped her hand into his—the hand from which the engagement ring had been withdrawn. "I don't mean to be forward...and I know we've just met. But these past hours I've spent with you are the happiest I've been in a long, long while."

To that he replied, "More than anything right now, I want you to be happy."

And he kissed her, ever so gently, and never before had any man made her feel the way she did.

"I should go," she said after awhile, pulling away. Her face felt hot, flushed. "I need to get a room in town."

"You can if you want to," he said softly, "but the guest room upstairs is free." And he kissed her again, and she kissed back, wrapping her arms tightly around him, pushing him back on the couch as the flames danced seductively before them.

Susan woke in the morning in the four-poster bed in Johnny's room. The early morning sun streamed in a nearby window and a cool breeze—with just a hint of the warm day to come—softly rustled the white cotton curtains.

She stretched. Never before had she slept so soundly! She'd woken once, in the night, but the sounds of crickets and wind rushing through corn stalks made a soothing symphony that lulled her back to sleep. Not to mention the afterglow of Johnny's tender love-making, first on the couch in front of the fire, and later during the night, in the four-poster bed. He hadn't tried to impress her, like other men she'd been with, Steven included. It was obvious he was so completely at ease with the act, that that put her at ease.

So had what he'd told her, when she said, "We've only known each other such a short time, Johnny...but I want to spend my life here with you, on this farm, in this perfect place."

And as those foolish words tumbled from her, she felt almost immediately embarrassed, until he said, "I want the same for you. I've found what I've been looking for...a perfect mate...."

Sometime very early in the morning, he kissed her cheek and told her he had to get up for chores, and she should go back to sleep. Which she did. Perhaps, after they were married, she would get up to help him.

Susan got out of bed and padded across the braided rug to her suitcase that lay on the floor, getting what she needed for the bathroom. Through the open window she could hear Johnny out in the greenhouse, whistling, as he tended to the plants.

It was when she bathed in the big old claw-foot tub that she noticed it—the scratch on her inner thigh. Was it a bug bite? Johnny's lovemaking had been forceful but not of the fingernail clawing variety. She shrugged it off and soaped herself with a bar of Ivory Snow.

Half an hour or so later, she emerged from the bathroom and stopped in front of a hall phone on its small half-circle table against the wall. Not impulsively, for she'd been thinking during her bath just what she would say; she called Steven's number at their apartment, knowing he'd be at work, and informed him the engagement was off, and he should pack her things, which she'd send for later.

Then wearing the same floral dress that she'd bought yester-day (she didn't want to scare him with all that black) she skipped down the stairs to the front hallway, and went back to the kitchen. There on the table was a glass of orange juice, and some muffins on a plate and a note saying there was coffee on the counter. Wasn't he thoughtful? She drank the orange juice, took two bites of a scrumptious muffin, then hurried out the back door to the green house.

When she got there, though, the greenhouse was empty. He was probably off to get something, and would be back soon, she thought. Smiling, she began to walk down one of the narrow paths between the tables (one table was set up like a mini-laboratory, with test tubes, Bunsen burners and the like), taking in the little green shoots coming out of the black dirt, which looked like rolled green dollar bills. Or fifties. That's what he told her they sold for last night.

Perhaps with her business savvy, she could help her new husband turn this farm into a real moneymaker; small-town life was fine, Prosperity was heaven, but money could always improve things. Giving half the proceeds of the harvest to the town, wasn't that a little excessive?

She stopped, noticing a little metal plaque on the side of the table, a plaque bearing a white card with a name and date. The card seemed to identify the month the seeds were started.

She moved along to the next table, which had a similar plaque. But this one read "Heather, May." The other had been "Jill, April." She continued to the last table, where rows of trays sat empty. Her eyes went to the plaque, its paper whiter, new than the others. It said, "Susan, July."

Johnny was going to name the next crop of plants after her! How romantic....

She touched the card and another one, which had been stuck behind it, slid out the bottom of the holder onto the floor. She bent down and picked up the weathered piece of paper, which must have been in there a long, long time because the paper was brown and stained. It seemed to say "Mother" and the date was gone.

The screen door of the greenhouse banking shut made her look up to see Johnny standing in the doorway, in faded jeans and a white t-shirt.

She let the old piece of paper fall from her hands and she hurried toward him.

"Did you sleep well?" he asked.

She was a little out of breath when she reached him. "Oh, yes! And thank you for the breakfast." She gestured to the back of the greenhouse. "I noticed that the last table had a card that said 'Susan'...Does that mean those plans will be named after me?"

"Oh, yes."

She squealed and threw her arms around his neck, and kissed him, but he didn't return the kiss. She brought her arms down slowly, and looked at his face, which wore a peculiar expression.

"I want you to know about the others," he said.

"The other what?"

"Those other names. Those other ladies."

Was that all? she thought, and breathed a sign of relief. She'd thought something was *really* wrong. "It doesn't matter," she said. "I haven't been an angel, myself."

He shook his head. "But you have a right to know. Just like the others."

She started to say something dismissive, but he continued, looking intently at her. "In April, there was Jill. In May there was Heather. In June there was Madeline...."

Madeline? She remembered the appointment book she'd found in the car...hadn't that woman's name been Madeline?

"...You see it all started seven years ago with Mother."

"Your *mother*..." she said, befuddled.

He moved forward, backing her against the table.

"You see," he explained, "my early attempts to raise Dionaea here failed. I studied the problem scientifically and came to believe the Dionaea could only survive in dry Iowa soil if it had first been given a nutritious start in soil high in nitrates...human nitrates with estrogen."

Her stomach dropped, like on the airplane. "What are you saying? You're not saying you used human...What *about* your mother?"

"She was heart-broken over dad's death. It was the humane thing to do."

She tried to move away, but Johnny's strong arms closed around her, and flailing away with her fists was like hitting a stone statue. And her strength was gone, she felt suddenly groggy...had that thoughtful breakfast been drugged?

"You heartless bastard! You said I was your perfect mate!"

"I didn't say you were *my* perfect mate. I checked your blood this morning..."

The scratch on her thigh!

"...and it's a perfect chemical match for the nutritional needs of my next crop. You're not my perfect mate, Susan—you're Dionaea's...."

And all around the little heads of the plants seemed to be nodding agreement.

"Why did you pick *me* out?" she asked, terrified. "You couldn't know that just looking at me..."

His smile was sickeningly sweet. "U-Save Car Rental is Prosperity's other successful business. They send me only their rudest customers...women so nasty they won't be missed."

And his hands went around her throat.

"But I've *changed*!" she managed to rasp.

Johnny shook his head, tightening his grip. "People don't change," he said. "I know I never could."

And his hands squeezed tighter, like the leaf of the Venus Flytrap when another poor fly haplessly enters its lair.

***

The Dionaea plant sat on a windowsill in an apartment on Seventy-third and Central Park West, warming itself in the late afternoon sun. It didn't even care if some idiotic insect came by and landed on one of its many thorned leaves, triggering that leaf to clamp shut, beginning the slow process of digestion...Because earlier in the day that nice woman who lived here alone fed it that special plant food from Iowa, making it feel big and strong.

It missed the farm. But across the street was a really big park and maybe some day, when it got too big for the little apartment, the nice lady would transplant it. There was always some activity going on in the park, although some of it was not very nice.

A knock came at the front door, and the woman went to answer it. The plant liked the woman.

"Steven!" the woman said to a tall, dark man who entered. "Thank you so much for the plant. Come and see it."

The man came over and bent his head down toward the plant. It didn't like him. It didn't know why.

"What in the world...?" he asked. "I just told the florist to send something exotic."

"It's a Venus flytrap," the woman said excitedly.

"No kiddin'? I've never seen one." His face came closer and the plant wanted so badly to clamp down on his nose.

"They're meat eaters," the woman said with a laugh. "Better keep your distance!"

"From the Susan series," he read from a little card that lay next to the plant. He made a disgusted sound with his lips.

"What's the matter?" the woman asked.

"That's the name of that flaming bitch who dumped me by leaving a message on my answering machine. I wonder what became of her."

"Well if she hadn't, dear," the woman said, "we wouldn't have gotten back together, would we? We might never get married."

"Sure we will," Steven said. "How could we not? We're perfect for each other."

Then, hand in hand, the couple left the apartment—off to eat at some expensive restaurant—and the plant sat alone, basking in the last rays of the late afternoon sun.

*   *   *

Why should someone come to Mayhem in the Midlands?

What the hell else is there to do in the Midwest?

DO HAVE A CUP OF TEA

by Rhys Bowen

Rhys Bowen is the creator of the Constable Evans mystery series, set in the mountains of Snowdonia, North Wales. She is British by birth and childhood summers spent with relatives in a little village in North Wales were the inspiration for her setting and eccentric characters.

Rhys grew up in England and studied at London University before landing a job with the BBC. While working in BBC drama, she began writing her own plays. She also sang in folk clubs with such luminaries as Al Stewart and Simon and Garfunkel. Longing for sunshine, she went to work for ABC in Australia and would have stayed had she not met her future husband who was California-bound. She has lived in Marin County ever since, raising four children there.

Finding nothing similar to the BBC existed in San Francisco, Rhys began writing children's books. Her first picture book, written under her married name of Janet Quin-Harkin, won many awards, including being named a New York Times best book of the year. More picture books followed, then Rhys moved on and up to young adult novels. She has written almost one hundred books for children and teenagers, including a number one bestseller, and many popular series of her own. She has sold about five million books worldwide.

Eventually Rhys felt confined by the limits of writing for children. She wrote several historical romances and sagas, also some TV tie-ins. Finally she decided to write what she likes to read. She took a big gamble, borrowed her grandfather's name and began to write the Constable Evans mysteries set in her grandfather's corner of the world. The series achieved instant critical acclaim. *Evan Help Us* was called "a jewel of a story" by Publisher's Weekly and was nominated for a Barry award for best novel. All of the titles have been Mystery Guild selections and have sold also in audio and large print editions.

The fifth book in the series, *Evan Can Wait*, comes out in February and has received great early response in the mystery community. Edgar-winner Laura Lippman says, "Few writers are capable of this deft combination of light and dark."

Rhys has just begun a second series, this one set in turn-of-the-century New York, and hopes to squeeze in two books a year, between conferences, tours and signings.

DO HAVE A CUP OF TEA

by Rhys Bowen

Dedicated to that obnoxious little twerp at the Liverpool Daily Post.

"My dear girl, don't get so upset. It's only a review. One person's opinion. It means nothing."

"Nothing?" she shrieked into the phone. "Edward, a million people read the Sunday Times. If their stupid review calls my new book trite and juvenile and says that I've never uttered a believable word in my life, are you telling me it's not going to affect my sales?"

"Do try and keep calm, Caroline. You know very well that the fellow prides himself on being ruthless and cutting. Why else does he call himself 'The Woodsman'? You made his column, that's the main thing. It means you're a player."

"A player who is trite, juvenile and unbelievable." Caroline pushed back her hair in a gesture of helpless frustration. She had had such high hopes of this latest book. Everyone had assured her it was her best yet, her breakout book. And now her first review in a national newspaper and she had been felled with one stroke of the Woodsman's ax.

"It will be all right." Her editor's voice was still calm and soothing. He had obviously been through this with a lot of writers before. "Trust me. In years to come you'll look back at this and laugh."

37

"Yes, when I've had to give up writing and I'm working as a bagger in Safeway."

"Will you get it into your head that this is not going to affect your sales, Caroline? All those little old ladies out there love Alice Malice. They don't care what one literary snob says." She heard him cover the phone and mumble something. "Listen, Cara sweetie, I have to go. I'm late for a meeting. But please don't get your knickers into a twist over this. Remember the old saying— there is no such thing as bad publicity? Why don't you go and prune a few roses in that delightful garden of yours? Very therapeutic, gardening."

"I know what I'd like to prune," she muttered. "A couple of vital appendages from that bloody Woodsman. Of course, he probably doesn't have any—that's why he's so aggressive and hostile in his columns. He's probably really a meek little twit who wears velvet jackets and lives with his mother."

"Cara. Go prune your roses." The editor chuckled. "I have to go."

She heard the phone click down. "Yes, to meet with one of your authors who isn't trite, juvenile and unbelievable," she said to the empty room. What did Edward care? He had a hundred up and coming writers who wrote brilliant, risqué, and noir. Far more likely to win fame and prizes than her elderly, lama-breeding sleuth.

She signed. Maybe a spot of gardening might not be such a bad idea. Working with the soil was a great way of bringing things into perspective and it looked like a lovely day out there. She put on her gardening gloves and her floppy hat and went outside. It was indeed a perfect summer day. The sky was a rich blue, dotted with white puffball clouds. The air was heavy with the perfume of a thousand roses and hummed with the drone of bees. From behind the hedge came the rhythmic clickety click of an old-fashioned push mower and the scent of new mown grass wafted to her nostrils.

She began to move down the front path, her pruning sheers flying as she dead headed roses. As she worked she felt the tension slip away and she began to hum to herself. The shears flew, the dead flowers dropped to the ground. Very satisfying. At last she came to the big climber that sprawled over the gateway. Goodness, how fast that thing grew! It was sending out straggling shoots in all directions again, making walking past her house a hazardous venture. She got out the step stool and started cutting ruthlessly.

The sound of footsteps coming down the lane made her look up. Foot traffic was a rarity as the lane came to a dead end and hers was the last house. A youngish man dressed in an open necked check shirt and khaki pants came into view, striding with the natural ease of a hiker. He nodded to her as he went to pass her cottage.

"Lovely day, isn't it?"

"Yes. It is."

They exchanged the conventional English weather report. He went to walk on, then looked into her garden and paused.

"What magnificent roses! And some quite old varieties, if I'm not mistaken."

Caroline came down from her stool. "That's right. The Damask and the Sally Holmes, and that sweet smelling one is called Invitation. Would you like to see them?"

"If you can spare a moment. I'm a great devotee of roses, especially the grand old varieties. There's something wrong with these newer ones, don't you think? Too perfect, almost as if they were computer generated..."

"For Walt Disney," she finished. "I agree completely. And most of them have no scent. The scent is very important to me. One of the pleasures of life is the scent of roses wafting in through an open bedroom window on a summer night."

"How very poetic." His eyes lingered on her face. He had nice eyes, she noticed—tiger eyes, green flecked with brown. And a nice smile, too. She forgot for a moment that she had sworn off men since Robert left her for a teenage bimbo.

"Do you live around here?" she asked. "I don't remember seeing..."

"No. I'm just visiting for the weekend." He smiled again. "I have a friend who owns a cottage on the green. It's quite charming down here, isn't it? One would never guess that London was only a brief train ride away. Are you a weekender too?"

"No, I live here all the time." For some reason she was stammering like a schoolgirl. And blushing, too. There was something about his frank, amused stare that was very unnerving.

"Lucky you. I'm stuck in the middle of London. It's unbearably hot and stuffy at the moment. Not conducive to thought."

"Look, I'm about to make a cup of tea. Would you like one?" The words just tumbled out before she could decide if they were rational or not.

"Thank you. I'd love one," he said. "My host is an early riser. It seems like hours since breakfast."

She led the way down the path. Her heart was racing and her cheeks felt as if they were on fire. What was she doing? She wasn't the kind of person who invited total strangers into her house. He seemed like a nice enough man, but then so did several serial killers...That was the trouble with writing about murder. Everyone became an instant suspect.

She opened the front door and he followed her into the cool darkness of the living room.

"What a charming room," he said, even as her eyes were sweeping round to see if discarded pantyhose or last night's supper were lying in view. "I do like these old traditional rooms with the ceiling beams and the big fireplace. Oh, and a window seat. I've always wanted a window seat. Do you curl up there with a book?"

"Often," she said, her eyes lighting up.

"I'm afraid I'd never get my work done if I lived here."

He followed her through to the kitchen where she plugged in the electric kettle. She dropped two teabags into the blue and white Cornish pottery teapot, then she put two matching blue and white mugs on the tray.

"So what kind of work do you do?" she asked casually.

"Me? I'm a writer of sorts."

"Are you? Me, too."

"Oh, what do you write?"

"Me? Oh, I write—" She had just remembered that there was a good chance he had seen the review in the morning's Sunday Times. Not a good time to reveal who she really was. "I dabble. A little of this and that."

"Me too. A little poetry, a few essays here and there. Oh, and a column in the newspaper."

They smiled at each other. The kettle boiled, she poured tea and carried in through to the low table by the window. "Now, what about some biscuits?" she asked. "Suddenly I'm very hungry, although..." she glanced at the grandfather clock in the corner. "Heavens, no wonder. It's after twelve. Look, I was going to make myself an omelet for lunch—a mushroom omelet, my specialty. I couldn't persuade you to join me, could I? It's such a bore making omelets for one."

"I'd love to join you. One rarely finds a well made omelet these days."

"Right, then enjoy your tea and I'll be right back. I've got freshly baked bread, too."

"Heavenly." He flashed her a wonderful smile.

Feeling warm and silly inside, she scurried back into the kitchen. She sautéed the mushrooms and green onions in butter while she whipped the eggs, trying to concentrate on what she was doing, for her brain was racing. A man after her own heart, a man of letters and good looking too, had just dropped onto her doorstep. It had to be fate. She must make sure that she didn't seem too keen and scare him off. The omelet had to be just perfect today.

She glanced across at the kitchen table and saw that the Sunday Times was still lying open where she had dropped it in horror. Better put that away, just in case he hadn't read the review yet. She went to fold it up, then stiffened and stared again. She had never noticed before but there was a photo beside the heading to the Woodsman's column. It was a grainy photo and very small, but clear enough for her to recognize that the man who now sat in her living room, waiting for a mushroom omelet was the same one who had just trashed her book.

"Oh, and I write a column..." the words echoed through hear head.

He was there, at her table. At her mercy. Her heart started racing again. Where was that book on undetectable poisons? No, that would be no fun at all. He would just cease to be, his death attributable to natural causes. If she was going to bump him off, she'd want him to know why.

Strychnine then? Didn't she have some rat poison out in the shed? But the police would discover that easily enough and she didn't want to spend time in jail, even though she was sure the court would rule it a justifiable homicide.

The sizzling mushrooms and the smell of butter about to burn made her race back to the stove. That was when she had the idea. A smile of wicked delight spread across her face. She finished the omelet and put it in front of him.

"How absolutely yummy."

She forced a smile in return. How could she have found him attractive? His smile was that of a self-satisfied prig, and the word yummy was totally pretentious.

"I hope you like it," she said, and watched him begin eating. "The mushrooms were picked this morning."

"Oh really?" He hardly paused in bringing the fork to his mouth.

"Yes, it's a new hobby of mine," she said. "Wild mushrooms have so much more flavor."

"They taste divine."

"I'm finding it fascinating. You've no idea how many kinds of edible mushrooms there are until you start. Some of them look absolutely fearsome, but they're quite harmless really."

He wasn't eating as quickly now. He looked up.

Another reassuring smile. "But don't worry. Mushrooming in England is very easy. Even a complete neophyte like myself can determine which ones are poisonous and which are good to eat. Some more tea?"

He took the last mouthful of omelet. "Oh, no thank you. Nothing more. Absolutely delicious though."

She put down her fork and got up, her own portion of omelet barely picked at. "I'd love to ask you to stay longer, but I'm afraid I have an appointment this afternoon," she said. "I really should think about getting ready."

"Oh, I quite understand. Some other time then? I'm sure I'll be coming down this way again now that I've discovered all the charms the village has to offer. Maybe next time you know of a little place where we could dine together?"

"Maybe." She let the words hang in the air.

He held out his hand. "I'm Justin, by the way. Justin Bates."

"And I'm Caroline Kirby."

They shook hands. His hand felt cold, clammy and distinctly weak. Rather like shaking a dead fish.

As he turned toward the door, she handed him a wrapped package. "A little goody bag in case you get bored this afternoon."

"You really are too kind. I must insist on reciprocating next time we meet, Caroline."

"And you must let me cut you some roses. Some of your favorites." She picked up the shears. Her hand trembled. She went down the row, snipping off the choicest blooms, then stuck them into a plastic bag. "These should survive until you get home."

"Wonderful. What a delightful day this has turned out to be. Au revoir then, Caroline."

He actually kissed her hand. The shears twitched in the other hand but she didn't move.

Then he was gone.

Justine Bates hummed to himself as he strode back to the village. He'd made a conquest there, all right. Good-looking woman. Nice eyes. Good legs, too. He'd had a chance to notice that when she was standing on the stool. He liked them with good legs. And she could cook, too. Yes, he saw himself taking up more of Trevor's invitations, even if he was a pretentious old bore.

"Had a good walk?" Trevor looked up from his deckchair on the front lawn, a lunchtime lager clutched in his hand.

"Yes, I have, actually. I met a charming woman. Name's Caroline something. Lives down that lane."

"Oh, you've met Caroline, have you? Of course you two would have a lot in common. She's our resident writer. Quite successful, so I understand. I don't read her kind of stuff personally—a lot of feminine waffle, but the women seem to like it."

"I think she gave me a book." Justin opened the paper package. "Wait, this isn't hers. Malice for Breakfast by Jane Sotherby. This was one of the books in my column this week. I loathed it. Surely she wouldn't think...?"

"But it is hers." Trevor interrupted. "Didn't she tell you she writes under another name, Jane Sotherby—a play on Agatha Christie, get it?" He looked up and the smile died on his lips. "I say old chap. What's the matter?"

"She knew." Justin stammered. "That bitch knew all the time—"

"Knew what? What on earth are you babbling about, man?"

"She knew who I was. She pretended she didn't. But why else would she have given me one of her books, hidden in a plain brown wrapper? She wanted me to know that she knew." He turned even whiter and beads of sweat broke out on his forehead. "And she served me mushrooms. My God, Trevor, I'm going to die."

Trevor jumped up from his chair. "What are you on about? Just because you ate some mushrooms. Are you allergic to them?"

"They were wild mushrooms!" Justin was yelling now. "She told me that she picked them this morning. She said it was a new hobby, but not to worry because it was really easy to distinguish the poisonous ones from the edible varieties. And she had a smile on her face when she said it."

He clutched at his throat. It was already beginning to close up. And his liver—he could feel his liver shutting down and his stomach churning. Once the poison got into his central nervous system he was a goner. If they could get him to a hospital in time to pump his stomach he might still have a chance.

"Where's the nearest hospital? Call for an ambulance. Hurry man, can't you see I'm dying?"

Half an hour later the villagers were startled by the wail of an ambulance siren. They came out of their cottages to watch the ambulance men come running out of Dove Cottage carrying a limp figure on a stretcher.

"One of them Londoners. Always getting heart attacks." Old Mrs. Finch at number twenty-three muttered to her neighbor before she went indoors again.

At her own cottage Caroline Kirby saw the flashing light and decided she had to go to the village shop to buy an extra loaf, just in case.

That evening Justin Bates lay in a haze of discomfort and disbelief. He had never imagined that pumping out a stomach was such an unpleasant business. And then, to crown it all, to find there was nothing wrong with him! The doctors obviously thought he was some kind of crackpot. They were keeping him in overnight for psychiatric evaluation tomorrow. When he'd try to tell them that someone had attempted to kill him he had seen the doctor write "Persecution mania? Possible schizophrenia?" on his chart. In any case, they had put him in a bed with bars on the sides and a nurse stationed at his door.

The pink twilight at the end of a beautiful day was fading as he lay there feeling wretched. What if the shrink didn't believe him the next day? What grounds did you need to commit somebody? What if it got into the papers? His reputation would be ruined if they thought he was a crazy.

He heard the neat tapping of feet along the vinyl hallway, then a low voice talking, then another nurse poked her head into his room.

"A visitor for you, Mr. Bates. This should cheer you up."

Caroline came in, looking fresh and lovely in rose patterned silk.

"Hello, Justin. I hear you were taken ill right after you left my house. I was terribly worried I might have fed you something that upset you. But the doctor assured me just now that nothing was wrong after all."

He managed a weak smile. "Thought it might have been food poisoning—a stray bad mushroom in with the good? You said yourself you were a neophyte. Anyone could have made a mistake. Perfectly understandable."

She was still smiling. Grinning, actually. "The mushrooms came from Safeway, Justin. I've never picked a field mushroom in my life. I wouldn't know how to."

"But you said..."

The grin broadened. "But didn't you write that I'd never uttered a believable word in my life? Obviously I can be quite convincing when I put my mind to it."

She bent to pat his hand, then swept from the room with a swish of silk and a waft of Ashes of Roses perfume.

*   *   *

The reasons the conference was so successful are:

1.   Small, intimate setting. It was easy to meet people.

2.   Excellent panels, different, fresh topics. As a writer it was wonderful to be on three or four panels for maximum exposure.

3.   Within walking distance of Old Town with some truly excellent restaurants.

4.   It fills the gap between Left Coast and Malice for those people who live in the Plains States and Canada.

EIGHTY MILLION DEAD

by Michael Collins

MICHAEL COLLINS writes the Dan Fortune detective series that began in 1967 with *Act Of Fear*. There are now 19 Dan Fortune books, the most recent being *Fortune's World*, Crippen & Landru, published in August, 2000, a collection of short stories spanning from about 1963 to 2000, that, with *Crime, Punishment And Resurrection*, 1992, contains all the Fortune stories prior to 2000. His most recent novel is *Cadillac Cowboy*, 1995. A collection of his non-Fortune stories, *Spies and Thieves, Cops And Killers, Etc.*, will be published in early 2002 by Five Star.

He has won the Mystery Writer's of America Edgar for one novel, been nominated for a second Edgar and three Shamus Awards, and been given PWA's Lifetime Achievement Award. His mystery and detective short stories have appeared in *Best Crime & Mystery Stories of The Year* many times. Under the names of Mark Sadler, John Crowe, William Arden and Carl Dekker, he has published another 18 crime novels and 13 juvenile crime novels. Under his real name, Dennis Lynds, he has published two novels and two collections of short stories. A third Lynds novel, *Pictures*, is with his agent now, and he is writing his 19th Dan Fortune novel, an as yet untitled thriller, his fourth Lynds novel, *Gung-Ho, Sam And Maxine*, and another collection from Crippen & Landru featuring his early series character, Slot-Machine Kelly.

His short stories have been included in *Best American Short Stories*. Born in St. Louis, raised in England and New York City, he now lives in Santa Barbara, California with his wife, best-selling novelist Gayle Lynds.

After writing crime stories for many years between the mid-Sixties to 1970, I stopped doing stories. There was more money in novels, and I had to support a young family.

But in 1984 Bob Randisi asked me to write a Dan Fortune piece for his first PWA anthology, The Eyes Have It. *I'd always wanted to rewrite a piece I'd written much earlier. It was the next to the last Slot-Machine Kelly story. The Kelly stories started out as something of a spoof, and, despite a growing core of seriousness, they remained light-hearted. But by the time I got to the last two they were neither spoofs nor light, and really called for a different approach and a different detective.*

The last became the first Dan Fortune novel, Act of Fear. *But the next to last remained in limbo. Randisi's request gave me the chance to rewrite it as a Fortune, and that's what I did.*

So here it is: a story first written in 1964 in New York, rewritten twenty years later in Santa Barbara.

EIGHTY MILLION DEAD

by Michael Collins

We have killed eighty million people in eighty years. Give or take a few million or a couple of years. Killed. Not lost in hurricanes or famines or epidemics or any of the other natural disasters we should be trying to wipe out instead of each other. From 1900 to 1980. The Twentieth Century.

That's a hell of a way to begin a story, except in this case it could be the whole story. The story of Paul Asher and Constantine Zareta and me, Dan Fortune, and I want you to think about those eighty million corpses. Most of those who killed them were fighting for a reason, a cause. A lot of those who died had a reason, a cause. You have to wonder what cause is worth eighty million ended lives. You have to wonder what eighty million dead bodies has done to the living.

I know what those eighty million deaths had done to Paul Asher and Constantine Zareta. Those were the names they gave me, anyway. They weren't their real names. I'm not sure they knew their real names anymore. It was Paul Asher who walked into my second floor office/apartment that rainy Monday.

"You are Dan Fortune? A private investigator?"

He was tall and dark. A big man who moved like a shadow. I hadn't seen or even heard him come in. He was just there in front of my desk: dark haired, dark-eyed, soft-voiced, in a dark suit. Colorless. Nothing about him told me anything. Only his eyes that looked at my missing arm proved he was alive.

"I'm Fortune."

"I am Paul Asher. I wish to hire you."

"To do what, Mr. Asher?"

"You will deliver a package."

He had an accent. One I couldn't place, and not exactly an accent. More a kind of toneless and too precise way of speaking English that told me it wasn't his native language.

"You want a messenger service," I said. "You can use my telephone book."

"I will pay one thousand dollars," Asher said. "I wish that the package is to be delivered tonight."

No one makes a thousand dollars a day in Chelsea, not even today. Most still don't make it in a month. It was a lot of money for delivering a package. Or maybe it wasn't.

"What's in the package?" I asked.

"I will pay one thousand dollars because you will not ask what is in the package, and because Zareta is a dangerous man."

He said it direct and simple, expressionless.

"Zareta?" I said.

"Constantine Zareta. This he calls himself. It is to him you will take the package."

"Why not take it yourself?"

"He would kill me."

"Why?"

"I possess what he wants."

"Blackmail, Asher?"

"No, I ask no money. You will take the package?"

I shook my head. "Not without knowing what's in it, and why you want to send it to this Constantine Zareta."

Paul Asher thought for a time. He seemed to look again at my empty left sleeve, but his face remained expressionless. He wasn't angry or even frustrated. I had presented him with a problem, and he was thinking about it. As simple as that.

He made his decision. "The package contains documents, nothing more. I am giving them to Zareta. They are of no value except to Zareta. For him they are of great value. The papers are not a danger, simply of value to Zareta. He would kill me to get them; I am tired of danger. When he has the documents I will not be in danger. Until then, I am not safe from him. I cannot take the documents myself, so? You will take them?"

"Let's see the package."

Asher produced a flat package from an inside pocket of his dark suit. It was about as wide as a paperback book, twice as long and thick. I took it. They make bombs smaller and better every day, but the package was much too light for even a plastic bomb. It felt like a package of documents and nothing else. Even a deadly gas has to have a container. I could feel the edges, the folds, the thickness of heavy paper.

"How did you happen to pick me, Mr. Asher?"

"From the telephone book."

For the first time I didn't believe him. Too quick? Something in his voice that wasn't quite toneless this time? I'm in the phone book, but I didn't believe him. Because he wasn't the kind of man who trusted to chance? Maybe and maybe. But if it hadn't been the telephone book, how and why had he picked me out of all the detectives in New York?

"I take the package to Zareta," I said. "What do I bring back?"

"Nothing."

"Who pays me? When?"

"I will pay you," Asher said. "Now."

He took a thin billfold from his inside pocket, counted out ten hundred dollar bills. He wasn't telling me the truth, not the whole truth, but I knew that. Warned of the danger, what could happen that I couldn't handle? If anything looked a hair out of line I'd toss the package and walk away.

I took the ten bills, crisp and new, straight from the bank. Maybe I wanted to know why he had picked me for the job. I wanted to know something.

"What's the address?"

"It is on the package."

"How do I contact you later?"

"You do not. You are paid. I will know if you do not do what you have been paid to do."

"Anything else?"

"Yes," Paul Asher said. "You will deliver the package at midnight. Precisely midnight."

He walked out. I tilted back in my chair. I was a thousand dollars richer. Why didn't I feel good?

***

The address was on the East Side up in Yorkville, far over near the river. Asher's instructions had been definite—midnight—and the slum street was dark and silent in the rain when the taxi dropped me. There was no one on the street. No one in sight anywhere, but I felt the eyes. When you grow up near the docks, start stealing early because you have to eat even if your father ran out long before and your mother drinks too much, you learn to feel when eyes are watching.

I walked slowly along the dark street in the rain and knew that I wasn't alone. I sensed them all around. The address was an old unrenovated brownstone with the high front steps. Two men appeared at the far end of the street. They leaned against a dark building. Two more appeared behind me where the taxi had dropped me. Two stood in the shadows on another stoop across the street. Shadows of shadows all around in the dark and rain. The glint of a gun.

I went up the steps to the front door and into the vestibule. There was only one mailbox and doorbell. I had my finger on the bell when I saw the man outside on the steps. He stood two steps below the vestibule with an automatic rifle. A short, powerful man behind a bandit mustache. There were two more behind him at the foot of the steps. They had guns, too. They stood there doing nothing. Too late I knew why, felt the inner vestibule door open behind me.

An arm went around my throat, a hand went over my mouth, another hand held my arm, and I was dragged back into the dark of the entrance hall. I didn't resist. The short one with the bandit mustache and automatic rifle followed us in. They dragged me into a small room, sat me in a chair, came and went in rapid groups. They barely glanced at me. They were busy. Except two I felt close behind me keeping watch.

"What's going on?" I tried.

"Do not talk!" He was the short, powerful man with the automatic rifle. He seemed to be the leader, sent the other men in and out with the precision of a drill sergeant. They spoke some language I didn't even recognize.

I didn't have to know the language to know what they were doing. They were all armed, and they were searching the street outside and the neighborhood for anyone who might have come with me. It was half an hour before the mustachioed leader sat down astride a chair in front of me. He still carried his automatic rifle, and the package Paul Asher had sent me to deliver.

"Your name is Fortune. What do you want here?"

"I came to deliver that package."

"Who are you?"

"You've searched my papers."

"You came to deliver this package to who?"

"Constantine Zareta. Is that you?"

"What is in the package?"

"Papers. Documents."

He studied the package a moment, turned it over in his heavy hands. Then he gave it to one of the other men.

"From who does the package come?"

"Paul Asher."

"We know no Paul Asher."

"It's the name he gave me."

"Your papers say you are a private investigator. We know what that means. A man who will sell his weapon to anyone. A hired murderer. An assassin. You came to kill Constantine Zareta!"

"I came to deliver a package," I said. "I don't have a gun. I don't even know who Zareta is or what he looks like."

"Of course not. They would not tell you who you kill or why. They have hired you only to kill. Do not lie!"

"If someone is trying to kill Zareta, go to the police. That's their work."

I had been watching all their faces as I talked. They were grim, unsmiling, and they didn't look like hoodlums. They were nervous and armed, but they didn't act like gunmen. They looked like soldiers, *guerrillas*. And as I watched them I saw their faces come alert, respectful. Someone else had come into the room somewhere behind me. A low voice with good English.

"The police could not help me, Mr. Fortune."

I felt him standing close behind me. His voice had that power of command, of absolute confidence in himself and what he did. Constantine Zareta. I started to turn.

"Do not turn, Mr. Fortune."

I looked straight ahead at the mustachioed man. "Maybe the police can't help you because you want to kill Paul Asher."

The mustache reached out and hit me.

"Emil!"

Emil glared down at me. "He's another one, Minister. I can smell them."

"Perhaps," Zareta's slow voice said. "Let us be sure."

"We cannot take the chance, Minister. Kill him now. If they did not send him, what does it matter?"

There was a silence behind me. A chair scraped. I felt hot breath on the back of my neck. Slow breathing. Zareta had sat down close behind me. That was fine. As long as I could feel his breath I was ahead of the game. As long as I could feel anything.

"A man sent you to me at this address."

"Yes."

"Why did he pick you?"

"Out of the telephone book."

"Do you believe that?"

"No."

I could almost hear him nod.

"What was his reason for not coming himself?"

"He said you'd kill him."

"Why would I kill him?"

"Because he had what you wanted. Documents, not dangerous to you, but so important you'd kill to get them."

"And these documents are in the package?"

"Yes. He said he was tired of danger, wanted to give them to you, but was afraid to come himself."

It was strangely unreal to be talking straight ahead into the empty air of the dark room, the silent face of Emil.

"This man's name was Paul Asher."

"Yes."

"I know no Paul Asher, but that does not surprise me. You will describe him."

I described Paul Asher down to the flinty calm of his dark eyes, his silent movement despite his size.

"I do not recognize him, but that does not surprise me either, Mr. Fortune. I do recognize the type of man you have described. It sounds true. You have saved your life, Mr. Fortune. For now."

Emil did not like my reprieve. "The risk, Minister."

"I think we can take some risk, Emil," Zareta said, his breath still brushing the back of my neck. "Mr. Fortune could be lying, but I think not. This Asher sounds like all the men we have known, yes? Mr. Fortune has acted exactly as he would have if his story is true, and you found no one else who could have been with him. Then, he clearly does not know what was in the package he brought to us, or he would have told a better tale, yes? And he has no weapon of any kind."

That seemed to stop Emil. I've said it before, most of the time a gun does nothing but get you in trouble. Sooner or later you'll use it if you have to or not, and someone else will use theirs. If I'd had a gun this time I'd probably be dead. I wasn't dead, and I wondered what had been in the package that would have made me tell a different story if I'd known.

"Why?" Zareta said. "I cannot understand what reason this Asher had to send you to me. That makes me uneasy. Tell me everything once more. Leave nothing out."

I told him all of it again. I was uneasy, too. Why had Paul Asher sent me if the package wasn't the reason? Or was it Zareta who was conning me now? Lulling me to get me to lead him back to Asher? If that was his scheme he wouldn't get far. I couldn't lead anyone to Paul Asher.

"I do not understand," Zareta said when I finished the story again, "but you have done me an important service. I know now what this Paul Asher looks like." The chair scraped behind me. "Take your money, Mr. Fortune, and go home. Forget that you ever heard of Paul Asher or me."

There was silence, and then a door closed somewhere in the dark brownstone. The troops began to disperse. The boss had spoken. Emil's heart wasn't in it, but Zareta was boss.

"Tonight you are a very lucky man," Emil said.

I looked around. I saw no one who looked like a boss, but I saw the package I'd carried lying on a table. It was torn open to show—a stack of folded papers. Just what Asher had said it was. Only there was something wrong, something odd about the package. Not quite right. What? They didn't give me time to look longer or closer.

They hustled me out into the dark hall. Then I was alone on the street where I'd started. I walked to the nearest corner without looking back. I didn't run, that would have been cowardly. I waited until I was around the corner. Then I ran.

By the time I got down to Chelsea and my one room office/apartment I felt pretty good. I had no more interest in Asher and Zareta and their private feud, whatever it was. I was a thousand dollars richer and still alive. I figured I was home free. I should have known better.

***

I awoke in the pitch dark to a violent pounding on my door. My arm was aching. The missing arm. That's always a sign. It's what's missing that hurts when the days become bad.

The pounding went on. Cop pounding. As I got up and pulled on my pants, a gray light began to barely tinge the darkness. Captain Pearce himself led his Homicide men into my office area. The men fanned out to look behind the doors and under the beds. Pearce sat down behind my desk.

"What's it about, Captain?"

"Paul Asher," Pearce said.

"Nice name. Is there more?"

"Asher is enough," Pearce said. "He was a client of yours? Or was there some other connection?"

"Was?" I said.

"Asher's dead," Pearce said. "You should give him his money back."

Pearce doesn't like any private detective much, but especially me. I was too close to old Captain Gazzo. Pearce took Gazzo's
place after the Captain was gunned down on a dark city roof. One
of the new breed, a college man, and he doesn't like me bringing
Gazzo's ghost with me. But he's a good cop, he does his job first.

"We found Asher an hour ago," Pearce said. "Dumped under
the George Washington Bridge. Shot up like Swiss cheese. Any
ideas?"

The George Washington Bridge is a long way from Yorkville,
but that I would expect.

"Constantine Zareta," I said.

I told Pearce about Zareta and Asher, about Emil and all
those silent gunmen. Pearce got up, signaled for his forces.

"Let's pick them up."

We went in the Captain's car. He sat silent and edgy as we
headed uptown at the head of his platoon of squad cars, drumming his fingers on his knee. He had no more questions. I had
questions.

"You said you found Asher an hour ago, Captain. How did
you dig up my connection so fast?"

"Your business cards in his pocket."

"Cards?"

Pearce nodded as he watched the dawn city, gray and empty
of people but teeming with trucks. "He must have had ten, and
your name was in his little black book with a thousand dollars
and yesterday's date noted next to it."

Business cards cost money. I don't hand them out without
necessity. Asher had found me, there had been no reason to give
him a card, not even one. I leave some with uptown contacts in
case anyone up there wants a kidnapped poodle rescued, so Asher
may have picked up the cards from whoever sent him to me
before he came down to my office. Or he could have palmed
them off my desk when he walked out. But why? And why ten?

In the dawn the Yorkville street was as deserted as it had been
last night. We parked all along the gray morning street. Windows

popped open in other buildings, but nothing moved in Constantine Zareta's brownstone. It was as dark and silent as some medieval fortress.

It turned out to be as hard to get into as a medieval fortress. Rings, knocks, shouts and threats failed to open the vestibule door, the building remained dark.

"Break it down," Pearce said.

His men broke the door open, and Pearce strode into the dim entrance hall. The mustachioed Emil faced him. Emil had his automatic rifle aimed at the Captain's heart. Other gunmen stood in the doorways of the rooms and on the stairs. We were all covered. It took Captain Pearce almost a minute to find his voice.

"Police, damn it! Put those guns down. We're the police."

Constantine Zareta spoke from somewhere behind Emil, out of sight in the dim hallway. I knew that slow voice by now.

"You will tell me your name, your rank, and your badge number. I will verify that you are police. You will make no moves, my men watch your people in the street also."

Color began to suffuse Pearce's face. The Captain isn't a patient man, and I wondered how long it had been since anyone had asked him to prove who he was. He opened his mouth, looked around the dark hallway at the silent *guerrillas* and their guns, and closed his mouth. If Constantine Zareta was as tough as he sounded, we could have a blood bath in the dark hallway and out on the morning street.

"Captain Martin Pearce," the Captain said through thin lips, and explained that a captain's shield does not have a number.

In the silent hallway we all waited.

I imagined the scene down at Police Headquarters when they got the call asking about a Captain Pearce, and would they please describe the Captain. It took some time, but whatever they thought down there they must have gone along with it and given an accurate description.

Constantine Zareta appeared in the dim light, and I saw him for the first time—a short, thick man as wide as he was tall, with a shaved bullet head attached to his massive shoulders as if he had no neck. He said something in his unknown language. The guns vanished and the gunmen disappeared.

"Very well, Captain," Zareta said to Pearce. "We will talk in the living room."

Pearce and Zareta faced each other in the same room where I had been interrogated earlier. The Captain stood. Zareta sat on a straight chair, Emil close behind him. Neither Zareta nor Emil had seen me yet.

"Just who and what are you, Zareta?" Pearce said. "Why do you need armed men?" His voice was controlled, but I heard the anger in it. No policeman can tolerate a private army.

"A poor exile, Captain," Zareta said. "My men have permits for their weapons."

"Exile from where?"

"Albania."

That was the language I hadn't recognized—Albanian.

"Was Paul Asher an Albanian too?" Pearce said. "Is that why he was afraid of you? Is that why you killed him?"

For a moment there was a heavy silence in the small living room lit only by a single lamp behind its drawn curtains. Then Emil grunted. Others made other noises. Constantine Zareta leaned forward in his chair.

"This Asher, he is dead? You are sure?"

"We're sure." Pearce said.

Zareta laughed aloud. "Good! He is one we will not have to kill! You bring me good news, Captain, I am grateful. But how did you know that this Asher's death would be something I would want to know? How did you know of Asher and myself? How...Ah, of course, Mr. Fortune. You have talked with Mr. Fortune. It is the only way." He looked around the small room. "Are you here again, Mr. Fortune?"

I stepped out into the dim light where Zareta could see me, flashed my best smile at the glowering Emil, and missed it.

I missed the whole impossible, monstrous plan.

***

Sometimes I wonder if there is anyone left who hasn't killed. I know there are millions, but sometimes it seems there can't be a man alive who hasn't killed. I've killed, but it always shakes me up, killing and death, and maybe that was why I missed what I should have heard in what Constantine Zareta said when I stepped out where he could see me and only smiled at him.

Pearce wasn't smiling. "You're saying you didn't kill Paul Asher?"

"We did not."

"But you would have."

"If he came here, yes."

"Why?"

"Because he would have killed me."

"Why didn't you ask for protection?"

"The police?" Zareta shook his head. "No, Captain, I am not precisely a friend of your government. I am a Communist. I have no love for your capitalist regime, they have no love for me. In my country the present leaders and I have no love for each other either. They want me dead, *must* have me dead, or someday I will destroy them. Six times they have tried. In four countries. Twice we had police protection. Once the police could not stop the assassin, once they did not want to stop the assassins. Each time I was close to death. I have survived. I have killed four of them, but they will not give up. If I were them I would not give up. One of us must kill the other."

That was when I first thought about the eighty million dead in eighty years. Zareta said the word *kill* the way other men say the word *work*—a fact of life. Neither good nor bad, just a tool. I remember when we used to say that a man who killed for the fun of it was an animal, inhuman, a monster. Today we kill without even having any fun from it. We just kill. A job, a duty, our assigned role. And it has nothing to do with being a Communist. It isn't only the communists who have swallowed those eighty million corpses like so many jellybeans.

Pearce said, "So you have your own army, trust no one to come near you, not even the police."

"That is why I still live, Captain," Zareta said. "But we do not kill unless we are sure a man is our enemy."

"You knew Paul Asher was your enemy. Fortune told you."

"Yes, but Asher did not come here."

"Someone else just killed him for you. A lucky accident."

"I ask no questions, Captain," Zareta said.

Pearce seemed to think. He glanced toward me. If Zareta or his men hadn't killed Paul Asher, it didn't leave many known candidates except me. I didn't like that much, but I couldn't think of anyone else to hand the Captain. While I was thinking about it, and Zareta and the glowering Emil had relaxed a hair now that they knew Paul Asher was dead. Pearce nodded sharply to his men. They grabbed Zareta, had their guns out before Zareta's men knew what had happened.

"Maybe you didn't kill Paul Asher," Pearce said. "But I need to know more. We'll go to headquarters and sort it out there."

"No!" Emil cried. "The Minister does not go with you!"

The police had the edge now, but if Emil and the rest went for their guns it could be nasty. It was a tense moment in the small, dim room. Zareta broke it.

"Very well, Captain," he said. He had little choice. He was an alien, they were the police, and his own chances of surviving a shoot-out would be slim. "But not alone. I will take Emil and two other men, yes? A precaution of safety in numbers we who do not come from free countries need."

"Okay, but they leave all their guns. My men will stay around here to help protect the rest of your people."

"Agreed," Zareta said.

"Minister!" Emil was uneasy.

"Come, Emil, they are the police," Zareta said.

They laid their weapons on a table, followed Captain Pearce out of the room.

I was uneasy, too. Constantine Zareta would kill any enemy, without anger or remorse. He seemed to draw the line at killing without some reason, and that had probably saved me the first time around, but it wasn't exactly high morality. Yet, as I watched them go out with Pearce I was suddenly sure that they had not killed Paul Asher.

Zareta wouldn't have waited to be caught if he or any of his men had killed Asher. He would have known that the moment Asher turned up dead I would tell the police all about him and his connection to Asher. No, Zareta would have been long gone before the police could connect Asher to me, and I could connect Zareta to Asher and lead the police to him, and this police...

And I knew the answer. The whole thing.

I knew what had been wrong about the package I had delivered. It was still there, open on the table next to the guns of Zareta and Emil and the other two men. The sheets of folded paper, the documents, were blank. I had been paid a thousand dollars to deliver a package of blank paper to Constantine Zareta.

And as I was thinking all this I was out of that room and running along the dark hallway to the gray dawn light of the front door. I thought it all, and grabbed Zareta's own automatic from the table, and was running out the front door into the morning like a racer coming around the last turn.

They had reached the sidewalk at the foot of the brownstone steps. The door of Pearce's black car was open. The man stood in the dawn not ten feet from the Captain's car. A stocky patrolman with an automatic in his hands. In both hands. A long-barreled automatic that was no part of the equipment of a New York City patrolman. An automatic aimed straight at Constantine Zareta.

I had no time to shout or even aim.

Zareta had seen the man now. And Captain Pearce. Emil had seen him. None of them could have moved in time.

I fired on the run. Three shots.

I never did know where the first went.

The second shot smashed a window of Pearce's black car.

The third hit the fake cop in the arm. Not much, a graze that barely needed a Band-Aid later, but enough. The assassin's arm jerked and he missed Constantine Zareta by inches.

Pearce, Emil and five real patrolmen swarmed the gunman under like an avalanche on the Yorkville street.

***

I never learned Paul Asher's real name, or who he really was, or where he came from. No one did. No one ever will.

No one will visit his grave in Potter's Field out on Hart Island in the East River. He's buried out there under a marker with only his false name on it. Nameless, even to his partner in the assassination plot, the phony patrolman.

The fake policeman never told us his real name either. No one came forward to identify him or even visit him. No one ever has or ever will while he serves his time up in Auburn. He never told us who sent them to kill Zareta, or what their cause was, their reason, but he didn't mind telling us the unimportant parts, and that it had been Paul Asher's plan all the way. A plan that had very nearly worked.

"Himself?" Captain Pearce said as we sat in his office.

It was late evening. Somehow it was hard to think that it was still the same day the police had pounded on my door at dawn. A century ago. The Captain looked out toward the distant East River as if waiting for it to rise up and drown us all.

"Himself," I said. "He had himself killed just to smoke Zareta out into the open where his partner could get a clear shot, to lull Zareta into dropping his guard for an instant. He died so Zareta would die."

"To do his job," Pearce said. "And he almost made it."

"Because I missed it," I said. "Missed that package of blank paper, and missed what Zareta really told me. When he asked how you knew about him and Asher, and realized that it had to be through me, I should have understood. I was the only one in New York who could have connected Asher and Zareta, and I brought the police to Zareta. He said it, and I missed it."

"We all missed it then," Pearce said. "Even Zareta."

Six killers had tried for Constantine Zareta and failed. So Paul made his own plan. The fake patrolman told us all about it. He was proud of the plan, proud of Paul Asher.

"He picked you," Pearce went on in the silent office, "because he heard you were especially close to the police through Gazzo. He sent you to Zareta so you'd know where Zareta was, and so Zareta wouldn't be alarmed when you brought the police. He put your cards in his pocket, wrote your name and the date in his book, and had his partner kill him and dump his body under the bridge. So we would go to you, and you would take us to Zareta, and we'd bring Zareta out in the open."

Paul Asher, dead, had sent the police to me, and I had taken them to Zareta where his partner lay in wait. Even a rat fights to survive, but Paul Asher died just to do his job. His life and death no more than a tool in his own plan for his cause.

I said, "Every assassin expects to die if he succeeds, maybe even if he fails, but Asher died without knowing if he would succeed or fail. Anything could go wrong. He died on the chance that his plan would work."

"He wasn't human." Pearce said.

There are people all over this world who will say that Paul Asher was a hero. The same people who can live with those eighty million dead, and maybe eight hundred million tomorrow or the next day, and go right on drinking beer and grabbing for a dollar. The Paul Ashers and Constantine Zaretas kill the way other men swat flies, and we let them. We've become used to it.

"He was human," I said. "That's the horror."

It's not the eighty million dead that really worry me, it's what those piled corpses have done to the rest of us in those eighty years. It's not the dead that scare me, it's the living.

THE EXISTENTIAL MAN

by Lee Killough

Lee Killough began publishing in 1970, but from the beginning she has been torn between science fiction and mysteries. The solution? Combine them. Though her short stories have usually been science fiction—her "Symphony For a Lost Traveler," *Analog*, 1984, garnering a nomination for a Hugo Award—most of her novels are equal parts SF and mystery. And a misspent youth addicted to cop shows like *Dragnet, Highway Patrol, Naked City,* and *M-Squad* has resulted in a particular fondness for cops: future cops Janna Brill and Mama Maxwell in three novels combined in an omnibus edition, *Bridling Chaos*...space-going cops in *Deadly Silents*...a vampire cop in two novels also combined in an omnibus edition, *BloodWalk.* A third Garreth novel, *Blood Games*, will be published in the summer of 2001 and she is currently working on a novel with a werewolf cop. She lives and writes in the unmysterious Manhattan, Kansas, where her significant other is a book dealer.

THE EXISTENTIAL MAN

by Lee Killough

The gun muzzle gaped like a cave before the condemned man's eyes. He screamed silently behind his gag...furious, terrified, disbelieving. I *can't really be about to die*. He struggled to breathe through his smashed nose. I *can't end here, not like this!* In the mud of a riverbank, trussed like an animal for slaughter. Someone would see them. A full moon shone overhead, for god's sake! Help had to come in time to save him!

He kicked at his executioner, but his legs, cramped from hours in the car trunk, jerked without control. The killer cocked his gun.

Terror and fury blazed to incandescence. The condemned man glared over his gag at the shadowed face. *No! I refuse to die! And I sure as hell won't let you get away with what you've done, you fucking bastard! Somehow, some way, I'll find a way to...*

Ripping pain cut off the thought.

***

Sergeant David Amaro shaded his camera lens from the glare of July sunlight off the river. Sweat trickled down his neck. What the hell had possessed him to volunteer for this floater call? Granted, it could be worse. At least the sodden body sprawled on the riverbank did not smell.

David focused the lens for close-ups of the shattered, exposed bone where a face had been, then on the large hole in the

69

forehead. "Do you mind repeating your story once more, Mr. Ballard?"

The fisherman sighed. "My hook snagged off my hat and the current carried it into this backwater. When I waded in after it I saw...his face just under the water." The fisherman paused. "Why dump him where the river's so shallow?"

David shrugged. "Intelligence isn't a prerequisite for crime. Thank you. We won't keep you any longer."

The fisherman hesitated, glancing from David to the coroner and ambulance attendants, obviously reluctant to give up the thrill of his part in a police investigation, before picking up his tackle box and trudging away.

David watched him pass the uniformed officers securing the crime scene perimeter, then turned back to the river. *Had* the killer dumped the body in shallow water? The woods marking the normal water level stood ten feet back from this year's shoreline.

"How long has he been dead, Doc?"

Dr. Miles Jacobs peeled open the shirt to expose the chest. "Hard to say. The fish have done a job on all the exposed flesh so he's been in the water a while. Looks like I'll find a lot of him gone to adipocere. Until the autopsy, my best guess is one to five years."

The skin under the shirt looked dark and leathery. One to five years...but it could be even longer. David remembered reading of adipocere, fatty tissues changed chemically to waxy material, preserving bodies for decades. "Do you suppose we can get fingerprints?"

Jacobs examined the clenched fists, cut loose from the wire binding the wrists to a concrete block. "Maybe. I'll see at the autopsy tomorrow." He stepped back. "If you'll finish we'll pack him up and be on our way."

David pulled on a pair of surgical gloves from the crime scene kit and reached for the nearest pocket of the dead man's trousers. But as he touched the fabric, a storm of emotions blasted him...furious anger, bowel-loosening terror, driving urgency.

Get him! a voiceless cry screamed in his head. *Burn the fucking scum who did this to me!*

"Amaro? What's wrong?"

David glanced up to see Jacobs eyeing him in concern. He ducked back over the body. "Nothing. Just a lunch hamburger versus the heat." No way would he mention the voice and have everyone accuse him of going wacko again.

The pockets contained nothing. The hands bore no watch or rings. Stepping back, David stripped off the gloves and scrubbed his hands on his trousers. But the voice continued in his head.

It raged on even with the body hauled away, and while he and the uniformed officers assisting in the crime scene investigation searched the area. They turned up trash and tracks, but none appeared more than a few months old, and all more related to fishing and canoeing than murder.

About what David expected. He had a better chance of winning the lottery than finding any relevant physical evidence of the murder after all the time and weather since...

The thought choked off in a new wave of terror. The scene blurred to a double exposure, the river running simultaneously sunlit and sheened with moonlight. Terrible chill gripped him...followed by an explosion in his head.

"Sergeant Amaro?"

The uniforms stared at him. David fought panic. Could he be going psycho again? He forced a grin. "I've had vision. Of air-conditioning. Let's pack it in."

Back at the Law Enforcement Center across the alley from the county court house, David nodded to a deputy coming out of the Sheriff's Office then pushed through the door into the detectives' squadroom on the PD side of the corridor.

He dropped into his desk chair and pressed the heels of his hands against his eyes, willing the voice to shut up. With all the victims deserving righteous wrath—high school kids killed by crack and meth, the Chaffin girl's strangulation still unsolved after two years—why did this one affect him so much more? The manner of death suggested an execution, a falling out of thieves.

"You all right, Dave?"

David made himself raise his brows at Lieutenant Christopher. "I'm fine."

His lanky commander rested a hip on the edge of the desk. "You look a bit like you did when..."

No need to finish. David knew what he meant.

Memory told David he kissed Jan goodbye that Tuesday two years ago and drove straight to headquarters. Except he walked in on *Wednesday* morning.

Fellow officers testified he had come in Tuesday, but left again to investigate the new influx of drugs in the area, and never came back. They found his car in the high school parking lot. Several students remembered talking to him. But what happened after that? He returned with a nightmare but no sign of physical injury, clean-shaven and neatly dressed...just stripped of possessions as well as memory...gun, ID, handcuffs, keys, even his watch and wedding ring. Investigation failed to trace him, and the shrinks to recover his memory.

He brought up a report form on his computer. "I'm feeling the heat is all. Do you want to know about the body?"

Christopher eyed him, then nodded.

David consulted his notebook. "Dead over a year. Male, black hair, about five-eleven, mid-thirties, average weight. Possibly Hispanic. Complexion...hard to tell with the skin discoloration. Not exactly a unique description; it stretches to fit even me. Shot through the forehead with a large caliber weapon, maybe a .45."

"What's your game plan?"

He shrugged. "See if the autopsy gives us anything useful. Check missing persons reports. Run his prints through NCIC. Contact informants about criminal disputes over the past several years. The regular routine."

But David knew he lied. The anger of the dead man beating him made this one anything but routine.

***

He fled down a long, dark tunnel. Heavy breath snarled behind him. Terror kept David from looking back at what pursued him, but every instinct screamed against letting it catch him.

Ahead glowed the end of the tunnel. The golden light there promised sanctuary and peace. David struggled toward it, breath scorching his throat.

Figures moved in the light ahead. David fought for breath to call. "Help!"

The figures turned. The breathing behind rasped louder with every step.

"*Please* help me!"

Why did they always just stand there! The terror behind blasted him with fetid, suffocating breath. Claws closed on his shoulder.

Bitter cold and white-hot heat spread out through his body from their touch. He screamed, fighting the grip. But as always the claws bit deeper, pulling him back...turning him. And as the terror came into view...

He woke thrashing.

Jan threw her arms around him. "David! It's all right! You've had a nightmare, but it's over now and you're safe."

He buried his head against her breasts, drinking in her familiar scent, the silk of her skin, clutching at the security of her reality. "I love you."

Her cheek rubbed the top of his head. "What was it about?"

"I don't know." The truth could only worry her. "It's the kind you can't remember."

Presently she went back to sleep, but David could not make himself close his eyes again. He lay awake the rest of the night, cold with remembered terror.

***

In daylight, the nightmare faded beneath the routine of investigation as David combed through missing persons records. Even a rat pack member must have people who cared enough to miss him. To be thorough, he went back ten years, and checked not only his department's records but those of the Sheriff's Office and the MPs at neighboring Fort Carey. Eight men fit his dead man's description.

By noon he sat at his desk going through the eight missing persons reports. At the desk back-to-back with his, Bill Purviance snarled over a file of his own.

David raised his brows. "Your drug case not going well?"

Purviance grimaced. "I can't get a hold on this Stacey kid."

David sympathized. "I never could, either."

"He's like Teflon!" Purviance slapped the folder closed. "He smells every plant, undercover officer, and wire a mile away. I'd try sweating the supplier's name out of him, but he'd just laugh at me. And then the supplier will find another dealer and we'll be back to fucking square one. How's your floater?"

"I'm trying to identify him." Anger swirled around David. He felt the pile of flesh and bone fuming at the hospital where it waited for today's autopsy. David gritted his teeth. *Back off! I'm doing what I can.* After waiting so long to have his death discovered, John Doe could wait a few more days for retribution.

But the demand for immediate action nagged at David until he scooped together the photographs of his possibles and headed for the door.

Most of the informants rose late. Only a handful held day jobs. Like Arlie Rudd at the European Motors garage. "Do you know any of these faces?"

Arlie wiped his hands on a shop rag before picking up the photos. "You think one might be the dude in the river?" He flipped through the stack. Twice he paused, giving David hope, but when he handed the photos back, he shook his head. "Sorry, man. None of them rings a bell."

"Maybe you can think of someone who might not be reported missing because of what he was into and with whom?"

Arlie picked up a socket wrench and leaned back under the hood of an MGB. "I haven't heard of anything recent."

"This wouldn't be recent. It could be anytime up to five to ten years ago."

Arlie hooted. "Ten years! Man, you're talking ancient history. No one remembers that far back!"

"The killer might. You listen around, like at that midnight chop shop of yours, and see if finding this body has made anyone nervous."

Two other informants he found had no better information. Neither heard of any executions. Neither recognized the missing man as linked to criminal activity that might be fatal.

David headed for Jacobs' office at the hospital.

The pathologist relaxed in his desk chair, still in scrub clothes. "We had a time unclenching the fingers but here are your prints."

"Yes!" David snatched up the card Jacobs shoved across the desk. The squares designated for the thumbprints showed only smudges, but the fingertips produced discernible ridge patterns...all ulnar loops except for a tented arch on the right index finger. With luck he would have an ID by tomorrow. "What else can you tell me?"

The pathologist sucked on an empty pipe. "He died of a bullet fired through his frontal bone and exiting through the occipital bone. No surprises there. He also sustained multiple facial fractures...a broken nose several hours before dying then malar and maxillary fractures post mortem. The fracture lines indicate numerous blows from something broad and flat."

Such as a concrete block? David's stomach lurched at the image of the killer pounding identity out of the dead face. "Any change in your estimate of the time of death?"

Jacobs shook his head. "Sorry."

So much for that. "What about distinguishing details?"

"He didn't smoke." Air hissed through the empty pipe. "X-rays showed retained lower wisdom teeth, very few fillings, and old healed fractures of the distal right radius and ulna and left second and third metacarpals."

The dead man broke a hand? Driving back to headquarters, David rubbed his own left hand, slammed in a car door by an angry motorist, and grimaced in displeasure. Just what he needed, shared trauma to give the dead man added hold over him.

At headquarters he wired the prints to the FBI's National Criminal Information Center, then began calling relatives of the missing men to ask about habits and medical histories. Had their husband...brother...father...son ever broken his right wrist and left hand? Did the missing man smoke? Would they please give him the name of their dentist?

The questions eliminated most of the men. They had the wrong number of wisdom teeth, and either they had never broken a bone or they broke different ones than the dead man. The three names left remained mostly because of unknown dental and fracture histories.

The watch ended without word from NCIC on the fingerprints.

***

The tunnel seemed darker than ever...colder, longer. David fled in even greater desperation, straining toward the light. Yet the horror behind gained just as fast. Its claws closed on his shoulder, and from beyond the excruciating cold and heat came the voice he associated with the dead man. *No you don't! First you have to nail that murdering bastard.*

The claws dragged David around.

He woke drenched and shaking but, this time, without screaming. Jan slept undisturbed against him.

He sat up and stared into the darkness. Now the dead man had joined the horror. Or...*had* he just joined? One to five years ago put the death within the time frame of David's lost day. Did the events connect? Did that account for the dead man's effect on him?

Which suggested a more disturbing question. Had his vision at the river been something seen through the dead man's eyes or...his own?

He had been hunting the drug supplier whose junk killed three kids, working the case with righteous wrath. In the darkness, David ran hands back through sweaty hair. Had he caught up with the scum and lost control? According to the shrink, amnesia resulted from an experience so traumatic that the mind rejected all memory of it. Violating his cherished belief in law and due process could fall into that category.

His gut knotted. What *had* he done that missing day?

***

The report on the dead man's prints came back from NCIC shortly before noon. David snatched the teletype from the secretary and read it with fingers crossed. But the charm failed. The FBI had no match in their criminal files. He slam-dunked the message in his wastebasket. This damned case refused to give him a break!

He teletyped back to Washington requesting that the prints be checked against the civilian files, then shoved on his sunglasses and headed for the parking lot. It appeared he must make his own break.

First stop...Rusty Ubel at the Easy-Cash pawn shop on the road west out of town.

Opening the door brought a welcoming wave of cool air and a two-tone chime. At the sound, carroty hair and a pair of eyes appeared above the rear edge of a display case. "Sergeant Amaro. I heard you were looking for me yesterday."

David nodded. "I need to know if any of these men look familiar." He held out the three photos.

A short arm reached up from behind the display case for them. "Ah. The body in..."

Screaming brakes interrupted him. David raced for the door. On Prairie Boulevard outside, a driver swore at a boy on a skateboard.

From under the arm David used to hold the door open, Rusty sniffed. "Crazy kids."

Agreed, David reflected, remembering his own skateboarding days. He and his friends not only darted through traffic, they caught tows on passing cars and trucks. It took a broken arm to convince him of the stupidity of...

The thought stumbled. That break had been in his right arm...the distal end of the radius and ulna. The same place the dead man broke his.

A chill slid down his spine. First the similarity of hand fractures, now this. What were the odds of him sharing not only physical description but medical history with a victim? And dental history. He, too, retained just his lower wisdom teeth. Still, it had to be coincidence. What else *could* it be?

David turned his hands palm up. Fingerprints would prove the coincidence. When he got back to headquarters he would...

The thought remained unfinished. The sunlight at the open door highlighted the ridges of his fingers enough to see the general pattern. David's breath stuck in his chest. The highlighting showed ulnar loops on finger after finger...except for the tented arch on the right index finger.

"Sergeant! What's wrong?"

The nightmare tunnel stretched before him. Fiery cold claws clamped on his shoulder. The pain sapped all his strength, destroying resistance to the pull. Inexorably, he turned, and saw...a man standing over him on the riverbank, silhouetted against the moonlit sky. A gun muzzle pressed against his forehead. He glared up at the silhouette, fury raging in him. *Somehow I'll get you.* Then the night disappeared in excruciating noise and pain.

David bolted for his car and gunned it out of the parking space. *No!* He could not be the dead man! He breathed; his heart beat; he bled when he nicked himself shaving. How existential could life be? *I think I am; therefore, I am?*

Yet the voice of the shrink two years ago murmured over his denials. He lost a day. Amnesia resulted from the need to forget some trauma. What trauma could be greater than his own violent death?

A blaring horn jerked his attention back to driving. He braked in mid-turn to avoid an oncoming car. After it passed, he saw why he turned, and grinned. Yes! The high school parking lot, the last place he had been seen his missing day. Tracking himself would prove that riverbank had nothing to do with him.

In the parking lot he sat on the hood of the parked car, concentrating, willing himself to remember. But his mind remained blank. Over and over, however, his gaze wandered to the sandstone wall on the north side of the parking lot, separating the campus from Memorial Cemetery.

That seemed little to go on. Still, what else did he have? David trotted across to the wall and vaulted it.

Standing in the cemetery felt...familiar. Encouraged, he started forward between the headstones, trying not to think, just move.

To his surprise, his feet took him to the gutted old bell tower in the middle of the cemetery. He stared at it. Why come here? Connie Chaffin had not been his case.

Then, why did he think of her? Because her strangled body had been found here?

She was running one time and saw them.

Someone said that to him, said it the day he vanished. A girl's voice. Who? Of course...Kim Harris, one of Connie's girlfriends. He had been asking about Brad Stacey and the Harris girl started talking about Connie. *"She saw Brad with someone."*

Saw him where? David looked around. Connie, a star of the girls' track team, ran every noon, often in the cemetery. Her failure to show up for afternoon classes started the search which ended at the bell tower. Did she see a meeting here?

She also ran along Deer Creek, he remembered hearing. The stream had cut a ravine behind the high school and cemetery and on north through a residential area.

David slid down the side of the ravine and leaped the stream to the path on the far side, worn hard and even by the track team and local joggers. In his head his conversation with the Harris girl replayed as though it had never been lost.

"When did she tell you about seeing Brad?" he asked.

"That morning...you know, the day she..." Tears cut off the sentence.

Had someone overheard? Did that conversation doom Connie?

That day David had followed the creek path, just as he did now...looking for places Connie could have seen Stacey and his supplier.

Passing the boundary of the cemetery and into the residential area, cold grabbed David's guts. His heart hammered. The trees arching together over the ravine reminded him of his nightmare tunnel. Balconies and windows of the Westminster Apartment complex looked down from beyond the trees on the eastern rim. Did Connie see Stacey up there? Or maybe around one of the houses along the western side? Steps led up from the ravine into most of the back yards.

Steps. Memory clicked. He had climbed steps. Stone steps. To...somewhere with bright flowers. He studied the houses. Several had stone steps, but only one a greenhouse. Sight of it brought a wave of fury and terror.

He savored the emotions with satisfaction. So, the horror began up there. He leaned against a tree and let memory flow.

Answering his tap on the glass had been a gray-haired man who carried himself with military erectness. Being this close to Fort Carey, a number of officers retired here.

David showed his ID. "May I talk to you, Captain...?

The firm chin lifted. "It's Major...Major Charles Burris, retired."

Behind the major, flowers in riotous colors filled the green-house. "Those are beautiful," David said.

The stiff shoulders relaxed. "Aren't they? I did some advisory work in Central America after my formal retirement and fell in love with the jungle flora. So I brought back seeds and cuttings."

Advisory work? Mercenary, he meant. It conjured up an interesting image...the major in camouflage fatigues and face paint pausing on a jungle march to admire flowers. David moved down the benches. "They must take a lot of work." Which would keep him in the greenhouse for long periods.

"Hours every day." Burris raised an eyebrow. "But I'm sure you're not here to talk about flowers."

"True. You have a good view of people on the ravine path from here."

"The joggers and dog walkers? Yes." The major nodded.

"Do you remember ever seeing Connie Chaffin?"

The major's face went grave. "The girl strangled last week? That was so...senseless. Yes, I saw her often. But not that day she was killed, as I told the detective who talked to me. Do you have a new lead on her death?"

An intensity in his tone had caught David's ear. He eyed the major more closely. "You know how these things go...check and recheck everything." He paused. "Have you seen a boy, tall, over six feet, very thin, white-blond hair? He would probably have been in street clothes, not running gear."

Burris had pursed his lips. "Offhand, no, I don't remember a boy like that. Sorry."

But the major's pupils dilated during the description of Stacey, and dilated again while denying seeing him. Every cop instinct in David snapped to attention. *Liar*, that dilatation screamed. What if Burris brought more than flower seeds back from Central America? The man deserved checking. "Well, thank you for your time." He turned to leave.

Just as a tall, thin, white-blond boy bounded through the door. "Major, that Harris bitch told..." He stopped short, staring at David.

Two thoughts collided in David. *Gotcha!* And *Oh, shit!* Movement flashed at the edge of his vision. He ducked too late. Burris smashed a flowerpot square in his face. David's nose flattened in blinding agony that paralyzed him long enough for the other two to pin, disarm, and tie him. They emptied his pockets and stripped off his watch and wedding ring, then carried him into the garage adjoining the greenhouse and dumped him in the trunk of the major's car.

The major slammed the trunk closed. "Now, what was it you were about to tell me, Brad?"

David missed the answer, but he guessed that Stacey told Burris about Kim Harris talking to their prisoner. Burris' crisp voice came back, "...so she won't mention her conversations with the girl and cop to anyone else, but without leaving any marks on her."

Leaning against the tree beneath the major's greenhouse, David understood why no one had tracked him past the high school. Fear kept Kim Harris from repeating what she told him.

So, now he had his day back...and had identified the dead man. He could no longer deny what he was. And with acceptance, fear disappeared. But not the hatred of his killer. What to do about Burris? He lacked proof the major killed Connie Chaffin, and he could hardly arrest the man for murdering David Amaro, despite the fingerprint evidence. Thoughts of nailing Burris on drug charges did not satisfy him at all. David wanted the major for murder, for his and Connie's and the kids destroyed by the major's drugs. He wanted Burris revealed to the world as scum, wanted him blackened, reviled, hated, and, most of all, dead.

And he knew just how to do that. David bared his teeth. It bypassed due process, but what the hell did a dead man care about due process?

A great sense of freedom filled him. Humming, David mounted the steps to the yard next to Burris and showed his ID to the woman who answering his rap on the back door. "May I please use your phone?"

When she showed him to an extension in the kitchen, he looked up Burris in the phone book and punched in the number. "Hello?"

The major's crisp voice sent a shaft of fury through David. He did not bother hiding the anger in his voice, just whispered to keep the residents of the house from hearing. "Major, I know all about your drug business. Meet me in your greenhouse in two minutes if you don't want me talking to the police." David jiggled the switch hook and punched the Law Enforcement Center's number. "Kate, this is David Amaro," he told the dispatcher who answered. "I've just learned that Connie Chaffin saw the Stacey kid's drug supplier. So the supplier killed her. He's a retired army major named Charles Burris. He also murdered my guy in the river. Send backup to 610 Franklin Drive."

He left the house, vaulted the fence into Burris's back yard, and opened the greenhouse door. Stepping over the threshold brought a shiver of remembered terror...quickly replaced by grim anticipation.

Inside, the major stood silhouetted against the glow of ultraviolet lights over the tables. "I don't know who the hell you are or what drug business you're talking about, but I don't tolerate being threatened."

David felt stunned. Burris did not *recognize* him? He hurled his badge case at the major. "The name is David Amaro, you bastard! Maybe you can forget a man whose head you've blown off, but I sure as hell haven't forgotten you? And your ass is mine, slimeball."

Burris opened the badge case. Now he remembered. David saw it in his face. But Burris remained composed. He tossed back the ID and shoved his hands in the rear pockets of his jeans. "You're raving. If I killed you, how do you come to be standing there? You surely don't expect me to believe you're a ghost." His right hand came back into sight...holding a .45 that must have been stuck in the back of his waistband. "Instead, I believe you're a trespasser who makes me fear for my life."

Fierce joy blazed in David. *Gotcha!* "You damned well should fear. I'm taking you down." He moved as though to reach for a gun.

As the .45 flashed fire, David reminded himself: *You're only as real as you believe. The bullet can't hurt you.* Sure enough, he felt no pain, though the wound spurted blood. Behind him, a section of the greenhouse wall shattered.

Grinning, David stalked toward Burris. "You're wasting ammunition, Major. You can't kill me again."

Burris tried, firing repeatedly. Amid splintering glass and spraying blood, David continued forging forward.

Burris's eyes went wild and white. "Fall, damn you!" He backed away, still firing.

Before the major emptied the clip, David forced him against the garage well and shoved the gun upward so the barrel pointed back toward Burris himself. The next shot, by now fired in convulsive desperation, entered the major's throat and exploded out the top of his head.

As the major collapsed, David heard the whoop of an approaching siren. Relief filled him. Good. He could leave everything else to the police.

***

It made a hell of a report to write. Officers arriving to back up Amaro met an hysterical neighbor with a story of hearing gunfire and running to her kitchen window to see her neighbor in his greenhouse firing bullet after bullet into a detective who had used her phone just minutes before. They found only the major's body in the greenhouse, however...amid a scene that belonged in a slaughterhouse, with blood splashed and smeared and pooled everywhere. Except for a bloody pile of clothing, Sergeant Amaro had disappeared. Lab tests showed most of the blood to be Amaro's type, and the bloody fingerprints on the edges of the tables matched his. The gun, however, bore only Burris's prints.

"What do you think happened?" the investigating officer asked Lieutenant Christopher. "Where is Amaro's body? He couldn't have walked away after losing that much blood."

Christopher had no suggestions, especially after NCIC's report on the fingerprints of the dead man in the river. They found a match in their civilian section...a law enforcement officer named David Douglas Amaro.

After comparing the dead man's prints to those in the greenhouse and Amaro's personnel file, Christopher showed it all to the chief. "What do you think about this? What should we do?"

The chief studied the prints for a long time, then returned the personnel file to Christopher. "I think we tell the press that the officer who solved the Chaffin murder has probably paid for it with his life, with his body being removed by some accomplice the neighbor didn't see. As soon as possible we'll make sure Amaro's family receives his pension. We bury the file on the river body. The rest..." He tore the NCIC teletype into confetti. "The rest we forget."

*   *   *

Why should someone come to Mayhem?

There's nothing more enjoyable than talking with people who share one's love of a particular subject. Mayhem provides the time and space for meeting fellow mystery lovers, both readers and authors. And I particularly appreciate the intimate size of Mayhem, which permits meeting and talking with all the other members.

SATAN'S TEARS

by Gayle Lynds

Gayle Lynds is the author of international thrillers *Mesmerized, Mosaic,* and *Masquerade,* and the co-author with Robert Ludlum of *The Hades Factor.* Her books have sold to some 20 countries overseas and been named in Murder Ink's "Best Thrillers of the Year." She is a former newspaper reporter, magazine editor, and think-tank editor with top-secret security clearance.

SATAN'S TEARS

by Gayle Lynds

Josie didn't like Uncle Walter living in the closet. It just wasn't right. She'd told Aunt Bertha again this morning, but Aunt Bertha had ducked behind the door to be with Uncle Walter so she wouldn't have to answer. Uncle Walter, of course, never answered anybody. He'd been in the closet three years, eleven months, and nine days.

Josie remembered exactly because of the record she kept on the Union Pacific calendar. She'd got the calendar in 1986 and kept using it because it was free and she'd never found another one. In 1997 the calendar had fallen right again, just like it would in 2003. She'd got excited when she figured that out. Aunt Bertha said she was slow, but when she figured out something, it stuck to her good. Now she looked forward to 2003. Everything was a lot simpler on the right calendar years.

For instance, in 1997 she'd understood why Uncle Walter had to go in the closet, even though she hadn't liked it. But now she wasn't at all sure. He'd been in there long enough. He'd been punished enough and she missed him... Besides, there were problems about having him there, like the smell. At first it'd been terrible, stinking up the whole shack, even her clothes, until she'd got to where she didn't dare go outside. Someone for sure would smell Uncle Walter on her.

Because of the stink, the three of them—Uncle Walter, Aunt Bertha, and Josie—had their weekly groceries delivered to the back porch. The grocery boy had been told to leave the sack next

89

to the old Kelvinator washing machine where Aunt Bertha iced down her beer. Aunt Bertha'd drunk twelve beers after she put Uncle Walter in the closet. She'd been pretty upset.

Josie had tried to calm her, but Aunt Bertha would have none of it.

"Mind your mouth, girl!" Aunt Bertha'd say. "Walt's where he deserves to be! Now he won't go sniffin' after every skirt he squints at. Bout time that man got out of Satan's hands!"

Then Aunt Bertha got the broom and dust pan. Somehow before Uncle Walter went in the closet, Aunt Bertha'd dropped a full bottle of beer. The beer and wet pieces of glass had been all over the linoleum.

Although Josie wasn't there for this last argument between Aunt Bertha and Uncle Walter, she'd heard enough earlier ones that she could run them through her head backwards and forwards. He'd say, "I didn't do nothin'." She'd say, "I saw you down the alley behind Daisy's, kissin' her!" He'd say, "But she had somethin' in her eye and I couldn't let it stay there, could I?" She'd say, "I'd better not catch you around her again!" He'd say, "Now, Bertha. Now, Bertha." Then he'd pat her shoulder because she'd be crying.

Once, before he could pat her, Aunt Bertha had hauled off and swung a fist at him. She didn't have very good aim, probably because her eyes were full of tears. The swing took her full circle and when she'd come around again, Uncle Walter put his arms around her and kissed her until she stopped crying. They hadn't had a fight again for three weeks.

Josie'd been cleaning at her people's house the afternoon Uncle Walter went into the closet. He'd given her one of his special hugs and kisses before she'd left. When she got home, Aunt Bertha was already locking the closet door. No matter what she'd said, Aunt Bertha wouldn't let Uncle Walter out. But then, he must've felt pretty bad about everything because he'd never even asked to get out.

She was the first to say Aunt Bertha'd been good about taking care of him. Aunt Bertha had all her meals with him, carrying two dishes in and two dishes and a slop bucket out. Josie guessed that Uncle Walter might be happy. He'd never had such good service before and now maybe he didn't feel Satan's temptation to chase skirts. At least, that was the way Aunt Bertha explained it.

Josie sighed and slid down the wall beside the closet door. It was lonely in the old shack when Aunt Bertha went into the closet. She stared across the kitchen, through the broken glass window at the Kelvinator on the porch. Course, it'd never washed any clothes for them. It didn't work, Uncle Walter'd said. As far as she knew, it never had. For as long as she could remember, it'd held beer for her aunt and uncle. She never got any. They'd said she was too young and, besides, it was medicine for Aunt Bertha when she cried. Funny, though, Aunt Bertha hadn't cried on the day she'd drunk twelve beers after putting Uncle Walter in the closet. And she hadn't cried since.

Josie slap-slapped her foot on the linoleum, watched the narrow naked foot lift up and flop down. Her legs were naked, too. She had on a muumuu that Aunt Bertha'd found in one of the trash cans behind the Savings & Loan. She'd got skinny since Uncle Walter went into the closet. She stretched out her legs and felt the bones that ran like boards along the tops of them. Well, there just wasn't as much money for food with neither she nor Aunt Bertha cleaning for their people any more. They'd had to stop when the stink got bad. She thought the stink had been gone for about two years and six months. She couldn't be more exact because it'd seemed to go away a little at a time, but Aunt Bertha'd said it still clung to everything, like a fly to sticky paper, and they'd just got used to it.

She stared at her legs some more until finally the closet door opened and Aunt Bertha waddled out backwards. Aunt Bertha had a hard time getting around these days. She'd got fat. Josie couldn't figure that one out—why Aunt Bertha was fat because she sure didn't get any more to eat than Josie did. Anyway, being fat hadn't slowed her down. She still went out every day to visit trash cans, only now she wore a greasy trench coat instead of a black dress like she used to at her people's. Just last week Aunt Bertha'd found two cans of condensed milk and a half loaf of white bread with green stuff on it. That'd tasted so good, pouring the candy milk over the torn-up bread. Course, they'd ripped off the green stuff first. They'd had the bread and milk for dinner, she by herself and Aunt Bertha taking her share and Uncle Walter's into the closet.

It was a good thing Uncle Walter still got his social securities. That way they could rent the shack and buy a few groceries and beer. Josie's social securities had stopped when she turned twenty-two. Even though Aunt Bertha had argued with the government man, he'd said he had Josie's birth written down and the money had to stop. Uncle Sam said so, he explained, and after all, Josie wasn't a re-tard and due more benefits. She remembered nodding. She knew there was no getting around it. Her head for figuring told her that.

Aunt Bertha stepped back from the closet, her eyes glued to it as she closed the door. She pulled the key from her apron pocket to lock it like she always did. Then she looked down, lifted her heels in a little jump, and squealed.

"Goodness, child! You gave me a start! What're you doin' sittin' on the floor there?" Her pale face quivered as she glared at Josie.

They hadn't been getting along lately because of Uncle Walter's living arrangement and now Aunt Bertha looked like she was just waiting for a remark about it. Josie decided not to disappoint her.

"When're you gonna let Uncle Walter out?"

Aunt Bertha's eyes narrowed and she shook her fist with the key in it. "Don't you start in on me again, girl!" she yelled. "Don't you do that!"

Josie stood up. "I'll bet he don't like it in there. *I* wouldn't!"

Aunt Bertha grunted and adjusted the trench coat under the apron. She hadn't taken the trench coat off since April 29, 1997. When she was going out to trash, she'd take off the apron. But now, since she was home, she wore it over the trench coat. She dropped the key into the apron pocket and gave Josie a look that would fry bricks.

Aunt Bertha snapped, "You're a fool, girl!" Then she wheedled, "Don't I feed you, take care of you? Don't I find you pretty dresses like that one there?" She pointed at the muumuu. "And look how you treat me, your very own aunt, the only one you got, the only one you're ever gonna get? Just what you think you'd a done if I hadn't took care of you after your Mam and Pap got themselves dead? Huh?"

Josie hung her head. Aunt Bertha was right. She didn't even remember her folks. That'd been twenty years, four months, and fourteen days ago that they'd been killed in a car smash. She'd come to Aunt Bertha and Uncle Walter with only the clothes on her back. Aunt Bertha'd told her that many times. Josie worried that she had nothing from her folks, no gift, no sign, no remembrance that they'd ever even lived, but what could she do? She didn't think she was smart enough to figure out how to get a sign or a remembrance, especially since she'd left school one day in grade three.

"Now, girl," Aunt Bertha announced. "I tell you what we're gonna do. We're *not* gonna fight about this again. Walt's happy in his closet. He's got more peace from Satan there than he ever did have out here. You don't want to upset his peace, do you?"

Josie hung her head lower. She didn't want to upset either of them. They'd taken her in, raised her. Still, she'd like to see Uncle Walter again, see his long bumpy face with the smile that made her tingle. He'd been so good to her, giving her red hots every night when he and Aunt Bertha settled down for their beers. Aunt Bertha never gave her red hots. Yes, Uncle Walter'd been nice to her, even nicer as she'd grown older. He told her stories and jokes, and she'd laughed, not so much about what he'd said, but because she was happy being with him and he looked just as happy being with her. She'd never felt like getting hugs and kisses from anyone else, not that anyone ever offered any, not even Aunt Bertha.

Yes, that was the thing about Uncle Walter and his closet, and that was the problem of these three years, eleven months, and none days. She missed Uncle Walter. She couldn't figure out to her satisfaction why he had to stay in that closet, and she didn't know where to start.

She watched Aunt Bertha shrug and plod towards the back porch and the Kelvinator. When Aunt Bertha was out of sight, she stared at the closet door. She wished she could spend a moment with Uncle Walter.

She touched the doorknob, watched her hand close over it. Had Aunt Bertha locked it this time? She didn't remember the key's ever finding its way into the lock. Maybe Aunt Bertha'd been too busy waving it at her...

She stared at her hand some more. It was moving, turning the doorknob. She wondered whether it was doing it all by itself or maybe Satan was making it do it. Satan. Sometimes he felt so good to her. She wondered why. When the door finally clicked open, she didn't care. So maybe Satan was making her open that door, but she didn't care.

She pulled it and at the same time heard the back door slam and Aunt Bertha screech.

"Josie! Don't do that!"

Josie pulled the door wide and heard a loud thud-bounce as Aunt Bertha's beer bottle fell.

"Uncle Walter!" she cried. "Come on out!"

The light from the kitchen spilled into the closet and Josie screamed and crashed to the floor, Aunt Bertha on top of her.

She screamed not from Aunt Bertha's weight, but from what she'd seen in the shadow of the closet. She twisted her head and looked again, her stomach going loose and shaky, her heart pounding, and then her aunt's hands closed over her eyes. In the darkness of her mind, she still saw him. She screamed again. Uncle Walter was skin and bones, dressed only in his under-drawers, black stuff caking and peeling all over his head, the bones in him poking through brown holes where his skin was gone. She didn't have to think hard to figure it out. Uncle Walter was dead. Her whole body ached with her loss.

"Josie! Josie!" Aunt Bertha bleated. "Why'd you have to see?" She seemed to soften and thicken over Josie. "Why'd you have to see?"

Josie tried to wriggle around, get some air. Her stomach did flip-flops and she had a pain right near her heart. It occurred to her that this was the first time she remembered her aunt's touching her.

"Josie! I had to do it! He had to be saved from Satan!"

Josie's mind had fixed on Uncle Walter's blackened head. What was that all about?

"I've kept you all these years, child! Don't forget that!" Aunt Bertha bellowed, her voice filling with tears. "I've kept Walt, too! He don't have Satan's curse any more. He's been saved! He's at peace! And we still got the social securities!"

Aunt Bertha dropped a hand from one of Josie's eyes and moved it towards the beer bottle on the floor.

Josie began to understand, just as she had with the calendar. Her breath came in short little bursts. She knew that Aunt Bertha was going to conk her with that bottle just like she'd conked Uncle Walter.

"Josie, honey! I don't want to do it, but you disobeyed me!"

A deep burning filled Josie. She was faster than her aunt. She grabbed the bottle and raised it.

"Satan's got you!" Aunt Bertha screeched, staring up at the bottle, her hands scratching the air.

Josie conked Aunt Bertha. Aunt Bertha yelled. Josie conked Aunt Bertha again and again. Aunt Bertha cried, moaned, and twitched. The bottle broke and Aunt Bertha lay quiet.

Uncle Walter used to have the best hands. Sometimes he'd let them slide along his overalls and she'd hear little snaps as the rough skin caught the cloth. Sometimes he'd cut his nails and yellow calluses with his pocket knife. When Uncle Walter touched her, she didn't feel the roughness and soreness of his hands, and she didn't think he did either. All she felt was good. He used to keep the red hots in the front pocket of his overalls. She wished he had his overalls on now. The red hots were always warm when he gave them to her.

Josie shoved Aunt Bertha off and went into the closet. She sat down across from Uncle Walter, said hi, and kicked the closet door closed.

*   *   *

Mayhem in the Midlands means great information, great camaraderie, and great fun for anyone who loves to read, for pre-published writers seeking guidance and tips, and for well-published authors who are ready to relax and hang out with fellow book-lovers in a beautiful, historic hotel in one of the Midwest's loveliest old cities.

STORMY WEATHER

by Susan McBride

Susan McBride is the author of *And Then She Was Gone*, nominated for a Reviewers' Choice Award for Best First Mystery, and *Overkill*, her second Maggie Ryan novel. Her essay "Getting It" appears in *Living the Writer's Life* (Tarcher/Putnam), and her regular column "From the Trenches" can be found at the Charlotte Austin Review on-line.

STORMY WEATHER

by Susan McBride

What a miserable day.

Helen frowned as she peered out the windshield, the wipers swishing back and forth with singsong regularity. Rain pelted the glass in thick sheets as the car glided through the wet streets. The old buildings in downtown Alton hovered on her either side like hazy gray ghosts.

Godforsaken weather, she thought, switching on the defroster to clear the condensation.

Cassie needs you, she kept telling herself, despite the voice inside her head warning her she should've stayed home. Her eyesight was bad enough without the rain to further dim it, and her reflexes weren't as sharp as they used to be.

She'd be seventy-five on her next birthday, though she felt no more than fifty on days when her joints didn't ache and her plumbing didn't kink. She'd lost her husband to a heart attack three years before and had seen more than a few of her friends fall by the wayside in between. That she still breathed with her own lungs, walked without assistance on her own two legs and kept her mind quick enough to win at bridge now and again was pretty good these days, she figured, when nearly everything you ate, inhaled or drank could do you in.

She crossed the bridge linking Illinois to Missouri, concentrating on keeping the car between the metal grids and the yellow line. Only once did her gaze stray from the road to the choppy brown waters of the Mississippi.

A pair of high-beamed lights swung toward Helen suddenly, briefly blinding her, and she swerved right, losing her breath for a moment until she straightened out the car again. Her heart pounded fiercely in her ears.

This is crazy, she told herself. Only fools and ducks were out today. But Cassie was in some sort of trouble. Something wasn't as it should be.

She signed, gripping the steering wheel like a lifeline as the truck in front of her threw back water in continuous waves. She flipped her wipers to hyper speed, half her mind on the road and the other half on Cassie.

The girl might've tried to hide her distress, but it was there all right. Helen had sensed it as clearly as she would a pebble in her shoe. She hadn't seen Cass much since she'd moved to well-heeled Frontenac in the suburbs of St. Louis. Her niece had seemed happy enough at first, taking a job as an assistant with an art dealer, jetting with him back and forth to Europe and the Far East all in search of, as Cassie put it, "another treasure."

Another treasure, hmm?

Sometimes Helen wondered if that fellow Cass worked for didn't like having her near for other reasons. Her niece was certainly pretty and smart, too. She'd graduated at the top of her class from the university, had gotten a job right off with a museum. And then she'd met up with...oh, dear, what was his name?

She scrunched up her brow, squinting at the foggy stretch of highway, envisioning the good-looking man Cassie had introduced her to at the gallery.

Jasper Cornwall.

That was it.

Helen smiled at herself, glad for proof that her gray cells hadn't deserted her so quickly as the dark hue of her hair and the narrowness of her waist.

Anyhow, Cornwall had needed a right hand, and Cassie had jumped at his offer. The two had rubbed shoulders once or twice at auctions, and Cassie had been thrilled that he'd chosen her to fill the spot.

Helen had been equally pleased when the girl had moved within an hour's drive of Chautauqua. "Keep an eye on her for us," her sister Marianne had called from Wisconsin to request. Helen did try, inviting Cassie to Chautauqua for weekends, even outings to the ballpark to see the Cardinals play, but Cassie was always too busy. She figured they hadn't seen one another more than three, maybe four times in nearly six months.

"Can't that man ever give you a minute off?" she'd grumbled when they'd gone shopping at Frontenac Plaza awhile back.

Cass had only laughed.

But just last week when Helen had phoned after not having heard from the girl in awhile, her niece hadn't sounded so cheerful. "What's wrong?" she'd asked. "It's work, isn't it? That fellow's a slave driver, I tell you."

"It's nothing," Cass had insisted. "Nothing you can help with. I've got to deal with it myself, in my own way."

Helen had felt instantly uneasy at her tone of voice, too soft and unconvincing. "Come on. Fess up," she'd prodded. "I'm not your mother, just your auntie."

"I can't talk now, all right? I've got to run." The girl had replied, sounding so pale and distant that Helen had started to worry all over again.

Then Cass had hung up.

Helen had tried calling the next day and the day after that, but had only gotten as far as Cassie's answering machine. Her messages had gone unreturned.

When Helen had finally caught her at the gallery yesterday morning, she'd ignored Cassie's protests, insisting they go out for Sunday brunch. That way, she could at least get a good look at the girl for herself and try to pry out of her whatever was amiss.

"Let auntie fix it," she used to say when Cassie was a child and had stayed with her and Joe up in Chautauqua during summer vacations. She only wished it were so easy now.

She exited the highway and headed south on Lindbergh, making her way cautiously through water-filled streets and finally pulling into a space in front of the townhouse where Cassie lived.

She parked the car and stared out into the downpour, deciding she'd better make a run for it. Joe wasn't there to come around with an umbrella to keep her dry. She was on her own now; though, after being wed for fifty years, it took some getting used to.

Tugging the hood of her raincoat up over her head and tucking her purse beneath, she pushed open the door and got out, her sneakers sloshing on the sidewalk as she hurried up to Cassie's door.

She rang the bell and waited underneath the overhang, pressing off her hood and wiping the damp from her cheeks. Then she shook the water from her arms and unzipped her jacket.

When no one answered, Helen tried the bell again, even knocking for good measure.

"Cass?" she called out. "Hello, Cassie?"

She had a key to the townhouse, one given her "just in case." She thought of digging into her purse for it, but tried the knob instead.

It turned in her hand, and she pushed the door wide.

"Cassie?"

The place was dark, the gloom of outdoors only adding to the dim. A light beckoned up the hallway, and Helen followed it to the master bedroom, her wet sneakers noisily squishing on the wall-to-wall carpeting. The girl was probably still in the shower or buried deep in the closet deciding what to wear.

"Cass, it's me." Helen stepped inside the stark black and white room, letting her eyes roam across the walls crowded with contemporary prints and the immense bed with its thick duvet covering. "Cassie?"

Seeing no sign of her, Helen went to the bathroom and opened the door.

"For heaven's sake, whatever are you do..."

The words stuck in her throat.

Blood stained the white bathmat and puddled on the white-and-black tiled floor around Cassie's body. Her wrists were slashed, the glint of a razorblade near her fingertips.

"Dear God...dear God." Helen backed out, bumping into the bed as she fumbled for the phone and dialed 911.

***

"She was your niece, ma'am?"

Helen opened her eyes to see the mustached face of the policeman leaning over her. He'd arrived with his partner half an hour before. Detective Archer? Was that it? Her mind was so fuzzy. She could hear the team from the medical examiner's banging about up the hall.

"You're her aunt?" he tried again.

"Yes." Her voice shook, as unsteady as the rest of her.

"Looks like suicide, ma'am." He shifted on his feet. "I, um, imagine you saw for yourself. Cuts on her wrists were clean and deep. No superficial scratches like we so often see in this type of situation."

Helen swallowed, not wanting to listen, picturing the girl lying there, still refusing to believe it was Cassie. She fought back tears, remembering her earlier fears, sure that Cassie was in trouble. But enough to do *that*?

"No," she struggled to get out, meeting his eyes despite her tears. "No, she wouldn't have. She had too much to live for. She was barely thirty...."

He pulled a hand from behind his back. Dangling from his fingers was a torn sheet of paper in a plastic bag. "This might explain it, ma'am," he said, holding it toward her; but Helen couldn't have read the words then even if she'd had the where-withal to fish her glasses from her purse.

So the fellow cleared his throat and did it for her.

"It's ripped at the top, see," he explained, "We couldn't find the missing piece. Anyhow, it says, 'I'm sorry, Jasper, but I can't go on like this. I hoped you would do the right thing, but you

made your choice. And I made mine. Maybe someday you'll for-
give me. Cassie.'"

Helen shut her eyes. Her chest tightened, making it hard to
breathe.

It couldn't be. It wasn't true. She would never have done
such a thing. Never. Not someone so bright, so ambitious.

"We've matched the handwriting against papers from her
desk, and it looks like she wrote it all right. Of course, we'll have
forensics double-check."

"There's no reason...she had no reason...."

"Everyone goes through it, ma'am."

"Through what?"

"Denial."

Helen turned away from him.

"Jasper. That's Jasper Cornwall, ma'am, isn't it? Your niece
worked for him at his gallery, right? We found her business cards
and an address book with his home number. I already called Mr.
Cornwall myself."

Helen stared at the tissue in her hands, wishing he'd stop
talking, afraid that when he did she'd fall to pieces.

"It seems your niece and him were, ah, engaged in a relationship. Mr. Cornwall claims he broke it off recently, and she
didn't take it very well. He mentioned she was pretty distraught."
He fiddled with the bag that held the note. "Did you know
Cornwall was married, ma'am? He said his wife's the jealous
type. Told me she stabbed him once when she thought he was
cheating. That's why he cut it short with Ms. Edwards, but he
never figured she'd take it so hard as this."

Helen pressed trembling fingers to her brow. Good God. An
affair with Cornwall? Is that what he'd said? Cass had never even
intimated such a thing. What other secrets had she hidden as
well?

"...we'll keep the place sealed off for the rest of the day, until
our investigators have tied things up," the officer was saying,
though Helen only listened with half an ear. "Still, the preliminary cause of death looks like suicide."

She sat quietly, shredding the tissue until it dissolved in white flakes.

"I'm sorry, ma'am." Detective Archer touched her shoulder gently. "I'll let you know when the ME's finished so you can, um, get on with the funeral arrangements."

Funeral arrangements?

Her heart lurched. She felt light-headed and covered her face with her hands.

Good Lord. She'd only come to take Cassie to lunch, not to bury her.

***

Though the rain had stopped during the night, the morning sun that slipped through the crack between Helen's drawn bedroom curtains did little to cheer her.

She had not slept at all. She couldn't bear to shut her eyes. Every time she did, she saw Cassie's body on the tiled floor, blood all around her.

So much blood, she recalled, shuddering at the thought.

She went into the bathroom and hit the wall switch, grimacing as the tiny space flooded with light. She leaned over the sink, avoiding the sight of her reflection in the mirror. Turning on the tap, she let the water run and splashed some on her face, trying to clear her head, to rid herself of the fog creeping into her brain.

Her sister's voice over the telephone, her devastation, echoed loudly in her mind, the sound of her cries so vivid even now that Helen felt herself tremble.

Marianne had been forty when Cassie was born. "My miracle," she'd called her, after years and years of trying, of thinking she and Jack would end up childless.

How cruel a thing to be rung up by a stranger and told your daughter was dead.

Procedure! She gave a snort, suddenly angry, wishing the police had let her tell Marianne and Jack herself, when the time was right.

But there was no right time, was there? No easy way to say Cassie was gone forever.

Tears filled her eyes, and she pressed the towel to her face to dry them.

If only Joe were here to talk to her, to put his arms around her and hold her until she stopped shaking. He always knew what to do, knew the proper things to say.

Deliberately, Helen steadied herself, put the towel back on the rack and finished up her morning ritual.

Twenty minutes later, dressed in a blue sweatsuit and sneakers, she left the house and set out for St. Louis. Marianne had asked that she pack up Cassie's things and send them home.

She rolled down the window as she drove. The air that blew into her face smelled of yesterday's rain. The river looked swollen, brown and rough.

She turned on the radio, but even that didn't drown out her thoughts. She kept recalling the last few times she'd spoken with Cassie. All she'd talked about was her job, the trips she'd made, the auctions she'd attended. When she had mentioned Jasper Cornwall by name, it had been with admiration...of a professional sort. Helen had never detected anything more in her voice. Certainly not love. But would Cass have confessed if she were sleeping with him? It hardly seemed the type of thing she'd confide in an aunt whose life she'd once said reminded her of cable reruns of "Ozzie and Harriet."

The postman was just leaving as she pulled the car into the slot in front of the townhouse and shut off the engine.

Helen retrieved the letters from the brass-lidded box and stood at Cassie's door, knees wobbling. She took several deep breaths before she let herself in, wondering if she shouldn't have brought someone with her.

She flipped on the lights and hesitated, summoning up her strength, knowing it would take all she had to get through this.

Her gaze drifted over the living room and its white walls filled with framed museum prints. "Until I can afford the real thing," Cass had said once, and Helen tried not to dwell on the fact that, now, she never would.

She settled onto the oversized sofa, the mail in her lap. She plucked her glasses from her purse, then looked over the small pile of assorted bills and letters.

Neiman-Marcus. Saks. Lord & Taylor.

Cassie had always liked nice things. Marianne used to joke that the girl's first word was "Gucci."

Helen glanced at a pair of invitations to gallery showings and a postcard from *Art & Antiques* magazine acknowledging a subscription renewal through the year ahead.

She frowned.

Why did that bother her as it did? Because Cass had been so organized? Because it didn't seem logical that someone suicidal would have taken the time to renew a magazine subscription?

She set the mail aside and went over to the rolltop desk. She ran a hand across the glowing reddish wood. Cherry, she remembered. She'd been with Cassie when she'd bought it at a shop on Rosebury.

Helen slid open the top and stared.

Papers lay in a jumble. The cubicles stood empty, as if someone had routed through them, searching for something.

Had the police done this when they'd looked for a sample of Cassie's handwriting? Everything seemed such a blur.

Beneath the mess was a dog-eared appointment book.

She slipped to the current date and went from there, running her finger down the pages. One meeting atop another. Gallery openings. Several dinner dates. A haircut and manicure two days hence.

Her pulse quickened.

Maybe there was more to her sense of disbelief than "denial," as Archer had suggested.

What if Cassie had not committed suicide? What if someone else had killed her?

But why?

Why would anyone want Cassie dead?

Helen couldn't imagine that any more than she could the alternative.

She wandered around the room, picking up one after another of the framed photographs set about on shelves and tabletops. Cassie with her mom and dad, Cassie at Christmas, Cassie in her graduation gown surrounded by college chums, Cassie in London, in Paris, in Japan. Cass and Helen. There were none of Jasper Cornwall, and the realization unnerved her, undermined all common sense, though she told herself that perhaps Cassie had felt it unseemly to put a picture of her married lover up on the mantel with the rest.

Helen forced herself to go into Cassie's bedroom, her eyes drifting toward the bathroom door, though she saw only slick black and white squares on the floor. Not a sign of what had happened. The bathmat was gone. Everything appeared scrupulously clean. Miriam Wright, she figured. Cassie's landlady. The police had no doubt been in touch with the woman, and she'd wasted no time in sending someone in to tidy up the place.

"She's compulsive, Aunt Helen, I swear to God. If she had her way, the Minute Maids would be over here twice a week, using white gloves to test the top of my refrigerator." Cassie's voice filtered into her consciousness, and Helen smiled for a brief moment.

If Miriam Wright was compulsive about the cleanliness of her renters, Helen was glad of it today at least.

She crossed the room to the closet, finding a pair of suitcases, and began sorting through the drawers. Sweatshirts and lingerie, jeans and sweaters smelling of rose-scented sachets.

She went through pockets, zipped up zippers, and buttoned up buttons, before she folded away the clothes, turning up a few coins, a ticket stub from a movie theatre, and a safety-pinned laundry tag.

A red dress lay crumpled on the closet floor, and Helen retrieved it and pressed it to her cheek, closing her eyes as she breathed in Cassie's scent, the trace of Chanel the girl had so adored. She pressed her eyes closed hard against the tears, determined not to break down now before she'd finished.

She carried the dress to the bed and brushed it smooth with her fingers. Something crinkled in one of the pockets, and she instinctively slipped her hand into its depth, drawing out several sheets of paper folded into squares.

She spread out the first page to look it over, setting her glasses down low on her nose to see more clearly.

It was a receipt of some sort. Or maybe an invoice. It was handwritten and dated two weeks ago. *The Storm on the Sea at Galilee*, someone had scrawled in less than perfect penmanship. Was it a painting? Seems it was destined for Tokyo.

She flattened out the second sheet, a page torn from a magazine. It was an article about an art gallery theft in Boston. The Isabella Stewart Gardener Museum had been hit in 1990 by a pair of thieves dressed as policeman. Among the priceless works stolen was a Vermeer and a Rembrandt....

Helen caught her breath.

...a Rembrandt entitled, "The Storm on the Sea at Galilee."

Her heart thumped in her ribcage.

Mere coincidence?

Or was there more she should be seeing?

Could someone at the gallery have dealt in stolen art? Jasper Cornwall himself, perhaps? What if Cassie had stumbled upon the invoice and put two and two together? Would she have confronted him? Was it enough to get her killed?

Was the story about the affair just a cover-up, and the torn "suicide note" something else entirely?

Maybe she'd watched too many late night reruns of "Perry Mason," but it was possible, wasn't it?

No matter, Helen couldn't let it go.

She snatched up the papers, the postcard about the recent magazine subscription renewal and Cassie's appointment book, hurrying out to her car, stopping at Exxon just long enough to ask directions.

She arrived at the police station not ten minutes later and tracked down Detective Archer after being shuffled from one person to another, then being told to wait in between.

"Oh, Mrs. Evans, I was about to, um, call you," he said as he led her to his desk and settled behind it. "A few things have come up that..."

"I'll say they have." She didn't let him finish. Dropping her armload in front of him, she told him of her suspicions, one by one. He said nothing, sat there so quietly she finally snapped in frustration, "Good God, won't you at least consider what I've said?"

He cleared his throat. "Like I started to explain, ma'am, a few things have come up. The ME's preliminary report on Ms. Edwards was faxed over this morning. He, uh, found some cotton fibers in and around her mouth and traces of petroleum distillate."

"Of what?"

"Paint thinner," he told her. "Someone knocked her out first and then cut her wrists. That's why the marks were so clean."

Helen nodded, feeling numb, knowing her sense of unease had not been unfounded. "What about Cornwall?" she asked, able to whisper. "You'll question him, of course?"

Archer leaned back in his chair. A muscle in his jaw twitched. "We can't do that, ma'am."

"Can't do it?" Helen felt as if he'd knocked the wind out of her. "For heaven's sake, why not?"

"He's dead, ma'am. Seems his wife overheard him talking to us about his supposed affair with Ms. Edwards. She shot him, Mrs. Evans. He expired on arrival at the hospital. She's downstairs being booked as we speak."

Helen stared at him. "Cornwall's dead?"

"Yes."

She shook her head. "No. No, he has to tell us the truth."

"We know that, ma'am." He picked up a pen and tapped it against his chin. "The truth is that your niece didn't kill herself."

There had likely never been an affair at all, she realized, believing now that Cornwall's story of breaking Cassie's heart was just that: a story. Nothing more than a smokescreen to cover up a stolen painting.

"I'm sorry," Archer said, and Helen nodded.

So was she.

*   *   *

Mayhem in the Midlands is one of my favorite mystery cons for several reasons: its smaller size gives writers and readers ample opportunity to mingle and the panel topics are witty and informative. Plus, I get to hang out with my friends who love Mayhem as much as I do! Omaha rocks, baby.

NEVER TRY TO CHEAT A CHEATER

by Wenda Wardell Marrone

I was born in Nebraska, raised in Montana, and spent (too many) years in New York City, editing and writing magazine articles and non-fiction books. My first mystery, *No Time for an Everyday Woman*, took me back to Montana. In my second book, *The Year 2000 Killers*, my heroine saved us all from the problems of Y2K. Now I'm back in Montana to stay, and I've hooked up again with the Reverend Abigail Butterfield and Claud Willetts of Merciful Valley, Montana.

NEVER TRY TO CHEAT A CHEATER

By Wenda Wardell Marrone

It was about 2:30 on a clear July afternoon when the big roan tore up to where Claud Willetts sat at a table beside a trail deep in the Heureux de la Chose Forest. Claud's was the final station on the Poker Ride. The first four stations were unmanned, marked just by their numbers. It was Claud's task to check the riders' badges and cards—to make sure they had paid their entrance fee and taken a card from each of the other stations—and to pass out the fifth and last card to complete a hand of five card draw. But the big roan was too twitchy for its rider to steer it anywhere near, so Claud stood, checked the guy's badge and cards, reached him up a fifth one, and ducked back fast.

The horse had caught its nerves from the rider, jobbing at its mouth till even Claud could tell, the way the poor beast jerked and rolled its eyes. Claud marked his name: Jack Farmer. He watched, scowling, as Farmer pounded on up the trail and around a curve out of sight. He was as bad at cheating as riding. The kind that gave cheaters a bad name.

This was the first Merciful Valley Poker Ride, proposed and organized by the Reverend Abigail Butterfield. Like most of her ideas, it seemed obvious after she suggested it. Other places in Montana already ran poker rides, and they were all pretty much the same. A hundred or so riders would gather from across the state and even out of state, pay a stiff entrance fee (for whatever charity Abby had in mind), and follow a trail through the woods marked by ribbons tied around designated trees, stopping at five

115

stations along the way to draw a card for a hand of Five Card Draw. No peeking: Abby apparently thought that possible. The goal wasn't to pass a finish line first, but to draw the best poker hand, for which there were prizes. Boots, a Stetson, somebody up in Demersville had even donated a saddle.

In Merciful Valley's Poker Ride, riders had begun that morning at the parking lot of Heroes Ski Resort (plenty of room for horse trailers) and spent the day winding through the adjoining Heureux de la Chose Forest, one of the prettiest places in Montana, Claud thought, or at least in Merciful Valley. They would end up back at Heroes for the prizes and a bang-up barbecue.

"I have the riding skills," Abby had said when she first brought up the poker ride to Claud.

He didn't doubt her for a minute. Since Abby had come from New York to Bitterroot Congregational Church in Merciful Valley, she had hacked trail for the Beargrass Basin, led camping trips with her youth group, strawbossed the construction of an immense playground behind the church, and organized a shoot at which she demonstrated her skill with a bow and arrow. If surprised by a blizzard, she could have switched her car for skis without missing a beat. She could braid leather and, for all Claud knew, tan it. In her five years in the valley, Claud had bit by bit decided that the goal of eastern girls' schools was to prepare their graduates to lead wagon trains.

Of course Abby had riding skills. How else could she lead a wagon train?

Claud himself wore cowboy boots; since his size dictated that his footwear be custom-made anyway, they were practical, as well as protective coloration in what was still, despite a growing trickle of newcomers, horse country. But footwear was as close to riding as he got. Any horse big enough to take his weight, Claud had far too much sense to go near.

"I can ride," Abby repeated, "but I can't play poker. That's where you come in, Claud."

"I don't play anymore, remember?" Claud said sourly. He liked getting his new trust fund check every month, but the condition under which Bandit Colman had willed him the money—that he give up his card games and scams in exchange—still rankled. All the tourist money pouring into Merciful Valley, none of it to line the pockets of Claud Willetts?

Worse, lying just for the hell of it didn't seem to have the same kick.

"The ride is for charity," said Abby, looking up at him over her half-glasses with her blazing blue gaze. "And you won't be playing, you'll be organizing. And only organizing, do I make myself clear?"

"Why, Rev," said Claud, perking up, "a person would think you didn't trust me."

"How right that person would be."

Which was how Claud came to be beside a trail in Heureux de la Chose Forest on a clear July afternoon, at a station accessible by all terrain vehicles as well as horse.

Truth to tell, he had enjoyed displaying his skills again, fanning cards effortlessly into a Gambler's Rose, shuffling decks with each hand separately. Being in charge, he could mark all the cards at all the stations; he knew everybody's hand without being shown and amused himself by the cards he passed out while people thought they were drawing their own. Bill Odegaard, for example, had needed new boots for months. As the ranger, he'd be sweeping the trail for stragglers after the race was officially over and collect his cards last. He'd get his boots, and no matter what Abby suspected, she wouldn't be able to prove a thing.

If he hadn't marked the cards, Claud wouldn't have known that Farmer, on the nervous roan, had taken two from the fourth station and none from the third. The funny thing was, so far he had been the only cheater. Horsepeople seemed to be almost as honorable as Abby thought. Maybe Farmer had planned to be last and assumed no one would notice. Wrong on both counts: two women plodded into sight, and just as they reached Claud's station, a man on a short-legged black caught them up, tipping his hat politely to the cuter one before Claud could himself.

"You're just in time." Claud said to them. "You want to get back in plenty of time for the barbecue."

The black horse made Farmer's twitchy roan look like a sleepy pony. It took exception to everything from butterflies to blowing weeds and obviously had been shying all afternoon; its dark coat was darker still with sweat.

This rider, though, had no trouble forcing the horse near to Claud and reaching down for his last card. He asked, "Are we the last?" as calm as if he wasn't keeping effortless control of a thousand-plus pounds of jitter. It was pretty to watch, even to a non-rider.

"I sure hope so." Claud showed his respect by letting the guy draw a ten of clubs to complete his full house. Just because the race wasn't about horsemanship didn't mean Claud couldn't pay tribute to it when he saw it. "Best get on, or the ribs will be gone. No sensible man misses Augie's ribs."

The black's rider tipped his hat, and the three of them trotted on together, the women swinging wide when the black decided to go up the trail sideways. It was heading straight again by the time they rounded the curve.

Three o'clock. Claud called the parking lot and asked Abby if his total matched the number of riders who had started out. "Yes!" she said in a voice that would have carried to the balcony of Bitterroot Congregational. "Come on in! The ribs will be done by the time you get here!"

It wasn't that simple. Two volunteers had to ride the trail to double-check, tidying up the ribbons as they went. Until they reached Claud, he couldn't leave his post. He knew the routine because he had set it up, copying the way ski patrolmen checked trails after the lifts closed at night.

But only one volunteer showed up: his nephew Stan, tearing along fit to break a leg to tell him that a body had been found off the trail. Bob Odegaard was waiting beside it until the sheriff could get there.

"Who was it?"

"Bob didn't know." Stan wheeled his horse to take off again. The horse had other ideas and kept right on wheeling. "He said the face was bashed to a pulp. He *said*. He wouldn't let me look."

Only a teenager could make that sound like he'd been insulted.

"Man? Woman?" Claud asked. "He must know that."

"Man. I don't know if I'm supposed to tell you. I only came to tell you because Bob's cell phone won't work from there—"

"Where's there?"

"What difference does it make, Uncle Claud? You can only reach it by horse." The expression on Claud's face must have warned him. He said sullenly, "Near station three, a couple hundred yards off the trail. So Bob says, will you please call Sheriff Neiderhoffer. I got to get back."

"Wait!" Claud grabbed a stirrup and then stepped hurriedly back as Stan's horse kicked out at him. "Have you found his horse?"

"Not when I left. Forget about it, Uncle Claud. Just call the sheriff."

This last was thrown over Stan's shoulder. He wouldn't have dared say it if he was still in Claud's range, mounted or not.

Since he couldn't think of an alternative, Claud did as he was told. By the time his ATV had reached Heroes' parking lot, he had talked to Sheriff Orry Neiderhoffer.

Abby came through the crowd toward him like a homing pigeon. "What's wrong, Claud?"

She was the one person he could never fool. "Did I say something was wrong?" he asked feebly.

She brushed that aside. "Do we need Doc Tilman?"

Tilman was a doctor up in Demersville as well as the coroner. Abby hadn't necessarily read Claud's mind; she might just remember Doc had done the ride, as Claud himself did. He was already craning over the crowd. "What's this *we* stuff?"

But she didn't hear; she was already off. And back again with Doc at her heels, cutting him out from the milling guests as neatly as a quarterhorse. She waited, too, forcing Claud to describe what little he knew to them both.

When he was through, he said, "Any extra horse show up? Anybody leave without waiting for ribs?"

"If there were an extra horse milling around, we'd all know it," Tilman assured him before he caught Abby's frown.

She switched the frown to Claud. "Forget about finding the killer. That's the sheriff's job. You stay here and hand out the prizes. I'll go with Doc."

"He don't need a guide, Rev, and it ain't your business any more than mine."

"We've had this conversation before, Claud, and you never listen. Death is as much my job as it is Sheriff Neiderhoffer's." She conjured up a horse and was on top of it by the time Doc Tilman was on his. "Concentrate on something you *can* do. Spin out the prizes as long as you can, and for once in your life keep your nose out of something that doesn't concern you."

Claud signed. If anybody had ever figured out a way to control Abby, it sure wasn't him. He shouted after her, "I'll have the killer tied up with a ribbon by the time you get back!"

She trotted away as if she hadn't even heard. In disgust, Claud bellowed everybody to silence, climbed on the back of his big old red pickup, and began to call out the prizes.

There were surprises. There had to be, since Bob Odegaard was otherwise occupied and couldn't complete his royal flush. The guy with the short-legged black horse was in the crowd, but his full house had mysteriously—well, not so mysteriously—migrated to the cuter of the two women he had ridden off with. Without Bob, hers was the high hand, and she picked the saddle. The boots went to a stranger, as did the Stetson.

Afterward Claud mingled, trying to keep the crowd in a party mood so they'd stay till after the sheriff had finished with the body and come to talk to them. After all, the killer might still be here, brushing shoulders and dripping barbecue sauce. Half Claud's mind pictured Orry and his men and Doc Tilman. And Abby. No need for yellow DO NOT CROSS tape back there in the woods. No way to look for prints on tree trunks, and assorted horses had been tromping on the pine needles all afternoon. Cameras, body bag, all the equipment would have to be packed in, and the body packed out again, plus they had to search for the victim's missing horse. All in all, Claud had a fair amount of time to work with.

There was no way to know why the man had been killed. People had come here from all over the state; the why lay back in somebody's home town. They wouldn't be able to identify him soon, either, not with a bashed-in face. If they figured out who the killer was, though, he could tell them who he'd killed and why.

By *they*, he meant Claud Willetts. Abby couldn't keep him from thinking, could she? Besides, it wouldn't be the first time he'd had to lead Orry Neiderhoffer by the hand.

They—he—would have to start with the one thing he knew for sure: Somebody had snuck into the Heureux de la Chose Forest before the Poker Ride with murder in mind. The same number of people had started and finished, all aboard horses, but there was now one more person than horses. The murdered man was an extra. Whereas, if the killing had been an accident involving two participants, horses and people would have come out even.

Claud was grateful that the horses were tucked up in the trailers with only their glossy rumps mooning the crowd. He'd never realized before that you could recognize a horse purely by his backside. The short-legged black was unmistakable, for example; surely Farmer's big sweaty roan would be, too. Claud set about to find it. And couldn't.

And this was the man who had missed station three but been back on the trail for station four. There were a couple of clues for you.

Claud tried and failed to get the sheriff on his cell; he must still be with the body. He called the sheriff's office instead, forty-five minutes away up in Demersville. Marcella, the telephone operator, couldn't patch him through, either, but she did agree, dubiously, to put out an All-Points Bulletin on a car pulling a horse trailer with a sweaty roan.

"Not to stop it, mind," she said, bossy as ever. "You aren't official, Claud. But we'll find him and keep tabs on him until we get hold of Orry. I mean, the Sheriff."

"You do that, Marcy, darlin'."

By the time Orry finally reached him to say the roan's owner had been stopped halfway up Route 42, Claud was irritable with the effort to keep everybody jolly enough to linger.

"Fetch him back here, will you, Orry?"

Even through the static, he could hear Orry go into a full frontal snit. "I hadn't planned to let you make the arrest, Claud. I'm just asking you to tell me what put you on to this man Farmer."

"For the Lord's sake, Orry, did you think he was the killer? He's just going to point out who it is."

There was a pause filled with plenty of off the phone conversation. Orry came back. "Farmer says he don't know nothing."

"Course he says that. He ain't exactly a hero, or didn't you notice? Fetch him back, Orry. You better block off the road here, too. Keep as many poker players penned up as you can."

Not another word would he say until the blue and whites arrived, fore and aft of a station wagon towing a well-maintained two-horse trailer. A cop was driving; the roan's former rider now sat sullen beside Sheriff Neiderhoffer in the front car.

"This Farmer says he's important," Orry said, the long ends of his mustache drooping. Important people always rattled Orry. "He says he's going to make trouble."

Maybe in another life. In this one, Farmer was so scared Claud was surprised his pants were dry.

"You saw one of these men in the woods earlier," Claud said to him.

Farmer stared here, there, everywhere but at the other riders. "I don't think so."

But then what Claud had hoped for happened. What Farmer did or didn't see suddenly didn't matter: somebody had seen him. The short-legged black and its rider broke for the trail, the horse's haunches bunching with the effort.

Well, not quite what he hoped for. Why hadn't he realized a horse was a means of escape? And Sheriff Neiderhoffer had driven, not ridden. But the parking lot was full of horsepeople, who seemed to know how to move fast. An instant posse took off in pursuit, with the Reverend Abigail Butterfield in the lead—of course she was in the lead—while Claud could only watch.

Here he had admired the guy as a horseman and a flirt, never seeing how both made him the likely killer. Doing without poker had made him rusty.

Orry said, "What put you on to him, Claud?"

"I wasn't on to him," Claud said in disgust. "I was on to Mr. Farmer, here. He never hit station three. He took two cards from station four to make up. I'd arranged the cards, see, so I knew."

Relief and fear gave Farmer a sickly color. "I wasn't trying to cheat—"

"I figured that out," Claud agreed.

"I was just following the ribbons to station three." With the black and his rider safely out of sight, Farmer suddenly found his tongue.

"I figured that out, too," Claud said. "The killer changed the ribbons to lead the black horse off the trail. He planned to kill the black's original rider and change the ribbons back before anybody found out."

The sheriff said, "He couldn't have been registered. Abby said everybody registered came through. And what happened to his horse?"

"Officially he ain't here, Orry," Claud said patiently. "He didn't need a horse. Give you any odds you like he has a nice alibi fixed up somewhere. He figured to let the black loose and slip away without anybody knowing he'd ever been here."

"But how could he guarantee he got the right man?"

"They must have arranged to meet late in the day. Just not quite late enough. Farmer, here, took the wrong trail, too." Farmer's own color had begun to come back. "How can you possibly know?"

"You saw it all, didn't you, son?"

"Not as much as you think. Station three seemed to be pretty isolated, so I thought I'd, well, answer a call of nature."

"Take a leak," Claud translated for Orry.

"I know what he means," Orry said huffily.

Farmer sounded calmer, safe enough now, apparently, to face what he had seen. "I was standing looking at nothing when I saw one man standing, and another on the ground, and the one on the ground wasn't moving. And then the first one looked over and saw me—and I saw him—"

Farmer scrubbed his face as if he could rub away the picture. "I've never ridden trail so fast. All I could think of was getting away, only I've never been here before, I didn't know how to get out. When I *did* find the trail, I had to follow it and pretend to play the game so you wouldn't remember me from anybody else. As soon as I got back to the parking lot, I got out of here."

Orry drew himself up, very much the sheriff. "You should've called us. Stuck around to identify him."

Farmer had regained enough confidence to be indignant. "Did I know he was dead? What if he'd just been knocked down? It was none of my business."

Farmer's fear had been too deep to come from a fistfight. Claud said, "What did I tell you, Hoff? Not exactly a hero. But it didn't matter. Once he knew he'd been seen, the killer had to change plans. Now his only chance is to pretend to be his own victim. Go through the motions as John Doe, leave with everybody else, and disappear someplace on the way back. Someplace far away from here. That meant making the victim hard to identify. It meant riding the victim's horse." It meant not claiming a prize that might get him photographed and identified as his victim.

Hoff said unbelieving, "You mean the horse saw the killing, and smelled blood and the death, and this guy got up him and rode it—"

Rode it well enough to impress an amateur like Claud Willetts. Claud nodded.

"Why did he do it?" Sheriff Orry Neiderhoffer.

Farmer gave an abrupt high-pitched laugh. "You're talking like he knows what happened. He could be wrong from beginning to end."

How much, how very much Claud would have liked to ask him to put some money on that possibility.

But Farmer's comeuppance actually came better from the sheriff, who said, "Like he was wrong about you being a witness, Mr. Farmer?"

He turned his back on the man. "Can you at least tell me how you knew Farmer was the witness and not the killer?"

"Easy," Claud said. "This started out to be a clever murder." He glanced disparagingly at Farmer. "Think somebody that clever would be such a lousy cheater?"

*   *   *

Midlands is the important part of this to me. Nero Wolfe is New York, Kinsey Milhone California...the Midwest has just as distinct a feeling of place, and we all reflect it. My characters tend to talk about it. (The prairie is "the biggest wheat field God ever made," said Bandit Colman in *Everyday Woman*.)

I think it's healthy for all of us, however different our styles and plots and success rates, to get together and celebrate this place we write about in common. Left Coast, fine, Malice Domestic, also fine—but I hope Mayhem soon rates just as prominent a place on the mystery calendar.

BLONDE NOIR

by Martin Meyers
and Annette Meyers

Martin Meyers, who is also an actor, is the author of five detective novels originally published by Popular Library, now back in print from iUniverse: *Kiss and Kill, Spy And Die, Red Is For Murder, Hung Up To Die,* and *Reunion For Death,* all featuring private detective Patrick Hardy. Meyers novelized the Cher movie, *Suspect,* for Bantam and wrote a young adult book for Scholastic Publications, *A Federal Case.* He also wrote lyrics for CAPTAIN KANGAROO on CBS-TV. In November 1992, Doubleday published *The Dutchman,* the first novel in a series of history mysteries, written in collaboration with his wife Annette Meyers, and using the pseudonym Maan Meyers.

The second book, *The Kingsbridge Plot* (1993) was followed by *The High Constable* (1994), *The Dutchman's Dilemma* (Bantam) (1995), and *The House On Mulberry Street.* The sixth in the series, *The Lucifer Contract,* was published in 1998. Maan Meyers' short stories, "The High Constable and the Visiting Author" and "The High Constable and the Rochester Rappers" have appeared in the anthologies *Crime Through Time* and *Crime Through Time II,* published by Berkley in 1997 and 1998. And coming up: "The Peculiar Events on Riverside Drive," in the Signet anthology, *Mystery*

Street, 2001. In 1998, a short story by Martin Meyers—"The Girl, the Body, and the Kitchen Sink,"—was published in the Signet anthology, *The Private Eyes*.

Annette Meyers spent sixteen years on Wall Street as an executive search consultant, and is currently an arbitrator with the National Association of Securities Dealers (NASD). She was formerly assistant to Broadway director-producer Hal Prince (for sixteen years), working with him on such productions as *Fiddler on the Roof, Cabaret, A Little Night Music, Company,* and *Follies. Murder Me Now*, Meyers' latest novel, is the second book in a new series, set in Greenwich Village, in 1920, featuring Olivia Brown, a young woman poet based loosely on Edna St. Vincent Millay. Olivia Brown was first introduced in *Free Love*, published in 1999, by Mysterious Press/Warner. Meyers is also the author of seven published Smith and Wetzon mysteries, *The Big Killing* (1989), *Tender Death* (1990), *The Deadliest Option* (1991), *Blood on the Street* (1992), *Murder: The Musical* (1993), and *These Bones Were Made For Dancin'* (1995), and *The Groaning Board* (1997).

With her husband Martin Meyers, using the pseudonym Maan Meyers, she writes historical mysteries set in New York in the 17th, 18th, and 19th Centuries. The first in the series, *The Dutchman*, was published in 1992. It was followed by *The Kingsbridge Plot* (1993), *The High Constable* (1994), *The Dutchman's Dilemma* (1995), *The House On Mulberry Street* (1996), and *The Lucifer Contract*, 1998, a Civil War thriller. Meyers' short stories have appeared in the anthologies, *Murder for Mother*, (Signet, 1994), *Malice Domestic 4*, (Pocket, 1995), *Lethal Ladies*, (Berkley, 1996), *Vengeance is Hers*, (Signet, 1997), in the German anthology, *Skrupellose Fische*, (Eichborn, 2000), and *Flesh and Blood*, (Mysterious Press, 2001). Maan Meyers' short stories, "The High

Constable and the Visiting Author," and "The High Constable and The Rochester Rappers" appeared in Berkley's 1997 history-mystery anthology, *Crime Through Time*, in Berkley's 1998 anthology, *Crime Through Time II*, in 1998, and in the Signet anthology, *Mystery Street*, 2001. Meyers' books have been published in German and Spanish. Her psychological novel, *Tracing Rose*, will be published as an e-book by Warner's iPublish Division in 2001. She is a former president of Sisters in Crime and is on the executive board of the U.S. chapter of the International Association of Crime Writers.

BLONDE NOIR

by Martin Meyers
and Annette Meyers

The sky is different in California.

The highway outside my window was a straight line away from the horizon.

I live and work in a squat two-story, fake pink hacienda on Ventura Boulevard in Van Nuys. Apartment upstairs, office down. The sign on the pebbly glass door of my office says, "John Marley, Private Investigations."

Don't go by the movie crap. I'm no Dick Powell, or Bogart. The one gun I own is a small .22 Colt automatic, and it only comes out of my desk drawer on exceptional occasions. Like if the Japs invaded.

I'm five-ten, a hundred and sixty pounds. And the only fights I win are the ones where I'm sneaky. Though, I must admit, I am pretty good at that.

That morning, light blue sky had mingled with white clouds, which, to the east, grew into a giant mass of ever darkening cotton balls. It all looked like a perfect backdrop curtain that didn't quite reach the desert floor. Between the space created by the bottom of the cloud curtain and the horizon was the emerging orange glow of the sun coming up from behind the foothills.

At the end of the road a stumpy, geometric block of a building stood between me and the foothills.

All of a sudden the blinding sun appeared beneath the cotton ball curtain and above the geometric block.

131

It was beautiful. And not quite real.

Like the blonde sitting across from me a couple of hours later.

She wasn't one of those Jean Harlow types that get it from a bottle. More natural. What they called dirty blonde: loose ringlets of light brown with glints of sunshine in them.

She had—the only way to say it is—pneumatic breasts. Even so she looked like somebody's kid sister, twenty at the most, come right off a farm, busting out with good farm girl health. Her skin was pink white. I wanted to touch it. Anywhere. Everywhere.

The girl had a small birthmark on her left cheek, just above the laugh line, which I wasn't seeing now because she was nervous as a wild cat in a pen. She smelled of Chanel #5 with an Ivory soap chase. She took off her sunglasses and abstractedly chewed one of the temple bars. Her dark eyes were bright, the whites were clear. This girl had a kind of innocent beauty. She was a humdinger.

On my desk the front page of the *L. A. Times* lifted and fell to the steady breeze from the fan overhead. In the center of the page, above the fold, was a four-column wide picture of Franklin Delano Roosevelt and the dates: 1882-1945. The headline was: FDR IS DEAD; TRUMAN SWORN IN; OUR OKINAWA GUNS DOWN 118 PLANES.

On the large Philco console standing next to my desk, I'd found the only station that wasn't talking about the dead President or the new one: Harry Truman. What they had was the Andrews Sisters singing "*I'll Walk Alone.*"

"Isn't it sad?" she said, her mouth pouting up.

"What? The song?"

"No. The President dying." She put on her sunglasses. "He's the President, for God's sake. Don't you have any respect?" When I declined to comment, she said, "Maybe I should go?" Her chair creaked but she didn't get up.

I reached over, turned off the radio, and waited her out.

She wasn't wearing a milkmaid costume. To the contrary, she was poured into a white sharkskin dress pressed and buffed to a bright sheen. Her white-gloved hands held a large white handbag in her lap and a thin green book. In spite of the desert sun she wasn't wearing a hat. She sighed and shifted in the chair, squaring her shoulders, giving me another angle of those magnificent breasts.

Her face was average, longish nose, sulky mouth. Her head was a little too big for her spectacular body.

"Stop that." She stood up. The book fell to the floor. She didn't stamp her foot, but it felt as if she had.

"Stop what?" I asked innocently.

"Stop staring at my breasts." Her voice was like a child's whisper.

"Sorry, can't blame a guy."

"Yes, I can. It's rude," she squealed. She was about five foot five or six—add two inches for heels—and all of it choice. She hadn't finished scolding me yet. "And I don't like it. I won't put up with it." Her upper lip trembled with the smile she flashed at me when she was done chewing me out.

Overhead the Hunter fan made a click-click noise. It didn't bother me. But it was annoying the hell out of the blonde, who kept looking up at it. I keep a pint bottle of Seagram's Seven in my lower right desk drawer. I brought it out. "Care for some?"

"I don't indulge." She plumped down hard on the chair. It creaked again in protest. Her face held onto a vacuous expression. Her lips were wet, pouty, over slightly protruding teeth, her mouth partially open. That delicious mouth put ideas in my mind. After a moment she methodically put on the sunglasses, not saying a word. This was going to be a barrel of laughs.

I shrugged. "Cigarette?"

The blonde had walked in off the street nursing a broken heel and a problem she was evidently reluctant to talk about.

She whipped off her glasses and frowned. The whole thing seemed rehearsed. She'd put on the damned glasses just so she'd be able to take them off like that. "I don't like cigarettes," she said.

I came from around my desk. We both leaned forward and reached for her book on the floor at the same time. I got there first. Our fingers touched. I tried not to look at her breasts. Oh, yes I did. Oh, my God. I wondered how it would be to have her on the floor right then and there.

I did nothing about my fantasy. Instead I placed the book on my desk. "Letters to a Young Poet" by Rainer Maria Rilke. I never heard of her. Him? I nodded at the book. "Good stuff?"

"I don't know." Each breathy word was rationed out as if in short supply. And each was given the same value as the others. "I haven't read it yet."

Since that was a dead end I said, "I can just make out the ridge of wedding band under those sweet white gloves."

She laughed. A queer kind of throaty sound. "It's a friendship ring."

"Makes no diff to me." I lit a camel.

She wrinkled her nose, lifted her shoulders, then let them settle. I enjoyed watching.

"You're right. I'm saving my modeling money in order to go to Las Vegas for a divorce. I want to be free, so I can become a starlet."

"A nice enough ambition. With money tight like that maybe you can't afford to hire me. What about that? You do want to hire me, don't you?"

She tilted her head up at me and pursed those wet lips.

I was sweating. I went back to my seat, feeling as if she'd won that round. "I charge ten bucks a day, and expenses. What can I do for you, Mrs...Miss?"

"My name is Norma Jeane...Mortensen." She laid the glasses on my ash dusty desk and sat up straight to give me the whole effect. Don't get me wrong, she wasn't throwing herself at me, but still, I got the feeling she wanted to please me. Make me like her.

I nodded at my door. "John Marley. At your service."

"Pleased to meet you." She was sitting in the chair like the good little girl in school, but her eyes were impish, as if her coming here was all a big joke. "I'm a model. Doing some stuff for the army."

"I'm 4F myself. Punctured ear drum."

"I didn't ask." Her sentences were short, breathless, and her voice was timid. "I'm staying across the road." She threw her arm out vaguely. "At the La Fonda Motor Lodge. I'd been working all morning with my photographer, David Conover. About an hour ago, there was a knock on my door."

I was fascinated by the way she chewed the red from her lips. She caught me watching her and widened her eyes. "Go on." My voice was hoarse, my throat gummy. "So, what happened?"

"I was just back from lunch." She snuggled into the chair with a shy smile. "Alone. I wanted to take a shower. After a shower I love walking around in the nude." This delightful little girl next door was absolutely luminous. And, obviously, a tease. "Don't you find that stimulating?"

I cleared my throat. "Walking around nude? Or hearing you talk about it?"

She blew some of the ash dust off my desk, wrinkled her nose at the inadequate results, set her elbows on the desk, and rested her chin in her cupped hands. "Take your pick."

I had to keep myself from getting lost in her. "Go on," I said.

"The young man told me he just wanted to show me his stuff. He was selling."

"I'll bet."

"Don't be fresh." She shook her finger at me like a schoolteacher to the class brat. "He was selling sterling silver carving sets on the installment plan."

"In a motor lodge. Sounds like a line to me."

"To me, too," she said in her breathy voice. "But he was cute, so I listened to what he had to say."

"And?" I snagged my handkerchief from my hip pocket and wiped the sweat from my lip and the back of my neck. My shirt was sticking to my chair.

"The phone rang. The room is a small hall and a bedroom. I went maybe ten steps into the bedroom to answer it."

"Without closing him out in the hall?"

The blond shook her head. She looked so sad.

"Not smart."

She took a deep breath, her nostrils quivered. So did those breasts. Oh, Lord, she was something else. I glanced down at Mr. Roosevelt. The sight of the dead President cleared my head. The doll was playing me. Every move, every gesture, every quiver was all deliberate. She knew what she was dong; yes, she did. Of all the dames I've ever met Norma Jeane, if that was really her name, was the world champion first class tease.

This time she waited me out. Since I saw she wasn't going to talk, I figured I'd better although I hadn't seen the color of her money yet. "I bet he's 4F, too."

"Bet he's not."

"Let's ask him."

"We can't. He's dead."

We were holding the drinks I'd poured neat into the two chipped coffee cups.

"Who was on the phone?"

She tossed back half the drink, about a shot's worth, and began coughing.

"Easy does it. You said you didn't drink."

"Did you think I was lying?" Those lovely dark eyes glistened with the suggestion of tears.

"Maybe yes, maybe no."

Surprisingly she nodded.

"Who called?"

"No one. The operator told me he hung up."

"That figures. He?"

"What?"

"The operator said he?"

"I think so."

"The body?"

"Lying in the hall of my room in the La Fonda Lodge." Her nostrils quivered. "With a knife in his back."

"Don't tell me. A sterling silver carving knife." She didn't tell me. "Why me? Why not call the cops?"

"I can't." A surprise. She practically screamed that. After all that controlled and sensuous banter, this dame suddenly seemed borderline hysterical. An hysteric. Hysteria made more sense than her earlier act. That's how most people would behave after having someone killed practically front of them. If her story was true.

"Why can't you call the cops?"

Her lips twitched undecided, hesitant, searching for the smile. But she didn't answer my question.

I returned to a previous tack. "How'd you come to me?"

"I was so scared that I ran out and jumped into my car. I was barely on the road when I crashed."

"Into what?"

"One of the palm trees."

"Oh."

"Some fellows in a truck stopped and pushed my car to your side of the road for me. I didn't know what to do, but God provided..."

"Yeah. You looked up and there I was."

Her lips trembled. Her hands. Her hands crushed the white purse. "It was gruesome," she said, "being there with a dead body." Her lips twitched. She found the smile, but couldn't hold onto it.

"While you were on the phone could you see...the salesman?"

"I c-c-c-could have if I l-l-l-looked. I didn't look. My b-b-b-back was to him." Now she was stuttering. This kid was a packet full of troubles.

"You're very trusting."

"I c-c-c-concentrate on one thing at a time. Besides I was brought up to trust p-p-p-people. I'm a Christian Scientist."

"Oh."

As if to prove the force and efficacy of her faith, she said, "Peter Piper picked a peck of pickle peppers," without a flaw. The stutter was gone as quick as it had come. "I'm an actress."

"Don't I know it?"

"You're being mean. Some day I'm going to be a big star."

"I have no doubt of that."

"If I bleached my hair, do you think I could be the new Harlow?"

"Why not?" Norma Jeane's case, if it was a case, didn't look like it was going anywhere. It sure wasn't putting any money in my pocket. But what the hell, the phone wasn't ringing off the hook, and sitting opposite this dame sure beat reading about Mr. Roosevelt or the War, winding down through it was, or listening to a bunch of kids from Van Nuys High School reciting "Oh, Captain! My Captain!", Walt Whitman's farewell to Lincoln, on the radio.

"I'm going to be a star." Now she gave me the full force of her baby face stare.

"I believe you."

"What about Beverly Hills?"

"What about it?"

"To live in, silly. No. Too snooty. But I do want to be rich. Maybe live in Brentwood. A small house will do me, Spanish sort of. With a pool. Kidney shaped. Like the stars have. A special place where I can be protected from the everything out here."

"That sounds nice." I drained my cup and poured a refill. I wondered what had really happened to the salesman. If he was a salesman.

"But I want my life to mean something. I want kids. Lots. And a poodle. Or maybe a collie, like Lassie."

"That sounds like a fair ambition."

"I had a collie once. Muggsy. She died."

"That's too bad."

The fan chugged overhead, putting out its muffled worthless breeze. I watched my seersucker jacket hanging on the peg on the wall moving to the fan's rhythms.

Somewhere outside somebody was yelling at a kid. Or a dog. My Camel smoldered in the thick glass ashtray. I lit a new one from the butt and stubbed the butt out. I got up, cranked open the blinds, and gave us both a limited view of the La Fonda Motor Lodge across Ventura. There was a beat-up old yellow Pontiac convertible at the curb. Hers.

The sunlight through the blinds cast bright stripes on her. I pictured her walking around in her birthday suit after her shower. In my fantasy her flesh was warm and alive. God, she was gorgeous.

The blonde looked from the window, to the fan, to me. All three were irritating her. "You have a soul, don't you?"

"Doesn't everyone?"

"I think you could be my best friend. And I do need a friend."

Wow. She was good. She was real good. Underneath the dumb blonde act was there a sparkling sensitive intelligence? I couldn't be sure. I studied her for a long time. My contemplation was a bit intense, I guess, because she flinched.

She was almost child-like in her desire to please. She was trying hard to be my friend. She stared at my shirt. "That's a beautiful shirt. A really wonderful shirt."

"Thank you." It was only a shirt. And one that had seen better days. "When are you going to tell me the real story?" I was losing patience and beginning to be annoyed by her little girl tricks.

She looked startled. "What do you mean?"

"I believe you about the dead body. But that's all I believe. Do you want my help? Just put twenty dollars on the desk and we can keep talking."

She fumbled with her purse. A tear rolled down her pink white cheek.

"Come on, cut it out." I pulled my handkerchief from my back pocket. It was clean; I shoved it at her.

"No, thank you," she whispered. She produced a wad of bills from the purse and counted out four tens on the desk. Then she dried her eyes with a little square of lacy pink cloth. "Take your money. Forty ought to get me twice as much."

I picked up the crumpled bills and slipped them into my shirt pocket.

"Do you believe me now?" She narrowed those beautiful dark eyes. "Is that the way it works? If I give you money you believe me?"

"Keep talking." My receipt pad was in the top drawer of my desk next to the little .22 Colt automatic. I wrote out a receipt and handed it to her. "Where'd you get all that money, Norma Jeane?"

"I...I..." She broke off with a startled hand to her mouth "I don't know," she said in that soft child's voice of hers. The words were so blurred that for a moment I couldn't make them out.

"Let's go across the road and have a look see," I said.

"I'm going to be a great movie star someday," she whispered, not moving. "I'm going to be a movie star. Whatever I do is an investment in myself. Do you like my dress? I've got to have nice things when I go out on a job. If you're dressed well, they pay higher fees."

"Let's go, Norma Jeane," I said. I held out my hand.

The blush bled through her pink white skin. She made a pleading gesture with her hands.

All of a sudden she thrust her right hand out. I took it. She shook my hand firmly once. Like something she'd seen in a movie. "Thank you."

"Lead the way," I said.

She winked at me and squealed her deep-seated laugh. "Walk this way," she said. But I couldn't. Not ever. I don't think there were even women who could emulate that rolling walk of hers. I don't know if it was the broken heel or what. Whatever made the walk work, she was as lovely aft as fore. And didn't she know it.

She was out the door singing snatches of "I'll Walk Alone."

After only a second's thought I grabbed my gun and rig from the desk and my jacket from the hook. This was an exceptional occasion. Not the Jap invasion, but it would do. I take dead bodies seriously. If there was a dead body. Hot as it was, I put the rig on and hid it by wearing the jacket.

My Ford coupe was in the little lot beside the office. I opened the passenger side and she hopped in.

"Ooh," she cried. Then she laughed in an altogether natural way. I was taken by the innocent awe in her face. "What a yummy car. I love red."

I closed her door. A lot she knew. I'd been nursing the coupe since '41. If the War lasted much longer I'd be getting around on a Schwinn. When I got in on my side I saw she'd put her sunglasses back on. I gunned the Ford and squealed it across the highway to the La Fonda. I was in that kind of mood. "Which is yours?"

"That one." She pointed to the last yellow cabin. I pulled in right next to a black Caddie.

I got out and opened her door. She didn't get out, she didn't even move. I couldn't see her eyes, but I knew she was looking at the Cadillac. "So how about it?" I offered my hand.

She removed the sunglasses and stared at me as if she'd never seen me before.

"I'm an orphan," she said in a tiny voice.

She was a real nut job. Too bad, I thought. "Norma Jeane, do you want to show me the dead guy?"

"Oh," she said. "I forgot." She got out of the car, then reached in for the white purse on the seat. Her dress rode up to her crotch. Jesus, she wasn't wearing anything underneath.

I must have made a sound because she straightened her dress and shot me a hurt look. I was sweating like a goniff under the lights in the back room of a police station.

"You go first," she said. "I'm scared."

"If he's dead, he can't hurt you," I said walking in front of her, imagining how she looked when I was behind her. The path was spread with little white stones. A phallic cactus leaned against her cabin.

The door was wide open. I drew my Colt, just in case. Just in case what, I thought. I had no idea.

"Oh, my God," she said. She was breathing down my neck, pushing up against me. I won't tell you what I was thinking. "Do you see him?" she whispered.

The little hall was empty. Measuring my steps I walked into the bedroom. Not a soul. Dead or alive. There was a sharp morbid smell in the air. The bed looked as if she'd just crawled out of it after an active few hours. The night table was full of bottles of make-up, some containers of pills, and a dusting of spilled powder.

A pair of blue jeans lay on the floor, a man's white shirt drooped from the doorknob of the bathroom door. The place was a mess. On the bureau was half a hamburger with raw onion and an empty coke bottle. The smell was coming from the hamburger, which was going green. But no dead man.

"Oh," she said, taking it all in, then giving me that tremulous smile of hers.

I holstered my Colt, reached into my shirt pocket, and handed her her forty bucks.

She gave me two back. "Because you were kind," she said.

The phone rang. She stared at me as if waiting my permission. I nodded. By the time she said hello, I was gone. Before I closed the door I heard her say, "What should I wear?"

It was one of those things, you know. I knew she wasn't all there, but I couldn't get her out of my mind. I just drove for a while. That was extravagant, what with gas rationing, but I needed to think. Or not to think. Still at a loss, I went to see a movie at a second run house in L.A. One I hadn't seen the first time around in '44. Edward G. Robinson and Joan Bennett in *The Woman In The Window*.

Here was a real bright guy, his life and career ruined because of a dame. So he tries to cover everything up and comes unglued. All because of a dame. There was a trick ending to the movie. When all was said and done, it turned out it was just a dream. But the point was made.

Ordinarily I would have wondered how Robinson's character could let a woman do that to him, but having met Norma Jeane and listened to her dead body story, I wasn't sure it couldn't happen to me. I was happy to be rid of her. After the movie I had a couple of beers and went home. But she haunted my sleep.

"I'm an orphan," she said. "There's something missing in orphans. We want everybody to love us." Her juicy red lips pursed and came close to me. Like an extreme close-up in a movie. "Do you love me?" The lips came even closer, all distorted like that Spanish fellow Dali paints them, begging me to kiss them. "He's dead," she whispered. "Why don't you believe me?"

The blonde was getting into the black Caddy bare ass naked when I woke up in a pool of sweat. I took a cold shower and put on yesterday's shirt because I forgot to get my other three out of the Chinese.

When I went down to my office, I saw that her Pontiac convertible was gone. I walked on out to the parking lot, got into my coupe, gunned the motor, and made a U and pulled up in front of her cabin. Her Pontiac wasn't there either. Neither was the Cadillac.

What I should have done then was pulled the car across the road, parked it, and got on with my life. But no, I had to know more.

I could see the maid running the vacuum in the next cabin. I got out of my car and walked to Norma Jeane's cabin. Again the door was wide open.

"Norma Jeane," I called. "You there?"

No answer. I stepped inside. The make-up and pills were gone. The clothes lying around, gone. All that remained was the rumpled bedclothes, the dusting of powder on the night table and a crumpled paper bag on top of the bureau. That and the sharp morbid onion smell mixed with just a hint of Chanel #5 with an Ivory soap chaser.

I sat on the bed. The temperature had already hit ninety and the heat was getting to me. Maybe, just like Edward G. Robinson, I dreamed the whole damn thing. I stood up and something shiny caught my eye from under the bureau. A piece of jewelry or something.

I knelt down. The case of the mixed-up blonde didn't exist. And the case that didn't exist was over with. Finished. Still, there I was, John Marley, real life private eye, crawling around a dead smelling cabin in the La Fonda Motor Lodge, waving his hand around under a dusty old bureau. Searching for whatever it was. I touched it, and quick pulled my hand away. I'd cut myself. Sitting on the bed again, I inspected the slice in my finger as the blood beaded up from it. "God damn."

I wrapped my handkerchief around the finger and got to my feet. This time I was smarter. I lifted the end of the bureau and set it down a few inches away, uncovering the shiny thing.

It was a silver carving knife. My blood was on it. From what I could see there were no stains to show that somebody else's blood had been on it, too. But that didn't prove anything.

I reached down and picked it up.

"Hello," someone called.

"Yeah," I answered. Quickly I uncrumpled the bag and put the carving knife in it.

The Spanish girl came into the room. "I thought you checked out."

"I did," I said. "I just came back to see if I forgot something."

The phone rang.

The maid looked at me. "Maybe it's for you," she said. She had no accent at all.

"Maybe?" I said. I picked up the phone, extremely conscious of the knife in the bag. "Yeah?"

But there was no one there.

*   *   *

Marty's first answer to the question: Why should someone go to a Mayhem in the Midlands convention? Is: that like Rick in

Casablanca he goes for the waters. When told his answer makes no sense Marty covers up by saying he was misinformed and says he goes to Omaha for the seafood. At this point Annette shoves Marty away and says the reason to go to Mayhem in the Midlands is the wonderful people, and the fact that the Omaha and Lincoln Libraries sponsor it.

Exactly what I meant to say, Marty shouts.

GENTLE INSANITIES

by Christine Matthews

"Christine Matthews" is a pseudonym for Marthayn Pelegrimas. Both were born and raised in Chicago, Illinois. In addition, she has lived in St. Louis, Omaha, Kansas City and back to St. Louis again.

Her first paying gig was freelance work for *Omaha Magazine*. She had a one act play, "Good Golly, It's Holly" produced at The Circle Theater in Omaha and also in Lawrence, Kansas.

But her heart lies in writing short stories. Starting off in Horror, ending up in Mystery, she has published over 50 short stories to date. Collaborating with Robert J. Randisi she has written two novels featuring amateur sleuths "Gil & Claire Hunt" (*Murder is the Deal of the Day*, SMP, 1999; *The Masks of Auntie Laveau*, SMP, 2002.) Her erotic thriller, *Scarred for Life*, is due out at the end of 2001.

GENTLE INSANITIES

by Christine Matthews

"They hired me because I'm a crazy lady." I squinted into the camera. Was my eye shadow smeared? Please, don't let me sweat through this new blouse—it's silk. God, I was enjoying my fifteen minutes of fame.

"A crazy lady? Is that what it takes to be a private investigator in Omaha?"

"It can't hurt."

The audience laughed.

The topic of today's 'Donahue' was *Daring People— Exciting Occupations*. I do admit I'm more exciting than the fire-eater sitting stage left. What does it take to douse a flame? Lots of practice and some sort of protective coating gargled inside your mouth. But I don't think I'm as daring as the eighty-seven-year-old sky-diving great-grandmother. Now that takes real guts.

"Have you ever had to use that?" He pointed to the .32. I didn't have the heart to tell him I'd worn it because the leather shoulder holster matched my skirt.

"Once." I hung my head, as though the memory was too sad to discuss.

Questions from the audience were coming in spurts: "I've read that being a private investigator is boring, lots of routine, paperwork, photographs of cracks in sidewalk...you know."

"The agency I work for specializes in people, not pavement. We track down deadbeats who owe child support, runaway kids...that kind of thing. And I've only been licensed a year; guess I haven't had enough time to get bored."

The next question dealt with the great-grandmother's sex life and I zoned off wondering if it was true that the camera would add an additional ten pounds to my hips.

When I got to the office the day after the show ran on TV, Jan and Ken stood beside their desks and applauded.

I smiled, took a slow bow, and blew them each a kiss. "Please, be seated. I'll walk among you common folk and sign autographs later."

"Roberta," Harry called from his office.

"Robbie," I shouted. I hate the name Roberta, especially the way my boss, Harry Winsted, says it.

I sat across from Harry, eased into the leather chair, crossed my legs, and waited for him to tell me how lousy I was on "Donahue." The more shit Harry gives me, the better I know I'm doing.

"Saw you on 'Donahue.' That number about your little ole .32. Great stuff. Makes us look like big time."

"Just doin' my job, boss."

"Yeah, well it's back to the real world, kid. I got a job that needs your special touch." He picked up a folder from the table behind him.

"Name's James Tanner. Seems the bastard skipped town with his three-year-old son and the wife's not getting enough help from the police to suit her." He tossed the file at me.

I reached out, caught it without looking away from Harry's beady little eyes. "Anything else?"

"Yeah. You look fat on TV."

"Love you, too." I made a point to slam the glass door as I exited Harry's office. The glass rumbles; he always flinches. With my back turned, I waved over my shoulder.

After reading through the file, I found that James Lucias Tanner was all of twenty years old. He'd gotten married when he was seventeen, to a pregnant sixteen-year-old from the right side of the tracks. It was that family money paying for this investigation. After a series of bad career moves, James finally landed work as a manager at the Touchless Car Wash over on Dodge.

I made a note to check out Kevin Tanner's preschool.

The next day I drove out to La Petite Academy, in Millard. I expected to see rows of toddlers all dressed in red uniforms. Good little soldiers with teeny, tiny swords tucked inside Pampers and baggy coveralls. Instead, I found a neat room full of partitioned activities. The smell of paste and warm milk reminded me of my own kindergarten class. I'd called ahead for an appointment with Kevin's teacher and made my way to her office, located in the back of the main room.

"Ms. Kelly?" I extended my hand.

"Ms. Stanton. I saw you yesterday on 'Donahue.'"

A fan. "That was taped weeks ago." I assumed a modest smile.

"Well, I enjoyed it a lot. Is being a private investigator really exciting?"

I shrugged, surveyed the room cluttered with Nerf balls and blocks. "I do get to go to some very exotic locales."

She laughed.

But her smile curved downward into a sad pout when I asked about Kevin Tanner.

"Oh, Kevin's such a sweetie. All the children and teachers miss him. But that father of his...what a creep. Always came in here dirty and mean. He had such a mouth on him. Tattoos all over his arms and a green and black snake on one hand spelled out the name 'Donna.' Kevin's mother is Lynn. The man's a pig."

Good, she was a real talker. All I had to do was sit back, nod, and wait for recess.

Ms. Kelly told me, down to the rip in his seams, what James Tanner had been wearing the day he kidnapped Kevin. She described how the backseat of Tanner's car was littered with Burger King and Taco Bell wrappers. But best of all, Ms. Kelly's anal-retentive memory recalled a bumper sticker. A Mary Kay pink design telling every tailgater that inside was a representative. And the pink coffee mug Ms. Kelly saw stuck to the dashboard was stenciled with the name AMY.

By the time I got back to my apartment it was eight o'clock. The red light winked at me from the answering machine. I punched the gray button. The tape rewound, then replayed. My father's voice shouted from inside the machine, frantic.

"It's your mother. Jesus, she almost died! We're at the hospital. What am I going to..." His sobs were cut off by the infernal beep.

The next message started. It was Dad again. "For God's sake, it's five. Your mother's in radiation. I'm at Christ Community; they've assigned a specialist. I don't know what..."

The beep disconnected his agony and before I could call information for the number in Chicago, the phone rang.

I grabbed the receiver, startled. "Hello?"

"Thank God! Where the hell have you been? I've called twice..."

"Dad, I just got home."

"We were having lunch; all of a sudden she couldn't breathe, she grabbed her chest, turned an awful color, and just crumpled."

"I got her in the car and rushed to the Emergency Room. She almost died." He choked on his fear. "I can't lose her."

I maintained an artificial calm, not even allowing the idea of my mother's death to seep into my brain. "Could it be pneumonia?"

"Haven't you understood a word I've said? She's in radiation. The x-rays show there's a spot on her lung. But the technician said we caught it in time and your mother's so strong. You know how strong she is, Robbie?"

Cancer.

"Yes, Dad. I know." Thirty-five years had taught me well. Agree and listen. That's all Dad ever required of me. Nod, smile, be Daddy's little girl. I played the part so well that sometimes I lost my adult self in the charade.

"Oh God, what am I going to do?"

"I'll come up and..."

"No, we'll be fine. We're fine."

"Have you called Delia?"

"I'll do that now, while I'm waiting. Talk to you later." The connection broke.

Tears welled behind my eyes refusing to roll down my cheeks. Mother always said she'd live to be one hundred.

"I'm holding you to that promise," I whispered to her from five hundred miles away.

After staring at my scuffed floor tiles for half an hour I couldn't wait any longer. I called my sister.

She sniffed. "Dad just called."

"Well, what should we do?"

"I couldn't go up there even if I wanted to. The shop's busy. With Halloween coming. I'm swamped with fittings and special orders. Then there's Homecoming gowns."

"And I just started a new case but if I can wrap it up, I'll go see what's happening."

"That'd be great. You know how Daddy gets. He blows everything out of proportion. Maybe it's not that bad."

"Maybe." I hoped, but deep inside I knew the truth.

The leaves seemed particularly vivid as I walked to my car. The apartment complex I live in offers covered parking, for an additional fee, of course. While my car is protected from the rain and ice, birds love to poop on it as they huddle above on steel beams supporting the ceiling. I cursed the black and white blobs covering my blue paint job and crunched dried leaves beneath my feet. The morning was mild and I could smell burning leaves. Someone dared defy the law and I applauded them. What was autumn without that toasty aroma clinging to orange and yellow leaves?

Ken was using the computer when I entered the office. He glanced up and grinned. "Get any last night?"

"Why do you ask me that stupid question every single morning?"

"Because I want to know if you got any."

"Sleazeball." I punched his arm as I walked to my desk.

"If you call me names, I won't show you a new program we just got in."

I admit it, I'm computer unfriendly. I admit, too, I've depended upon the knowledge of others when accessing or exiting a screen. I still needed to pick Ken's brain.

"I'm sorry. You're not a sleaze ball. You're just scum. Better?"

"I knew you'd come around. Take a look. This is great."

Reluctantly, I stood behind him as he pushed keys with the artistry of Liberace. "All we have to do is punch in a last name and we practically get a pint of blood."

"Could you try 'Tanner' and see what comes up?"

Before I could turn for the file, the screen displayed twelve Tanners in the Omaha metropolitan area.

"First name?" Ken asked.

"James L."

"Bingo! We got your credit ratings, places of employment, marital status, number of children, pets, even a ring size from a recent purchase at Zales."

"Can you print it out for me?"

"No," he scolded. "I showed you how to print something. So do it yourself."

"Kenny," I pulled his ear. He loves it when I pull his ear. "Kenny, sweetheart, you're right there, in front of the thing. Please?"

"Just this once. This is the last time." He pushed some more keys and the printer started to life.

"Thank you very much," I said in my best Shirley Temple voice. He also loves it when I talk like a little girl. Hell, if it'll get the computer work done, I'll talk like Donald Duck. I sat up straight behind my cheap desk and studied the printout. In between reviewing blue and white lines of tedious, boring statistics, I suddenly remembered Amy and let my feet do the walking to the yellow pages. I flipped to "Cosmetics." There were four "Independent Sales Directors" listed. One of them was named Amy Schaefer. I jotted down her number and address and stood to return the book to its shelf. Passing Ken's desk, I poked his shoulder. "I bet I crack this case and don't even have to use a computer. Brains, ole bean. Human brains beat your computer friend any day."

"God, you're the most bullheaded broa—"

"Careful," I warned.

"—woman I've ever known. You belong back in the dark age."

"Where men were men..."

"Careful," he warned right back.

Omaha has a small-town feel to it. Tractors frequent busy streets, cowboys visit from out west when there's a cattle auction or rodeo. People are friendly and move in second gear instead of third. But with a population of half a million, a symphony, ballet company, museums, and great shopping, it also has a big-city mix.

I turned onto "L" Street and took it to Seventy-second. Making a right onto Grover, I found the apartment complex where Amy Schaefer lived. I backtracked to the Holiday Inn and dialed her number from a phone in the lobby.

After three rings a timid voice answered.

"Amy Schaefer?"

"Yes. Who's calling?" She was a regular church mouse.

"Let's just say I'm a special friend of James."

"Oh? Where do you know Jimmy from?"

"We've been friends a long time, met at..." *Think, think.* I looked across the street and saw a sign for a lounge named Jodhpurs. "...Jodhpurs. It was a twofer night, ladies were free. You know how cheap he is." Was she buying any of this? From all the fast-food wrappers in his car, I figured the guy was not a big spender.

"Why are you telling me all this?"

"Well, Jimmy's been begging me to come back to him but after he told me about you..."

"You know so much about me and I don't even know your name." She waited.

"Oh, I'm sorry. It's Donna."

Suddenly her schoolmarm act exploded across the phone line. "That son of a bitch!"

"Now, calm down. The way I figure it, us wome...broads should stick together."

My head felt as though it had been fired at, close range, when she slammed down the receiver. She was hot! Hell hath no fury and all that jazz.

I dashed to my car and swung back onto Grover. Parking across from the Grover Square Apartments, I saw a woman come stamping across the lot toward a pink Cadillac. I followed as she screeched into traffic, flooring the accelerator as the light turned yellow. I raced after her.

Then a Trailways bus pulled out of the McDonald's parking lot. Amy swerved, the car between us rammed into her rear bumper, and I jerked my steering wheel to the right, hoping no cars were in that lane or riding my tail. Last thing I saw as I passed the accident was one screaming woman, a busload of Japanese tourists snapping pictures, and a salesman-type man calling the police from his car phone. I hate those things.

"Damn," I hissed, rubbernecking as I passed the scene. I was hungry, frustrated, and had a headache that wouldn't quit.

While I hate the plastic trappings of twentieth-century life, I do love the simple pleasures. Like mail for instance. And as I poked through my mailbox and found only an ad for a new beauty salon, I felt cheated.

The apartment seemed cold; I hiked up the heat. Rummaging through the refrigerator, I looked for the chili left over from last night. The bowl had worked itself to the back of the middle shelf. I scooped a heaping portion into a smaller bowl and put my lunch into the microwave.

The microwave is another of those simple pleasures I referred to. I know, it also fits under the category of "twentieth-century conveniences." Oh well, I use it anyway but each time give thanks that I don't get contaminated from the radiation or whatever flies around in there to produce heat. And, if I should one day wake up to find all microwaves have disappeared, I'd survive. See, I don't depend on the convenience. That's the difference: the mind-set. I enjoy the convenience while knowing full well that one power outage will not upset my life. Dad taught us that. Don't depend on anything or anyone and you'll never be disappointed.

Dad.

I looked across the room. The answering machine was blinking. As I programmed the time into the oven, I realized my headache was fierce and went for some aspirin before listening to messages.

After gulping the last swig of water, I reluctantly pressed the gray button.

Beep.

"This is Mrs. Calhoun from American Express. Your account is now two months past due and we were wondering if a payment had been made. Please call me at 800-555-9100."

Beep.

"Ro-ber-ta," Harry whined. "Some guy, says he's your father. He's been calling every fifteen minutes. Sounds weird. Give me a call, okay? Roberta?"

Beep.

"Just got a frantic call from Dad." It was Delia. "He's kidnapping Mother from the hospital. Call me!"

Beep. Rewind.

I pulled the phone over to the table, set my place for lunch, then poured a Coke over lots of ice. I dialed Delia's number. She answered on the first ring.

"Are you okay?" I asked.

"Oh Robbie, thank God. I don't know what's going on. I talked with Mother's nurse—the doctor wasn't available. She said when Dad brought Mother in, she was barely breathing. They thought they'd lose her right there. What the hell have they been doing all this time? I've called and called and no one's home. I'm scared."

"Calm down," I advised with my mouth full. "If the doctor let her go home, she wasn't kidnapped. I'll talk to him and call you back."

"I think one of us should go up there." She was suddenly the frightened little sister and I knew which one of us would be going to Chicago.

"Your father needs help, Miss Stanton." That's the first thing Dr. Blair said after I'd identified myself.

"I've known that for a long time." I bet he thought I was kidding. "But right now I'm more concerned about my mother."

"I can appreciate your position. Well, your mother's a heavy smoker. Maybe if she'd come in sooner." He took a breath then dove right it. "Your mother has cancer...lung cancer."

"Should she be home now?"

"She responded very well to treatment and your father understands how important it is she came in twice a week for it. When she regains some of her strength, we can start her on chemotherapy."

"And then? After the chemo?" I really didn't want to hear his answer.

"Six months, a year. A year and a half—tops."

I had to hang up, quickly. "Thank you."

I ran to the bathroom unsure if I was going to cry or collapse but feeling the bathroom was the direction to head. I ended up sitting on the edge of the tub, holding my head in my hands, rocking back and forth until the panic passed. I thought I was going to die.

Delia took the news better than I had, or maybe she just pretended. It's hard to figure her out sometimes. While she stands five feet seven, I barely reach five feet four inches. She has dark hair—I'm light. She explodes over situations I find amusing and laughs when I want to scream.

We had agreed that I would fly to Chicago; I'd have to be the eyes and ears for both of us now.

I called Harry and told him about my near-miss with Amy Schaefer. He grumbled until I added in the news about my mother.

"Geez, kid," he signed. "You just do what has to be done. Family comes first, that's what I always say. I'll sit on this Tanner case until you get back."

"Thanks, Harry. Thanks a lot."

"Hey, no skin off my ass."

I couldn't tell if Dad was happy to see me. He'd always made me feel as thought I was intruding. Most times he looked annoyed.

"What are you doing here?" He stood behind the storm door, talked through the screen.

"Can I come in?"

"Well, sure." He held the door open. "It's just this is such a surprise."

I set my suitcase down and wrapped my arms around him. He felt thinner, bony. I whispered into his ear. "How's Mother?"

Tears welled in his eyes. "Not too good today."

I held him at arm's length, surprised at how old he looked.

"Let me go tell her you're here."

He walked away from me, went down the hall, and I stood waiting, feeling like a salesman calling on the lady of the house. Then I followed him. "Hi." I said softly. She lay on her side, on top of the bedspread. She was wearing a pink sweat suit, her feet tucked inside a pair of white cotton socks. She didn't turn to look at me. I walked to her side of the bed and knelt down. And then she whimpered.

I threw myself on top of her and we hugged. When my eyes adjusted to the light, I saw how swollen and misshapen her face was. She reminded me of one of those Betty Boop dolls.

"Why didn't you call me? Or Delia?"

"What could you do?" she asked, puzzled.

What could I do? Love you. Comfort you. What does a family do for one another? I knew then that she hadn't the slightest idea.

I couldn't get any information out of them and for two days watched my father dole out vitamins, steroids, and antibiotics. He cooked; he helped her up; he helped her down. I was in the way most of the time.

When I asked about Dr. Blair, I received mixed reviews. So I decided to check out Blair for myself. Telling my folks I was going shopping, I headed for Christ Community Hospital and the two o'clock meeting I'd set up the day before.

He looked like Elton John. Dark hair cut in bangs across his forehead, a toothy grin and oversized glasses. I agreed with Mother; I liked him.

"Her mental attitude is wonderful. And your father takes excellent care of her." His compassion assured me he wanted Mother to be well as much as I did. But doctors can't guarantee miracles.

I called Delia from a pay phone in the hospital lobby. She seemed relieved and encouraged. I felt better about the relieved part but cautious about the encouragement.

I packed my suitcase as my father trailed behind me. He walked in a clipped step and waved his arms as his voice rose. "How dare you."

I folded a blouse, keeping my back to him. "I'm her daughter. I have the right."

Words came in slow, deliberate syllables. "You're trying to turn your mother against me. We were doing fine until you came."

Hot, angry tears dripped down my face. I bent over the suitcase, quickly fastened the clasps, and turned to get my coat.

"Now what are you crying about? I can't say two words to you without you bawling. You're too goddamned sensitive, Robbie. Always have been. We're just having a conversation and you get hysterical."

"I gotta go." My eyes scanned the carpet as I walked toward Mother's room. I crept in and kissed her check. She breathed slowly, never acknowledging my presence. Confrontations were not her forte.

My father followed me to the front door, all the time telling me how I didn't understand, how selfish I'd always been.

I called a cab from the store across the street and waited, staring out the window.

It was worth one more try. I dialed Amy Schaefer's number. Timid as ever she asked, "Hello?"

"Amy, just thought you'd like to know we're taking Kevin and going to Disneyland for Christmas." That seemed like the kind of thing Tanner would do. At least I hoped it was. "Sorry if that screws up your holiday, doll."

"You're full of shit! Jimmy ain't going nowhere."

"Jingle bells, jingle bells, jingle all the..."

Slam.

I dashed out of the Holiday Inn and got in my car. Sure enough, after a ten-minute wait, Amy Schaefer came out of her apartment and this time she carried two shirt boxes wrapped in Christmas paper, tied with red ribbons.

I giggled. "Oh, goody, someone's gonna get their Christmas presents early."

Once again we headed up 72nd Street. Turning west on Dodge, we passed the Touchless Car Wash. She made a right on 120th and turned into an apartment complex. Amy got out of her pink car, and opened the door of apartment number forty-nine with her own key.

I knew I'd have to sit and wait. And I admit, okay, it would have been nice to have a phone in the car.

I checked my watch against the bank's huge read-out. My watch showed two-ten; the bank displayed two-twenty. I decided to compromise. It was two-fifteen.

Around three o'clock the door of number forty-nine burst open and I saw those two Christmas packages come flying across the parking lot. Amy Schaefer dashed for her car, followed by a short guy with dirty hair. I'd seen his driver's license photo and recognized James Tanner.

I called the police from the Taco Bell across the street, identified myself, and gave them the address where they could pick up James Tanner.

Within ten minutes a squad car pulled in behind me. They'd kept the siren off as I'd advised, but Tanner spotted the car just the same. He ran for the apartment while Amy stood screaming after him. "Run! You lying son of a bitch. I wish I would have called the cops myself. Coward!"

The police knocked at number forty-nine until Tanner answered. By that time several neighbors had gathered and traffic slowed to catch a glimpse of the action. I waited while an officer escorted James out. A female officer went inside and after a few minutes came out holding a frightened little boy in her arms. She patted his back, talking softly into his ear. The boy clung to her.

I opened my car door. I just couldn't resist.

"Amy?"

She spun around, relieved to see I wasn't wearing a uniform. "What? How'd you know my name?"

"Santa told me, said you'd been a real good girl. Jingle bells, jingle bells, jingle all the way." I kept singing as I returned to my car. "Thanks for all your help. We couldn't have done it without you."

"You bitch!" the timid church mouse screamed. "You fuckin' bitch!"

Some days are like that...you get no appreciation.

"Here you go." I dropped the papers onto Harry's desk. "All wrapped up, neat and tidy. Tanner's in custody, Kevin's being reunited with his mother as we speak, and Amy Schaefer is selling Passionate Pink blusher with a heavy, yet cheerful heart. Life just keeps—"

"Your mother died this morning."

It took me a minute. "What did you say?"

He stood as I fell into the chair. Coming around his desk he bent to touch my shoulder. "Roberta...Robbie, I'm so sorry."

"But I just saw her." I was angry. No, I was upset. I was going to cry. No, I was going to faint. Don't let go. Hang on.

"Your sister's been trying to get you all day. She broke down, couldn't say another word after she told me. I offered to break the news...I didn't want you to feel, you know...alone."

My grief started slowly and built into deep gulping sobs. Harry knelt in front of me, hugging me against his chest.

As the funeral procession wove down the street my parents had lived on for the past eighteen years, I noticed the Christmas decorations. A brick house on the end of the block had a life-sized wooden Santa, painted a hideous red and white. I hated it. The tree lights twinkling around doorways and windows seemed to accentuate our sadness.

Dad stood by himself at the cemetery. Bitter. He told anyone who would listen that now he had no family. Friends reminded him he had two lovely daughters. But he didn't hear. He repeatedly told Delia and me that he was alone and no one had ever loved him but my mother. I was too empty to fill him with reassurance.

"We've gotten through Easter, Mother's Day, Father's Day. I really don't think he should be alone for his birthday." Delia worried. "We'll make a cake, bring some presents."

It was August, and once again I found myself back in Chicago. The birthday party had been a good idea. But the pressure of having a normal celebration had tired us all. Delia had gone to bed early. I sat in the living room, rocking and watched a "Fawlty Towers" rerun. John Cleese always made me laugh.

Dad walked into the room, grunting.

"What's so funny?" Before I could answer, he attacked. "How can you laugh? Your mother's dead! You know, come to think of it, I haven't seen you or your sister cry."

"We've cried a lot." My agony was all that would comfort him now.

"Well, I've never seen it."

I stared at the TV.

When he realized he wasn't going to get me to play, he changed tactics. Reclining in his chair, he signed. I glanced sideways at him and he smiled. When I turned to look him full on, he smirked.

"I've got to tell you something." He leaned forward, confiding. "This is just between us."

"What?"

"I hired someone...to kill the doctor."

This had to be one of his lies. The kind he took back later claiming he had only been kidding.

"Your mother's doctor. That cocksucker, Blair."

"A hit man?"

"Yes." He sat back, satisfied his announcement had knocked the laughter out of me. "Money can buy anything, Robbie. That bastard is to die on the anniversary of your mother's death. At exactly eleven-ten in the morning. And if he's not alone, his wife or children, whoever's with him, are to die, too. Slowly, in agony. I want them to suffer like I have—like your mother did."

"Mother told me she was never in any pain."

"That's beside the point," he almost shouted. "But what about Delia? And me? You could ruin our lives—our futures. There'd be headlines, reporters, we'd be humiliated. You'd end up in prison."

"It'll be done right."

"Don't you care about any of us?"

"He killed your mother. You expect me to let him get away with that?"

I walked over to him. Softly I tried to reason. "No one killed Mother. She had cancer...and she died."

"She didn't have cancer. She was getting better. You heard what they said. It was that doctor; he killed her. And I'm going to kill him."

"I can't talk to you now." I walked down the hall and went to the room I shared with Delia. In the morning I'd tell my sister that our father was crazy. She'd laugh and say, "So tell me something I don't already know."

By the time I returned to Omaha, it was late. The nine-hour car ride had allowed time for lots of thinking. I called Delia.

"I really think we should take Dad's threat seriously."

"Me too." She offered no resistance.

"Before we do anything, I've got to be sure. I'll try to trip him up or get him to admit he lied."

"Do it now, please," Delia asked. "I can't sleep until you do."

"Right now."

I made a cup of tea to warm my hands, spirit, and mood. All the time wondering when things would get back to normal. But as Delia had said at the funeral, "Normal will never be normal again."

Finally I placed the call.

Dad spoke in a calm and serious tone. "I meant every word. Everything's been take care of; there's nothing you can do now."

Then I lost it. All of it; my composure, my logic, my last shred of loyalty. "How can you do this?" I screamed hysterically. "How can you do this to us?"

Slowly, he explained. "Nothing will go wrong. No one will ever know. Just forget about it; it doesn't concern you."

"Please," I was crying now, "please..."

"You don't owe this man anything. He's a murderer."

"No..." I stopped. And that proverbial straw, the one that broke the camel's back, had finally been hoisted upon my own. I hung up the phone.

"From here on out," I later told Delia, "we're taking care of ourselves because no one else will. I'll go see a guy I know—a criminal lawyer. I'll pick his brain."

"You're the mother now," she said. "Please. Don't let Daddy hurt us."

"I won't," I said, and swore silently to protect us both.

Our lives had suddenly taken on a soap opera quality and I did not like being cast in the role of victim.

Bradley Johnson has this great office located in the Old Market area. A bricked passageway, flanked on one side by restaurants and on the other by shops, is illuminated by large sky-lights. Bradley's office is at the top of four flights of wood stairs.

His secretary, Lucy, sits behind a small desk and greets clients with a cup of coffee.

"I heard your mother died. Harry told me. I'm so sorry." She buzzed Bradley.

"Thanks."

Brad escorted me into the large room that serves as his office, meeting room, and lounge. We sat next to the tall windows he prefers to keep free from draperies. He shifted his legs and leaned back in an overstuffed chair.

I confided everything. Bradley reacted with a raised eyebrow.

"Legally, there isn't a thing you can do, Robbie. It's your word against his."

"What I wanted, I guess, was more of a favor. I thought maybe you could contact my father, tell him we've talked. That might scare him enough to call everything off—if there really is a hit man. This way I'd be covered, the doctor would be safe, and my father would have to forget about all this."

"My advice is to call Dr. Blair yourself. Explain the situation, see what he suggests. That's the best you can do. But, Robbie?"

"Yeah?"

"None of this is your fault. You know that, don't you?"

"I guess. It's just that I feel so...dirty. It's hard to explain."

The hospital receptionist said Dr. Blair was with a patient and would get back to me. I knew he kept late hours and told her I'd wait up for his call, no matter what the time.

Around ten o'clock he called.

He was kind and my hands immediately started to shake. I finally worked the conversation around to where it should have started.

"My father told me he holds you responsible for my mother's death."

"Your father has been through a lot. You mother and he were married forty-some years. It's only natural he misses her."

"I know. But...Doctor?" Nothing would ever be as difficult as this moment. "My father told me he's hired someone to have you killed."

Silence.

"Le me take this call on my private line, Ms. Stanton. Hold on a minute."

When he came back, his tone was hushed. "You don't really think he's serious?"

"Yes I do. It's to be done in four months, on the anniversary of my mother's death." My voice trembled. I felt sorrier for all of us having to go through this than I ever could for my father.

Dr. Blair said he wanted to think about things. He'd get back to me.

Sergeant Danta of the Oak Lawn Police Department contacted me two days later. Dr. Blair had filed a complaint.

I'd talked with police before. Lots of times. But this was about me...my life. I repeated my story for what seemed like the hundredth time and for the hundredth time I didn't believe it myself.

"We'll have to proceed with this as if it were truth. But tell me, Ms. Stanton...would you be willing to testify against your father in a court of law?"

I thought about all the years I'd worked for Dad's approval. I thought about all the agony Delia and I were going through so soon after losing our mother. And I answered.

"No."

"Call on line two. Pick it up, Roberta," Harry barked.

"Miss Stanton? I'm Detective Carter, with the Chicago Police Department. A report has been filed with us concerning your father."

"I've already been through this with Sergeant Danta."

"Danta's out of Oak Lawn, where the hospital is located. We need something filed in your father's precinct."

"Oh." I repeated my story from the day before.

"I have to tell you, Miss Stanton, when he first opened the door—"

"What a minute. You spoke to my father? You confronted him? In person? What did he say about Dr. Blair?"

"We had to get his statement. He said he thought the doctor killed your mother."

I suddenly felt as though I'd been strapped into a roller coaster and was slowly being hauled up to the top of Anxiety Mountain. I could hear the gears clicking. And I prayed I wouldn't crack before Christmas reared its holy head.

"Your father's in bad shape."

"We all are."

"There's nothing else we can do."

"I know."

Detective Carter apologized and promised there would be no need to disturb my father again.

"Get any last night?" Ken asked as I walked through the door.

I punched him on the shoulder. "Scum."

"You may think I like it when you call me that, but I don't," he complained.

"Sorry. I had an awful night, didn't sleep at all."

He waited for the punch line and when none came, he shrugged and sat down at the computer.

Harry came banging in from outside and a frigid gust slammed the door. "Roberta. In my office. Now."

I followed behind, a little spaniel, and watched as his boots tracked wet black prints along the dirty carpet.

"Close the door." Harry pulled his gloves off and stuffed them into his pockets. Without removing the snowflaked overcoat, he abruptly turned.

"The body of one Dr. Blair, practicing out of Christ Community Hospital, in Oak Law, Illinois, was found this morning in the trunk of his car. The car was parked in the doctor's reserved space in the hospital lot. He had been beaten to death. They think it was one of those aluminum baseball bats. Very sloppy. I spoke with Sergeant Danta. He said it definitely was not a professional hit."

Click...click...hang on.

"Your father's in custody."

"Was anyone else with the doctor?"

"No."

I turned and we just looked at each other for a minute.

"What do I do?"

"Go home. The police will be calling you."

"Don't tell anyone. I feel so ashamed."

"It'll be all over the news soon enough." Harry shook his head in disbelief. "Go on, get your butt out of here."

After talking with the police, I booked a flight into St. Louis. Delia was in shock when I told her. "Oh God, oh God, oh God," she repeated. "He really did it. Oh God."

"Will you meet me at the St. Louis airport at ten-five tonight?" Springfield was only a few hours away and I knew the distraction would be good for her.

"I guess. But why St. Louis?"

I didn't want to scare her, to tell her that soon reporters and television crews would be camped out on her front lawn.

"We need to be together now," I said.

When my flight finally landed, I spotted Delia standing by a fat man in a blue sweat suit. I could tell she'd been crying. I smiled a hello.

We walked silently to the baggage claim and then she said, "Oh, I almost forgot. Your office called. Ken somebody. He wants you to call him tonight. Here's his number."

After we registered and fought over who got which bed, I called Ken from the hotel.

"You lose our bet."

"What bet? What are you talking about?"

"Computers versus brains." He sounded so sad.

"That was months ago. The Tanner case."

"No, now...the Stanton case."

"I'm tired and..."

"The computer. I was playing around with it today and punched in your name, Robbie. It showed all your credit card charges for the past year."

"And?"

"There was this code number that looked familiar. When I cross-referenced with the police computer, we came up with 'Freedom, Inc.' They offered a very unique personal service. Geez, you can buy anything with a Visa card. It's really disgusting."

Click...click...click...

"We plugged into the airline computer and know you're in St. Louis. Even the phone number you're calling from is being recorded...Why'd you do it, Robbie? Your own father?"

"Ken...Kenny." I know he loves it when I talk in my little girl voice. Daddy always did. "I had to protect all of us. Delia and I don't want Daddy to bully us anymore. And this way, he won't be alone. Maybe the doctors can help him now."

It's those gentle insanities that bring such clear insight. The huge problems only come once in a while. They're easy to fix. But the small, everyday, constant, infuriating irritations drop you over the edge.

Click...click...click.

*   *   *

Everybody should go to Mayhem in the Midland Convention because it's in Omaha, and Omaha is smack dab in the middle...of everything.

A FAVOR FOR SAM

by Robert J. Randisi

Robert J. Randisi is the author of over 360 novels under 14 different names in the mystery, western, horror, fantasy and men's adventure genres. He is the sole founder of the Private Eye Writers of America, and the creator of the Shamus Award (an award for which he has received four nominations, but has never won.) He is also the co-founder of both *Mystery Scene Magazine* and The American Crime Writers league with Ed Gorman. He is the former mystery reviewer for *The Orlando Sentinel.*

Among his series protagonists are private eyes "Miles Jacoby," "Nick Delvecchio," "Henry Po," retired Police Detective "Truxton Lewis," and Police Detective "Joe Keough." He created and has written The Gunsmith western series for Berkley Books at the rate of one book a month since 1982. He is also the editor of more than 25 print and audio anthologies, including the very first all original audio anthology, *For Crime Out Loud.* His anthologies also include the *Deadly Allies, Lethal Ladies* and First Cases series. In 1993 he was presented with a Life Achievement Award by the Southwest Mystery/Suspense Convention.

Delvecchio's Brooklyn, a collection of Nick Delvecchio short stories, was published by Five Star Books in 2001. His new

"Gil & Claire" novel, *The Masks of Auntie Laveau*, written with Christine Matthews, will be out late in 2001. The new "Joe Keough" novel, *East of the Arch*, will be out in 2002. Next year will also see publication of his first horror novel, *Curtains of Blood*, a tale of Bram Stoker and Jack the Ripper.

A FAVOR FOR SAM

A Nick Delvecchio Story
By Robert J. Randisi

1

"Sam! You're a day early. You weren't due back from Chicago until tomorrow."

She was sitting on the floor with her back against my door as I came down the hall. She was wearing jeans, a T-shirt, and she was barefoot.

"Oh, Nick!" She started to cry.

I stared at her, unsure what to say, so I slid down and sat next to her. She looked at me and then wiped at an errant tear as it worked its way down her face.

"Lisa's my friend...a writer who I see at these conventions. When she didn't arrive I called her and...and she told me on the phone that she tested positive for...for the HIV virus."

She was talking very fast, the way people who are upset do. I'd never seen her this upset. She just about collapsed in my arms and started sobbing. You have to understand about my neighbor, Samantha Karson. She's smart, gorgeous, sensitive, and confident. I'd never seen her cry before.

"And...and that's not the worst part. She really loved this guy, Nick, the guy who...who gave it to her. At first she didn't want to believe that she got it from him, but there was no one else."

"Did she confront him?"

"On the phone. She called him and told him that she had AIDS, and do you know what the son of a bitch said to her?"

"What?"

"He told her it was her fault, that she should have been more careful."

"What? He gave her AIDS, and *she* should have been careful?"

"That's what he said."

"What a shit."

"He also said it wasn't his responsibility to tell her."

"Then whose was it?"

"He told her that she should just treat everybody like they have AIDS."

"That's good advice—funny, too, coming from him. What kind of shape is she in?"

"She said she's on some kind of medication and she's responding well to it, but you know that will only put the inevitable off for a while. She's going to die, Nick."

"I'm sorry, Sam."

"There's something else."

"There's more?"

Sam nodded.

"She found out from another girl that the same guy gave her AIDS."

"Before or after your friend?"

"Before. She was his girlfriend before Lisa."

"Too bad Lisa didn't meet her earlier."

"I feel terrible."

"Why?"

"I wish there was something I could do."

"Like what?"

Sam shrugged. "I don't know. Something."

"Well, I wish there was something I could do to help you, Sam."

Sam looked at me sharply and said, "There is."

I looked back at her and asked, "Did I just walk into that with my eyes wide open?"

"Nick, Lisa wants to confront the guy—face-to-face."

"So?"

"She doesn't know where he is. She can't find him."

"I repeat. So?"

"You could find him. You're good at that."

"Sam—"

She stopped me by putting hand on my arm.

"Please, Nick. There's so little that can be done for her. If she could confront him..."

"Aw, Sam..."

She kept staring at me, her eyes pleading. How could I turn her down? And what would it cost me to try? It would probably make *her* feel like she was doing something, which would make her feel better.

"Okay, Sam, I'll see what I can do. Where does your friend live?"

"St. Louis."

"Saint—Okay, well, where does the guy—what's his name—live?"

"His name is Ted and he lives in St. Louis, too."

She had a wary look on her face, like she was waiting for me to explode.

"St. Louis? Sam, that's in Missouri. That's all I know about St. Louis—"

"What do you have to know? If you're looking for a missing person, don't you do the same things, no matter where he lives? Check his home, his work, and...and whatever else you check?"

"Well, sure, but I don't know my way around St. Louis—"

"Lisa said she can tell you how to get anyplace you want to go."

"Lisa said—you already told her I would come?"

"Well...you don't think I expected you to pay your own airfare, do you?"

2

Sam and her friend Lisa didn't have much money but she did have enough to pay for airfare from New York to St. Louis. Of course, I had to lay out the two hundred and forty-eight dollars and she'd reimburse me later. Oh, and Sam said there was a catch—she was coming, too. She said she wanted to spend some time with Lisa. Since I considered that I was doing the whole thing as a favor to Sam, I didn't argue as long as she did what she was going to do while I did what I was going to do. She agreed.

Lisa Carlson lived in a suburb of St. Louis called Shrewsbury. Well, they didn't call them suburbs, they called them cities. That meant that within the city of St. Louis were all these other little cities such as Shrewsbury, Webster Groves, Clayton, and others. Being from New York, it was confusing to me, so I preferred to think of them as suburbs, or even boroughs.

We rented a car at the St. Louis Airport, which was the biggest airport I'd ever been in. One entire section of it was the TWA hub and we seemed to walk miles before we left the gate area and got into the area with the ticket counters, shops, and transportation.

When we got in the car I got behind the wheel and asked Sam where we were going. That's when she explained about all the little cities and told me the one Lisa lived in.

"How do we get there?"

"She gave me directions."

She started telling me about I-270, and something called the inner belt and that was also known as I-170, and then there was Highway 44—I let her get that far and stopped her.

"I'll drive," I said, "and you just point."

"Okay."

With her pointing we only went the wrong way twice but we finally ended up in Shrewsbury, getting off the highway at a street called Laclede Station Boulevard. Lisa lived in an apartment complex on Big Bend Road, and when she opened the door to greet us she and Sam embraced warmly. Lisa seemed genuinely touched by Sam's presence, and at that point I was glad I was helping both of them.

Sam made the introductions and then we sat down at Lisa's table with coffee and cookies and I took a good look at her. Outwardly there were no indications of the disease. She was slender and attractive, with brown eyes and long dark hair.

"You can't see it," she said to me.

"Oh, I'm sorry." I thought I'd been staring and she caught me.

"It's all right. Actually, I don't have AIDS, I simply tested positive for the HIV virus."

"But that will become AIDS, won't it?" Sam asked.

"Maybe," Lisa said, biting her bottom lip, then, "probably. It depends on how well I continue to respond to the medication."

We were silent for a while and when it became awkward, Lisa broke it herself.

"I'm glad you came here to help me, Nick. What do you need?"

"Well, Sam says the guy's name is Ted. I need his full name, his home address, where he works, who his friends are—if you know them—and some other women he might have seen."

"His name's Ted Drew. I can write down his address for you. I know the last place he worked, but I don't think he works there anymore. Umm, I know one or two of his friends, but I don't know their addresses."

"Maybe you could give me some idea where they hang out"

"Sure, I can do that. As for other women, there's his former girlfriend—"

"Sam mentioned her. I definitely want to talk to her."

"I have her address and phone number. We're kind of, uh, well, members of the same club."

"What condition is she in, Lisa?"

"She's showing some signs, Nick. She's lost a lot of weight."

"What about medication?"

Lisa looked down.

"She was on the same medication I am. It worked for a while, but now she's getting worse."

"And how about Ted? What kind of shape is he in?"

"The last time I saw him you couldn't tell he had anything wrong with him."

I frowned at that. What kind of justice was there when he could go around infecting innocent, trusting women and not be suffering himself? AIDS is not something I know a lot about. Okay, I'm ignorant, like a lot of other people. I know that safe sex is advised, and I've had those kinds of conversations with women, but I didn't know that someone could have it, pass it on, and not show any sign themselves.

That sucked.

"Why don't you write all that information down for me, and anything else you think might be helpful?"

"All right."

Sam and I waited, drinking coffee and munching without appetite on cookies, while Lisa got a lined pad and wrote for almost ten minutes.

"There." She stopped writing and pushed the pad across to me. I tore off the sheet, scanned it, folded it, and put it away.

"I want to ask you something, Lisa."

"All right."

"Do you think Ted is deliberately infecting women with this AIDS virus?"

"Well, he knew he had it when he slept with Kitty—that was his girlfriend before me—and then when he and I were together. I guess that means it's deliberate."

"If that's the case," Sam said, "he could be brought up on charges."

"No, what I mean is, is he the kind of man who is looking to infect as many women as he can on purpose?"

She frowned.

"That would make him...evil."

"I guess it would."

She thought for a moment, then shook her head slowly.

"I really don't know, Nick."

"That's okay." I stood up. "I'd better get started. Do you have any pictures of Ted?"

"I thought you might ask."

I'd noticed when we arrived that she was limping slightly. Now she limped over to the counter and took a picture from where she'd left it. Coming back she saw me looking at her.

"I stepped on a nail a couple of days back. Here."

It was a wallet-sized head shot. Drew was a good-looking man in his late thirties, brown hair falling down over his forehead. I could see where a woman might want to brush the hair back, maybe run her fingers through it. He was smiling, looking for all the world like Beaver Cleaver all grown-up. The All-American boy, passing AIDS along like a bad joke.

Before I left, I came up with one more question.

"How long has it been since you saw him?"

"The day I told him I tested positive was the last time I saw him. That was about a month ago."

I walked to the door with Sam, followed by Lisa. I opened the front door and walked out, then turned and saw that Sam was still inside.

"Come on," I said, "we have to get a hotel room."

"Oh, we do?"

"Well, sure..."

"One room?"

"Well...it would be cheaper that way, wouldn't it?" I have to admit, the prospect of sharing a room with Sam was...interesting.

"I suppose it would, but I have a better idea."

"What?"

She smiled and said, "Get my bag out of the car. I'm staying here with Lisa."

"You had this planned all along, didn't you?"

She just smiled, so I got her bag from the car, gave it to her, and told her I'd call when I got to a hotel.

3

I found a Best Western nearby, off of Highway 44, and checked in. In my room I took out Lisa's sheet of paper and read it. I had gotten a map of St. Louis from the car rental, so I spent the next fifteen minutes finding addresses and marking routes in pen. Before I left the room I called Sam and told her where I was staying.

"Why don't you come back here for dinner?" she suggested.

I agreed, and we planned for me to arrive at six.

The first person I wanted to see was Kitty Marks, Ted Drew's former girlfriend. I had her phone number and called her. She had spoken with Lisa, and said I could come right over. She lived in Brentwood and since I had her on the phone I asked the best and most direct route to her. Armed with that, I got to her apartment in twenty minutes.

Her illness was obvious because she was at least five feet ten and seriously underweight. There were also dark hollows beneath her eyes. Her hair was dirty blond, almost brown, and listless. She kept her arms folded, with her elbows in the palms of her hands. I noticed that her right hand was bandaged.

"I can't tell you much," she said, "except that the son of a bitch gave me AIDS."

"I hope you'll excuse me if I ask you how you know it was him."

"I was with only him for six months, Mr. Delvecchio."

"Nick, please." Even as I spoke it sounded inane to me. I'd probably never see this girl again in my life—or hers.

"Nick...and before that I hadn't been with anyone for over eight months."

"Did you or he have an AIDS test before you started seeing each other?"

"I mentioned it, but he refused. He said how could I claim to love him and think he wasn't clean?" She looked ashamed. "I bought it."

"After you found you had AIDS did you tell him?"

"You bet I did. You know what the bastard did?"

"What?"

"He moved out the same day. Quit his job and moved out."

"Did he express...remorse? Say he was sorry—"

"He said I should have been more careful."

Same thing he said to Lisa.

"You know what pisses me off? He's probably out there right now giving it to some other poor unsuspecting girl. I'd like to cut off his dick!"

I couldn't blame her for that.

"Can you give me some idea of where to find him? Who he hung out with?"

"I can tell you who he hung out with when we were together, but I don't know where he goes now."

"That'll be good enough."

I left Kitty Marks's place with a couple of more hangouts I could try in my search for Ted Drew.

I went from her house to the home address I had for Ted. It was an apartment complex on Manchester Road. I knocked on the door, but no one answered. I went to the office to find out if he still lived there. The woman there told me he didn't, because he was two months behind in the rent. Even if he returned, she said, he wouldn't get back in. I asked if he had left anything behind and she said no. She added that the apartment was furnished, so the furniture wasn't his. I thanked her and left.

My next stop was the place where he was working while he was seeing Lisa. It was a print shop, and when I asked for him the owner angrily told me that Ted had simply stopped coming in, with no notice at all.

I left there and stopped at a Hardee's to eat. There are no Hardee's in New York, but there are Roy Rogers, and since Hardee's owns Roy's, I tried the fried chicken and found it the same. I think Roy's has better chicken than KFC.

Over my lunch I thought about Ted Drew. Why would a man who has a disease make the conscious decision to spread it? Did he figure he'd gotten it from a woman, so he was trying to pay all women back? As I understood AIDS it was statistically more likely that a woman would get it from a man than the other way around. Also, the people most susceptible to contracting AIDS were gays and drug users. I'd have to call Lisa and ask her if Ted used drugs.

The fact that Drew had abandoned both his home and his job fit the man's pattern. When he found out that Kitty tested positive, he moved out and quit his job. Lisa hadn't been living with him, but he left his apartment anyway and stopped going to his job, in effect quitting.

How far back did this pattern go? I wondered. Did he sleep with women until they tested positive, then move, quit his job, and start over? Was he doing this all over St. Louis? If he did it long enough, wasn't he bound to run into an old girlfriend or boss?

Since he'd infected two women I knew of, I wondered if Ted Drew hadn't already left town, moved to another city where he could start fresh with new victims.

Jesus, I thought, if women started dying because he was infecting them, did that make him a serial killer?

4

I hit a couple of bars where Drew hung out when he was with Kitty Marks. I didn't see any way around asking for him. I didn't have the time to start staking places out, waiting for him to show up.

I tried to be casual about it, but bartenders these days are a suspicious bunch. As soon as you say, "Hey, Ted Drew been around lately?" they want to know who you are and where you're from. If you happen to tell them that you owe him money and want to find him, that's the end of it. They shut up. You're better off saying that he owes you money.

In the third place I tried I caught a bartender's interest.

"Owes you money, huh?"

"Yep."

"A lot?"

I played with my Busch bottle and said, "Enough to make me want to find him."

"Gambling, huh?"

I looked him in the eye and said, "He picks the wrong teams."

"Don't I know it. You're shit out of luck, pal. He already owes a couple of regulars money and he don't come here no more."

"Any idea where he does hang out?"

He didn't mince words. "What's it worth to you?"

"You sell the information to your regulars, too?"

"Fuck them. He owes them forty, fifty bucks from a one-night bet. They ain't making book."

He assumed I had booked bets for Drew, and consequently figured that Drew was into me for a lot.

"I'll go ten."

"Make it twenty."

"Fifteen."

"Twenty, and I think I can tell you where to find him."

We matched stares for a while, and then I gave in.

"Okay, twenty."

"Let's see it."

See? What'd I tell you. A suspicious lot. I handed him the twenty.

"Check the Landing. I heard from a guy that he saw Drew down there."

"What landing?"

"Laclede's Landing, by the river."

"What river?"

"Where you from, pal? The Mississippi."

Yep, that was a river, all right.

I got back to Lisa's place at six. She and Sam had prepared dinner and while we ate I told them what I'd been doing. When we were done Lisa gave me directions to Laclede's Landing. "A lot of people hang out down there," she added. "There are lots of clubs and restaurants and you can walk along the river."

"The Mississippi," I said to Sam.

She gave me a funny look and said, "I know."

Sam wanted to come to the Landing with me, but I vetoed the idea. I figured when I found Ted Drew he wasn't going to be real happy, and I might just find him in his own turf, with his friends around him. I explained that to her. She walked me to the door.

"If you find him like that," she said, touching my arm, "be careful. Don't approach him."

"I'll just tail him and find out where he lives. That's all."

"That's all she wants."

"I'll remember."

I left the house and got into the rental car. Lisa just wanted to confront him. I'd started this thing as a favor for Sam, but the more I thought about Drew deliberately infecting women with a deadly virus, the more I just wanted to smash his face in. How the hell could somebody justify doing that? I just couldn't understand it, and I doubted he could ever explain it to me.

5

There were plenty of bars and restaurants down on the Landing, as Lisa had said, but I'd already been to three places where Ted Drew used to hang out, and they were all of a type. They all served food, but none of them could have been called restaurants. With that in mind I walked along and stopped at bar and grill type places, had one beer and looked around. A couple of them catered to a younger crowd, so after a single beer I rejected them. Both Lisa and Kitty were in their thirties, so I figured that was the kind of girl Drew would go for.

I didn't ask questions this time, either. If he was currently hanging out in any of these places I didn't want to scare him off.

If he was the barhopping type—which he seemed to be—then if I didn't spot him this night, I would the next, or the one after that. He wouldn't be able to stay away.

I worked the Landing for three days and nights until the bars closed, staying away from Lisa and Sam until dinner. I'd made up a list of the places I thought Ted Drew might show and I had a beer in one, then moved to the next one, and so on. On Friday, I caught a break, which is usually the way my job finally gets done. I was in a place called The Big Muddy, sitting at the bar nursing a beer. When the beer was done I was going to move on to the next place on my list. A woman in her early thirties with long brown hair came up to the bar and stood about five stools from me. She was wearing a light blue shirt and dark blue jeans. She stood there and waited for the bartender to notice her.

"Has Ted been around?" she asked, and my ears perked up.

"Not yet," the bartender said.

"Come on, Maury, he's not home, he must be—"

"He ain't been in, Lynn, I swear."

"Is he coming in?"

The bartender, a beefy man in his forties, just shrugged.

"He's hiding from me—"

"He's not hiding, Lynn. Why don't you just give up?"

"I don't want to, Maury. Do you think he's at the Rock?"

"I don't know. You could try."

The Rock was another bar that was on my list. When she left I decided to follow her.

Walking along behind her I couldn't help wondering if she'd slept with Drew yet, if she'd been infected. From her conversation with the bartender, it sounded like she wanted to find Drew, but he didn't want any part of her. Maybe there was something I could do before anything happened.

She went into the Rock and I stepped in behind her, remaining just inside the door. She went up to the bartender and talked to him, and I saw him shake his head and shrug. She slammed her hand down on the bar once and he spread his hands in a helpless gesture. As she turned to leave, a patron sitting at the bar said something to her and she spoke sharply, cutting him down, and started past him. He reached out and grabbed her arm and I saw her wince.

The man was in his late thirties and big, but he was carrying some extra weight around his middle that would slow him down. This looked like my chance to meet Lynn.

I moved toward the bar and stopped just on the other side of the man.

"...think you're too good. You ain't even that good-looking."

"Then let go of my arm." Lyn's voice sounded calm, like she'd dealt with this kind of thing before. Up-close I could see that the man was wrong, though. She was kind of cute, and I'd walked along behind her from the Muddy and knew she filled her jeans out okay. He was just smarting from being brushed off.

The bartender came over to me and I said, "Busch, in a bottle."

Lynn was trying to soothe the man's wounded ego now, telling him she was sorry but she just didn't have time.

"It didn't sound to me like your man was gonna be around, so why not have a drink with me?"

"Look, I'm trying to be nice—"

"No, you ain't," the man said, cutting her off. "That's the problem."

The bartender brought my beer, cast a look at Lynn and the man, and walked to the other end of the bar.

I picked up my beer in my left hand and with my right I tapped the guy on the shoulder.

"Huh?" He turned his head to look over his shoulder at me. With my rigid index finger I poked him in the eye.

"Ow, Jesus!" He released Lynn and put both hands up to his face. I pushed my beer in front of him and looked at Lynn.

"Come on," I said.

She looked unsure, but I took her hand and led her outside.

"T-thanks."

"That's okay. With that kind of guy you just have to give them something else to think about."

She examined my face, then smiled and said, "That makes sense."

"I heard you asking for Ted. Would that be Ted Drew?"

"Do you know Ted?"

"No, but I'm looking for him, too."

Now she looked suspicious.

"Oh, yeah? Why?"

"Are you his girl?"

She bit her lips a moment, then said, "I thought I was."

"And you'd still like to be?"

She stared at me a moment, then nodded.

"Let's go someplace and talk."

"I don't know—"

"There's something very important you should know about Ted."

"I thought you said you didn't know him?"

"I don't," I said, "but I know something about him."

"What?"

"Let's get a drink, Lynn."

I figured she was going to need one.

6

There was a McDonald's on the Landing so we went there to talk instead of a bar. We both got coffee and found a table.

"What do you want to tell me about Ted?" she asked.

"First, can you tell me where he lives now?"

"What for?"

"I want to find him, Lynn."

"Are you a cop?"

"Is Ted afraid of the cops?"

"No, why should he be?"

"Why are you asking me if I'm a cop?"

"You look like a cop."

I looked at her and smiled. "How many cops do you know?"

"None."

"Lynn, how...close are you and Ted Drew?"

"We're...tight."

"That explains why you can't find him."

"We had a fight. It's nothing serious."

"But he's avoiding you."

"So what? He...he loves me. I know he does."

"Lynn..." I leaned forward. "Have you slept with him?"

"Sure I have."

She said it too fast. I sat back in my chair.

"Lynn, I'm a private detective. I know two girls who have been infected with AIDS by Ted Drew."

Her eyes went wide. "That can't be true."

I took the picture Lisa gave me from my pocket. "Is this Ted?"

She looked at the picture and nodded.

"Then it's true. He's given two women AIDS that I know of. There could be many more. I'll ask you again. Have you had sex with him?"

She looked drugged.

"No." Her tone was listless. "I wanted to, but he didn't want no part of me."

"You're a lucky girl, then."

She rubbed both hands over her face, then looked at me.

"Is it true?"

"Yes, it's true."

"Jesus. I never thought I'd feel so glad a guy dumped me. But...he doesn't look sick...except he wasn't feeling too good the last time I saw him. He said he had a...a bug, or something."

He had a bug all right.

"I've got to find him, Lynn. Will you help me?"

"I can give you his address. He wasn't home when I banged on his door."

"When was that?"

"All week."

"Give me the address and I'll check it out."

I took a small pad out of my pocket and she wrote his address on it, then told me how to get there.

"Count yourself lucky, Lynn. Be more careful in the future who you pick."

She laughed ironically and said, "You know the first day I went to his place I thought he was cheating on me. I mean, I felt like he was."

"Why?"

"I saw two women coming from his apartment."

"Coming out of his apartment?"

"No, just from that direction. I banged on his door and when there was no answer I figured I was wrong. Besides, there looked like something was wrong with one of them."

"Like what?"

"She was holding her arm stiff, and the other woman was supporting her."

"What'd they look like?"

"Well...they looked like me, sort of. Long dark hair, slender, about my age. I thought maybe Ted liked that type, you know? He wasn't home, though, so they weren't coming from his place. I guess I ought to thank you, mister. You probably saved my life."

"Maybe. From now on, though, make sure you save your own, all right?"

She nodded and I left, feeling like a commercial for safe sex.

I followed her instructions to an apartment complex on Gravois and Grand. When I got to Drew's apartment there was no bell, just a knocker. I used it a couple of times, then peered in the window next to the door. I saw furniture, but if he rented furnished apartments that explained that. There was other stuff around, though. Magazines, newspaper, some fast-food wrappers on a coffee table. It looked to me like someone still lived there.

The apartment was one of six in this building, and it was on the first floor. I walked around to the back and saw that there were patios, and sliding-glass doors. The gate was on a latch and easy to open. When I got to the sliding-glass door I found it locked. I couldn't see any way to get in short of breaking the glass, and that wasn't my place to do. I peered into the room. It was a kitchen, with a cheap aluminum table and two metal folding chairs. I was about to give up when I spotted something else. I moved all the way to my right to give myself a better angle and saw what it was. Sticking out from behind the kitchen counter was a shoe—with a foot attached.

7

Ted Drew was dead. He'd been stabbed in his kitchen. The place was a mess behind the counter, which I was unable to see from outside the door. There were pots and pans and glass all over the floor, and a lot of blood.

I told the police the whole story. There was no reason not to. I also told them I was doing a favor for a friend, not working for a fee. After all, I wasn't licensed in the state of Missouri. They took my statement, my name, address, and phone number. After that they let me go. I drove directly back to Lisa's house.

"How was he killed?" Lisa asked.

"He was stabbed. Well, actually, it looked as if he was stabbed during a fight."

"So then he didn't..."

"No, he didn't die of the disease."

"That's too bad. I'll call Kitty and tell her."

She was cold, real cold, but who could blame her? She just wanted him to die of the same disease she knew she was going to die of.

"I guess there's not much more to say, Nick. Thanks for trying to help."

She made it sound like I had failed. Hell, she wanted me to find him and I did. It wasn't my fault she and Kitty had killed him.

"Sam, it's time to leave."

"But—"

"I really think it's time to leave. We can change our tickets at the airport." We'd been scheduled to leave in two more days, but I didn't want to stay any longer.

It took Sam fifteen minutes to pack. She and Lisa embraced, but over Sam's shoulder Lisa's eyes met mine, and I think she saw that I knew.

"Stay in touch, please," Sam said.

Lisa promised she would, but it was a promise she never kept. Ultimately, she locked herself away from her family and friends and just waited to die—or go to jail.

On the way to the airport I explained it to Sam.

"I don't believe it," she said. "How could you think that Lisa and Kitty killed him?"

"They're members of the same club, remember?"

"Nick—"

"It all fits, Sam. Lynn saw two women walking away from Drew's building last Monday. According to the M. E., Drew would have been dead about then. That's why he didn't answer the door when Lynn knocked."

"So how does—"

"Let me finish. She said one of the women was supporting the other, and one was holding her arm. I don't know who was supporting who, but Kitty has a bandage on her hand. I think she got cut during the fight."

"And Lisa?"

"She's limping. There was broken glass on the floor. I think that's what she got in her foot, not a nail."

"But why would she kill him, and then ask me to help?"

"Did she ask you for help? For my help?"

"Well...no, now that I think of it. I offered to have you help her, but that was only when she said she wished she could find him."

"She knew he was dead when she said that, Sam. She just thought that was what she was supposed to say. When you offered to have me find him, she must have thought it would sound suspicious if she refused. Besides, it'll make a good argument when they arrest her. She'll ask the cops why she would have me searching for him if she killed him."

Sam folded her arms across her breasts.

"I don't believe it."

"Well, I do."

We drove in silence for a while and then she asked, "What are you going to do?"

"Nothing."

"Nothing? You think they committed murder and you're not going to say anything to the police?"

"No."

"Why not?"

"Because if I figured it out the cops will, too, eventually. Let Lisa and Kitty think they got away with it a little longer."

"Why would you do that?"

"Because they don't have anything else. Besides, I don't think they went there to kill him. I think they went there to confront him, and things got out of hand. Maybe he ridiculed them and there was a fight, and the two of them were able to kill him. He was only stabbed once, so it could have been an accident. If they'd gone there to kill him I think they would have both stabbed him several times before stopping."

We drove a little more in silence before Sam spoke again.

"I still can't believe it."

At least she didn't say she "didn't" believe it.

"Forget it, Sam. Let's just get back to Brooklyn."

*   *   *

For readers, attending a convention the size of Mayhem in the Midlands is a rare opportunity to meet the authors they've been reading up close. For the authors, a chance to really connect with their readers and with other writers. As solitary as the actual writing is, it's important for the writer to reach out and touch readers and other writers on occasion.

THE MULBERRY RIDE

by Laurel B. Schunk

Laurel Schunk was born in Illinois in the Forties and moved to Wichita in 1976. She began writing, secretly, at her grandmother's antique secretary desk at the age of seven. A lover of books, she never expected to become a writer; a private person, she felt too reserved to let her thoughts become public, but she overcame that fear in order to tell stories about child abuse, racism, and other social justice issues. She has a bachelor's degree in French from the University of Illinois as well as a second major, in psychology, from Wichita State University.

Her books in print include *Black and Secret Midnight, The Voice He Loved, The Snow Lion, Rocks in My Socks,* the Regency mystery, *Death in Exile,* as well as the first book in the Callie Bagley Gardening Mystery series, *Under the Wolf's Head.* Her newest book, a mystery about a man striving to live a normal life under Nazi and then Soviet oppression in Lithuania, is entitled *A Clear North Light* and will be published this spring by St. Kitts Press.

THE MULBERRY RIDE

by Laurel B. Schunk

Luke Brookings said:

It would have been a perfect crime if I hadn't gone to her funeral. As I stood beside the casket, I wanted to touch her hair, with all the shades of gold that hair comes in, intermingled in the braids that fell across her shoulder. It was her hair that caused it all.

I stood fighting my impulse to touch her when a man and a woman with older, faded white-golden hair approached the bier. The man said, "Cassandra was so lovely. She was destined for greatness, in spite of her problem." Her mother's reply—it flayed me.

I first saw Cassandra in May. She was riding a buckskin mare down the road toward the bridge. The mare's coat looked gold from one direction and silver from the other. As they rode among the aged mulberry trees, the sun caught and lost them in the branches. Sometimes the two of them shone gold in the sun and sometimes they gleamed silver in the shade.

The beauty of them there in that vernal light pained my heart and made my throat ache. They didn't see me. I lay hiding in a copse of elders, there beside the river, to see where the pheasant and deer hid. I planned to come back early the next day to hunt.

Her hair was braided with the plaiting begun on each side of her heart-shaped face. The colors dazzled, three different golds

199

plus fair brown and pale red and even pink. I wanted to call her to me, to come and lie with me in the soft grass under the elders, to listen to the river burble over the white boulders in its bed. Small yellow-hearted daisies starred the grass, and I wanted to bite them, so much did my heart hurt to have her.

I didn't hunt the deer or the pheasant the next day. Instead I returned every day to hunt her and her golden hair. Soon May warmed into June, and the mulberry trees hung heavy with purple fruit. She would come on her mare and ride into the trees and reach up for the fruit, to eat them as she laughed to the horse. I wished then that I was her horse, that I held her up to eat the mulberries.

Then when the juice of the mulberries stained her lips, I wished I was the fruit she lusted after and ate, one by one, off the emerald trees.

June melted into July, and still I watched from the grassy copse. The grass was sharp and scratchy now, drying in the summer heat, and so was I. She rode the mare she called Citron across the fields of lupine and Queen Anne's lace, and I wished she'd ride across me.

July baked into August, and still I watched. Snow-on-the-mountain and purple thistle sprang up by her ride, and she leaned over to pull long stems of big bluestem grass to thrust between her lips. Oh, how I ached to cross her lips myself!

Late in August I burned brave, and I began to call to her, softly, as she rode past. She never turned that golden head or smiled a golden smile for me—she saved it all for the horse and the wildflowers. Once I even stood up as she passed and called out loud to her. The mare skittered away, but still Cassandra didn't deign to turn and look at me.

August flamed into September, and my pain flamed into hatred. She knew I was there. She knew I was nobody. She wouldn't speak, wouldn't even look at a nothing like me! I despised her.

On the day before the last day of summer there along the mulberry ride, she stopped up the road to pick sunflowers, and she looked like a bride with her arms full of long stems of golden blooms. I resolved to stand in front of her and make her speak. Just before she and the mare reached the bridge, I jumped out of my copse of elders and yelled to her. "Look at me, speak to me! Admit you're not too good for me!"

The mare reared and snorted and she dropped her armloads of flowers. Color flamed in her cheeks. "Oh," she said with a tuneless voice, "I hope we didn't startle you."

"Say hello to me," I bellowed, wanting to cry, to throw myself on the ground and scream.

Her eyes widened and her nostrils flared. She was frightened, of me! "We'll just go around you on this side," she said.

I turned to watch her cross the bridge, and then I made my plans. Only recurring thoughts about that strange, flat voice disturbed me as I plotted.

I was there waiting for her on the last day of summer. Rain clouds piled high on the western horizon, and it seemed the right day to quench all golden light. I leaned over the strut under the bridge to view myself in the placid river. I wasn't ugly—she had no call to treat me like some monster. I would show her my true nature today.

I felt rather than heard the drumming of her mare's hooves. I positioned myself against the heavy wooden struts under the bridge and braced my gun against my shoulder. I didn't want its kick to dash me down on the boulders below.

She was running the horse flat out, probably afraid she'd have to face me again. When I judged she was ten feet short of the bridge, I pulled the trigger and blasted a hole through the floor of the bridge. The horse screamed and jumped the twenty feet over the side of the bridge. She never made a sound. I heard a sob and a laugh, and they came from me.

Then the rain came and washed away my prints.

As I said, it would have been a perfect crime if I hadn't gone to her funeral and heard her mother say, "Cassandra couldn't hear, you know."

*   *   *

Why go to Mayhem? Mayhem is an exciting convention to attend. It's very accessible, being in the Midwest. Its size means one can meet great mystery authors and fans there without being overwhelmed by the huge numbers at a couple of other major conventions. In addition, the people who run the convention are very professional and helpful.

ANGELS

by Gretchen Sprague

Gretchen Sprague is a retired attorney who grew up in Nebraska and once lived in New York City. Her series sleuth, Martha Patterson (*Death in Good Company*, St. Martin's Press 1997; *Maquette for Murder*, St. Martin's Minotaur 2000), is a retired attorney who grew up in Nebraska and lives in New York City. Gretchen's young-adult suspense novel, *Signpost to Terror*, won an Edgar in 1968. Her present home, the Hudson Highlands town of Philipstown, somewhat resembles Phillip's Landing, the setting for "Angels."

ANGELS

by Gretchen Sprague

The day started hot, with a hazy July glare, but as they headed down the blind curves into Phillips Landing, the afternoon dimmed as if a cosmic hand had turned a rheostat. Wind lashed the leaf-heavy treetops; lightning flashed; thunder rolled. Raindrops spattered the windshield and on the narrow blacktop, splotches joined into a black slick.

Ben eased up on the gas and switched on wipers and headlights. Sara, sitting on Frieda's lap beside him, squealed as rain spattered her. Frieda laughed and cranked up the window. In the back seat, Jody said, "It's about time."

Movement in the rear-view mirror caught Ben's eye: a big pickup grill coming up fast behind them. It tail-gated for a few seconds, then veered left. *Passing* them, the idiot, on a blind curve in the rain. Ben muttered, "Son of a bitch," and tapped the brake. The pickup roared up beside his left ear.

In front, light raked the trees beside the road, solidified into headlights slicing into view around the curve.

"*Son of a bitch.*" Ben stood on the brake as the pickup veered toward their hood. His seat belt grabbed and he heard Frieda cry, "*Ben!*" But the oncoming car took the shoulder and cleared the pickup, and the pickup cleared their hood and roared on down the road. Their headlights caught the red tailgate, streaked with brighter red where rainwater cascaded through the caked dirt.

Ben's stomach registered the first fishtailing swerve. The car slewed toward the unguarded embankment. A jolt traveled from his buttocks to his shoulders as a wheel dropped off the blacktop.

He had time to think *We're going to roll* and to shout, "Hang on!" and to hear Frieda cry out once more, and then their center of gravity heaved over and battering jolts shredded his awareness.

#

His senses re-ordered themselves one at a time: his weight suspended sideways; the windshield crazed; the rain drumming.

The car had come to rest on its right side. Only his shoulder harness restrained him from crushing down on Frieda and Sara beneath him.

"Frieda," he ventured. "Frieda?"

Behind him, Jody quavered, "Sara?"

"Jody." He fought disorientation. "Are you hurt?"

"I'm all *right*. What about *Sara*?"

Below his suspended shoulder, he could just see Frieda's breast bulging her rumpled yellow blouse below the curve of her bare arm and the pepper-and-salt bun of hair against her slack neck. Of Sara, only the back of her head over the protective curve of Frieda's arm, the soft curls on the delicate little head that rested at an impossible angle against the spiderwebbed window.

"Jody..." Dread blocked his voice. He cleared his throat. "I think they're hurt."

The steering wheel caged him. Knives stabbed his rib cage as he tried to reach the door handle above him. Then through the crazed windshield and the pounding rain, figures took on form, two men slipping, staggering, down the sodden embankment from the road.

#

The windowless waiting room smelled of Lysol and air freshener. The deputy's wide-brimmed hat lay beside him on the flowered sofa. In a flowered armchair, Ben breathed shallowly within the strapped stiffness of his ribs and said, "The son-of-a-bitch must have been doing seventy. On those curves, forty-five limit, in the rain..."

Jody came through the door. The left side of her face was puffed, dark red, the eye nearly swollen shut.

Ben hoisted himself upright. "Did you get Herb?"

Her voice flat, she said, "It's nine-thirty at night in London. He could be anywhere. I don't know what to do with myself."

"Honey..."

"I don't know what to do with myself. I never lost a child before."

"Honey." Ben laid an arm around her unyielding shoulders.

The deputy had got to his feet. "Ms.—uh—Cutler," he said gravely, "if you don't mind, just a question or two?"

Her voice still flat, Jody said, "Fire away."

"Professor Whitehead says—your father says a vehicle passed him just before the accident. Did you see it?"

"I didn't see anything. The rain started, and then we started banging around and I hit my face on the kiddy seat."

"Your daughter wasn't in the seat?"

"No." Her voice turned harsh. "She was sitting on my mother's lap. I was tired..." Tears spilled. "It was hot as hell and she was being a complete pain in the ass. She wanted to sit on Mom's lap, and I *let* her." Her voice cracked falsetto. "I *put* that seat in the car, and then I *let* her." She said, "I don't know what to do with myself," her voice skidding up and down.

"That pickup," said Ben to the deputy. "Can you nail him?"

"Can you identify it?"

Ben said, knowing his words were useless, "It was red. A big dirty red pickup." The county was full of big dirty red pickups.

At the door, someone in white said, "Mr. Whitehead? Your wife is asking for you."

He dragged in breath. "Yes. Thank you." Jody shrugged off his arm and followed a step behind.

A plump little blue-uniformed aide, tip-toeing out of the room, nodded to Ben. Above the sheet, Frieda's face was slack. Strands of hair straggled across the pillowcase from her half-undone bun. One hand lay on top of the sheet, an IV needle taped to its back.

"Frieda," Ben said.

Her eyes opened. Her face tautened into focus. Careful of the IV, he took her hand and felt her fingers liven. "Ben," she said, her voice slurred. "I have the most stupid headache. What happened?"

"You got a bump on the head. How do you feel, sweetheart?"

"Dim." A hazy hint of vigor. "Stupid. I hate it. Was it..." Her voice thickened. "Stupid headache. Wasn't inna car?"

His heartbeat slow and heavy, he said, "Yes."

Frieda's hand clamped with sudden strength. "Sara! She should go in the seat, darling."

Half a pace back, Jody made a wordless sound.

"Jody?" Frieda tried to lift her head. "*Jody! Where's Jody?*"

"I'm here, Mom."

"Jody! Your face! What *happened?*"

Ben said, "We had an accident."

"Jody's hurt." Frieda tried to sit up. "Where's Sara?"

It was intolerable. Ben tightened his grip on her hand and said, "We had a terrible accident, sweetheart. Sara..." Between them, concealment had no place, but his voice locked and he couldn't force the words through the wall.

No need: knowledge smudged Frieda's face. "Oh, Ben. Oh, *Jody!*"

The partnership was intact, and at last, Ben wept.

#

Waiting while the doctor scribbled a prescription for sleeping pills, Ben said, "I hate to leave Frieda."

"Don't you worry, Perfessor." The plump little middle-aged aide was sitting in the nurse's station. "I'm meaning to stay right with her. You go get your rest."

Only then did he look properly at her. Cake sales, white-elephant booth...one of Frieda's fund-raisers. He dredged up *Colleen*. McCarthy, Mulcahy...something like that. He said, "Thank you, Colleen."

"You rest, Perfessor. The little girl's with the angels." Her plump hand sketched the sign of the cross. "You tell her, you tell Jody; the little girl's with the angels now."

#

Jody spurned the sleeping pill. Ben sat up in an easy chair while she paced. When Herb called, nobody mentioned that three-thirty a.m. Eastern time was eight-thirty a.m. in London.

Then they tried to sleep. They were up again in less than four hours. He had, of course, spared Jody any talk of angels.

#

At the nurses' station, the doctor put down the phone. "Ben. I was just calling you." Behind his glasses, the skin around his eyes was pouched.

"Something's wrong."

"I'm sorry. She's up in intensive care. It was a stroke."

Protestation was futile. "Her chances?"

"There've been big advances in therapy," the doctor said.

#

Matthew brought condolences from his lover in Frankfurt. At the hospital, he kissed his comatose mother's slack cheek and spoke to her as if she could hear him; outside he wiped his eyes and blew his nose. The next morning they drove to Northampton in Frieda's old subcompact. Matt shook hands soberly with Herb; he hugged his little sister and cried and bandied with her the fierce raillery of their connection. The swelling had gone down, leaving a purple and yellow bruise that Jody disdained to mask with makeup.

The speech department rented out its little theater; a philosophy professor read soothing secular paragraphs; the faculty string quartet played Bach. The ashes of Sara's delicate dead flesh were scattered from a windy Massachusetts hilltop.

Matthew and Ben drove back to the Highlands the next night, Ben mired in lassitude until they stopped for coffee. Enlivened by caffeine, Matt said, "Dad, are you thinking what I'm thinking about that marriage?"

"Mm?"

"Without Sara, I don't see much glue."

"Mm."

"I didn't feel good when she abandoned the doctorate."

Ben forced himself into speech. "She chose to carry it through, and it was Sara. Can we say she shouldn't have?"

Matt said, "I admit I'm biased against instructors who bed their students."

Ben said, "It's Jody's life."

A long silence later, Matt said "Shit," rousing Ben from a doze. "So it shouldn't be a total loss?"

"Mm?"

"Now she's free to do the field work."

Ben didn't answer.

"Putting Sara in the category of a mistake that got wiped out? Shit." Another couple of minutes of silence. "You and...you and

Mom may end up without grandchildren. Jody's clock could run out."

"Matt, she's only twenty-nine."

"Still. Would you mind? Not having your...biological immortality?"

"You're entitled to your lives. Both of you." He fought despair as if prying loose the jaws of an attack dog. "You must be tired," he said. "Pull off at the next rest stop. I'll drive."

#

The first dreams were flashbacks: the pickup grill looming in the rear view; the oncoming lights in his eyes; the streaked red tailgate dwindling down the road as they lurched into the skid.

He learned to lie quietly, letting the heavy insect-loud night fill his senses, once or twice blessed with the *hoo-hoo hoo-hoo, hoo-hoo hoo-hoough* of a barred owl deep in the forest. When his heart quieted, he would fumble his way out of bed and down the stairs in the empty house and read until his body clock circled once more into drowsiness; then he could fall away again into sleep, safe for that night from more dreaming.

In one dream, they did not skid; they drove on and on forever untouched down the green avenue of leaves. From that one, he woke weeping; his mind refused the words in the book and he slept no more that night.

But most often it was the knotting of his right calf as he stamped the brake, and the terrible swerve, and the pickup dwindling down the road in front of him. The pickup was a blur at first, but as week dragged after week, he began to see it whole, strangely familiar: dirty red, with a yellow bumper sticker on the tailgate, which he could not quite read.

#

Six weeks after Sara's funeral, Ben identified the pickup.

He was half-way from their house to the county highway, approaching the biggest house on the dirt road, when a blast of rock music assaulted his ears. The handyman's pickup was parked in the drive, a boom box blaring from the truck bed. Rage punched his rib cage. It wasn't the first time that yahoo had left his boom box unattended while he rode the roaring mower around the grounds.

Frieda was funny about this place. She disliked the weekend showplaces, of course—alien lawns wrested from the forest, eight-foot deer fences guarding imported shrubbery, the blue sizzle of bug zappers invading the summer nights. Why, she would storm, did they spend all that money on a place in the country, only to war against all that the country was?

And yet, and yet...her exasperation would melt into laughter. This place drew birds—forest birds, meadow birds, edge-dwelling birds—mingling in this spot where lawn battled forest. Ben had been listening for birdsong to carry to Frieda. She was beginning to respond a little; he could detect some new little tension in her muscle tone when each day he brought her these gifts from their world.

But birdsong today was drowned in electronic blasphemy. Drawing a deep breath to thin out anger, he eased past the end of the blaring driveway.

And saw the tailgate. Red, filmed with dust; a peeling yellow bumper sticker on the tailgate.

He braked, shifted into reverse, and inched back until he could read the sticker: MAKE MY DAY. He took the dog-eared little notebook from the glove compartment and wrote down the license number.

#

Harry Jacobs, who had handled their closing and their wills, was to handle the lease. "How's Frieda?" he asked.

"A little better," said Ben. "She's in a wheelchair. She doesn't seem to be in pain, but she's aphasic. She can feed herself, but she doesn't seem to be able to write."

"It stinks." Harry clasped his hands on top of the folder in front of him. "Ben," he said, "are you sure you want to rent the house?"

"We've already had this conversation," said Ben.

"We're having it again. I can't visualize you in one of those apartments for the handicapped."

"Harry, it has to be. You know how the house is built, against the side of the hill. I couldn't get her up and down those stairs safely. She'd be in jail. She needs stimulation. People around her. I'm not asking how we got this vacancy, but they must have jumped Frieda up the waiting list. God knows, she's done enough for them. If I fool around, I'll lose the apartment."

"It stinks." But Harry unclasped his hands and started to open the folder.

"Harry," Ben said, "before we talk lease, I have a question."

Harry clasped his hands again. "What's on your mind?"

"Assuming I could identify the pickup that cut in on me, would there be any chance of nailing the bastard?"

Harry's eyebrows went up. "How do you make this ID?"

"I've recognized the truck."

"Have you now?"

"It came to me this morning. I saw the back of the truck and it clicked."

"Mm. Did you describe the truck to anybody at the time of the accident?"

"Sketchily. Big and red. It only really came to me this morning. I saw the back of the truck and it clicked."

"Did you see the driver at the time of the accident?"

"I have his license number. It shouldn't be that hard to find out the son-of-a-bitch's name."

"How do you know he was driving it that day?"

"Oh."

"Anybody else see it? Your daughter?"

"Jody didn't see it. Maybe the third car? The one that was coming toward us? The driver would only see headlights, but what about a passenger? Maybe I could put an ad in the paper, asking for witnesses?"

Harry said, "Mm."

"I suppose criminal charges might iffy. Could I file a suit for damages?"

"Anybody can file a suit for damages," said Harry. "You make out a check for a hundred bucks to the County Clerk and file the papers. If you want the judge to keep a straight face, you make out some more checks and a lawyer draws up the papers."

"Money isn't the issue. I just want to nail the son-of-a-bitch." He didn't realize his voice had risen until Harry held up a hand.

"Ben," Harry said, "listen. Sit still for a minute, Professor, and listen to a lecture for a change. There are major problems with this issue." He took off his glasses and swung them by the earpiece. "First, your identification of the pickup. You first saw it in the rain while you were distracted, trying to control a major skid. You didn't get the license number. You didn't describe it to law enforcement. You first recognize the vehicle—what is it, a couple of months?"

"Six weeks."

"Six weeks later. There's no corroboration, and you don't know who was driving it. Any half-way competent trial attorney would grind that ID into a McDonald's quarter-pounder and feed it to you in full view of the jury." Harry swung his glasses some more. "Then there's what we shysters call 'proximate cause.' The s.o.b.'s lawyer says, "Now, Professor Whitehead, you admit the vehicle passing you made no contact with you? You admit it was your own abrupt braking that caused the skid?"

"Harry, for God's sake, I wouldn't have braked like that if that son-of-a-bitch..."

Harry raised his hand again. "Okay, for argument's sake, let's suppose you succeeded in making a credible case that it was the s.o.b.'s violation of the double yellow line that caused you to roll. You're seeking damages for Frieda's pain and suffering, your

emotional distress and loss of consortium. The s.o.b.'s insurer
retains a nationally known expert in the geography of the brain,
who says it wasn't the accident that disabled Frieda, it was the
stroke she had afterward. The accident only caused the concus-
sion, not the stroke. You pay a lot of your state-college history
professor's salary for your own nationally known expert. Your
expert says different. You've written a lot of checks and now it's
up to a jury. Juries are crazy."

Ben breathed in and out. "Sara."

"Okay, Sara. First off, that's Jody's lawsuit, not yours. What
would she receive? For Sara, a minute or two of pain and suffering, wrongful death. Wrongful death of a little kid brings peanuts;
no loss of earnings. Jody's got pain and suffering, emotional distress big-time. Okay, Jody's on the stand and the s.o.b.'s lawyer
said, "Now, Ms. Uh, where was the little girl when the accident
occurred? Not in a safety-tested child seat as required by New
York law?"

"Harry..."

"Guaranteed."

"Damn it, Harry, you're telling me the son-of-a-bitch gets
way with murder."

"So? All the time, people get away with murder. Remember,
oh, years ago now, deer season, that idiot in Maine blew away a
woman outside her own back door? Young mother with twin
baby girls? Oops, accident. Thought she was a deer. High-pow-
ered telescopic sight and he thought she was a deer. Hey, it was
her own fault, she was wearing white mittens, looked like a deer
tail. She wasn't one of us anyway, moved in from somewhere in
the big out-there. It took two grand juries to indict him, and when
they did, the trial jury acquitted him. I'm no ambulance-chaser,
Ben. Let's talk lease."

#

Vengeance is mine, saith the lord. Ancient words, resounding
like organ music across five decades.

Vengeance is mine.

#

September came. Five mornings a week, Ben left Frieda to
Colleen Mulcahy and the physical therapy appointments and
drove Frieda's car to the state college across the river, met his
classes, kept his office hours, ate lunch with accustomed col-
lages, treading the deep-worn ruts of academic gossip. There was
no room in the handicapped accessible apartment for his desk or
his books; he did his professional reading and writing in his
office at the college.

Saturdays and Sundays, he pushed Frieda's wheelchair up
and down Main Street on invented errands. Out-of-town anti-
quers glanced carefully away; locals stopped to speak. He would
see them probing for the old vigorous laugh, the flashing good
sense. Speech, like walking, had abandoned Frieda, but her eyes
would focus on the speaker and tiny muscles in her face would
tauten. He tried to learn to read those flickers of comprehension,
the movements of her eyes. As the months wore on, there were
panicky times when he could no longer remember the challenge
of her voice.

This, he thought, is what the lawyers call "loss of consortium"; this is what you sue the bastards for.

#

He saw the red pickup parked here and there, the son-of-a-
bitch in the hardware store, the pizzeria, shooting the breeze in
the 7-11's parking lot, truck and man sharp in his vision as if
pinned by a spotlight. He studied the stocky body, shirt open to
the navel over a matted chest, the shag of hair curling to the col-
lar, the hook-nosed face with deep-brown long-lashed eyes; he
learned the voice, the slurred consonants of the local studs. He
learned the s.o.b.'s NAME: Vinnie Mazzarola. He learned his
age—twenty-two—and his marital status—single. Firehouse

gossip informed him that Vinnie Mazzarola had not attended Phillips Landing High School, was related to nobody anybody knew. An intermittently employed odd-jobs man, he seemed all the same not to want for ready cash. Firehouse gossip speculated about controlled substances, but the sheriff's drug unit was concentrated in the population centers at the other end of the county. Ben saw the gun rack across the rear window of the pickup and learned that Vinnie Mazzarola was a hunter of deer.

#

Matt flew in for Christmas and lodged at the Hudson Inn. He helped Ben bake a chicken and helped Frieda eat it. Jody phoned from Herb's parents' house.

The night after Matt left, Ben dreamed they were back in the house. He was in his study; snow was deep on the ground outside. He heard Frieda open the back door and felt the draft seep around the corners. He heard Frieda exclaim, "Sara!" and Sara's thin excited voice call, "Gramma, come look at my snow angels!"

Dear God, maybe it was over.

He hurried to the kitchen and found Sara, bundled in her snowsuit, standing in the open back door. He could smell the damp wool of the lumber jacket Frieda was pulling on. "Sara!" he cried, kneeling and reaching out. "You're back!"

She let herself be hugged, delicate but solid in his arms. "Come on, Grampa. See the angels."

"Does Mommy know you're back?" he asked, marveling. "Go tell Mommy you're back. Show her your angels."

"Not real angels, Grampa. Snow angels." She began to fade.

"Sara!" His arms held mist. "Sara, stay!" But she faded, drifting like winter wood smoke.

#

The next morning he walked down Main Street to Earl Beattie's gun store.

He'd been served venison a while ago, he lied, and thought of trying to get some of his own. To his surprise, a bookish guy like him, he'd enjoyed the rifle course, years ago, in ROTC. Maybe it wasn't too late to get his eye back.

"It's never too late." Earl stroked a gunstock. "The population's too heavy for rifles in this county. You'll want a shotgun and a deer slug load. A deer slug's accurate enough at forty or fifty yards."

Ben ran his hand over steel and walnut and learned about gauge and length, over-and-under, bird shot and deer slugs. At length he said, "Well, thanks a lot, Earl. I'll have to give it some thought."

#

Early in June, two days after he turned in his final grades, Frieda had her second stroke. In the morning, fumbling just awake from his narrow bed, Ben found her no longer sleeping, but dead, her skin clammy to his touch, the room where she slept smelling of her emptied sphincters.

His hand shook on the phone. Only then did he realize how deeply he had hoped.

#

People overflowed the historic chapel whose Restoration Commission Frieda had chaired. Jody came alone. Afterward, eating carried-in casserole in the sterile apartment, she said, "I'm not going back to Herb, Dad."

Frieda would have had the necessary words. He said after a while, "Are you thinking about going back for the degree?" but knew even before he saw Matt shaking his head that the question was untimely.

Jody said, "I'm not thinking at all. Everything's a fog. It's like I got tired and threw Sara away...." She choked and went back into the bedroom to lie on the narrow bed and cry.

#

He terminated the lease and a month later his tenants moved out. He removed the furniture from storage and re-built his bookcases. He traded Frieda's little car and the insurance money for a Jeep. At the end of July, he went back to Earl's and bought a Remington smooth-bore 21-gauge with rifle sights and a box of Number 9 shot shells for the trap range, and a box of deer slugs.

Vinnie Mazzarola, outsider though he was, belonged to the Rod and Gun Club. Ben joined the Rod and Gun Club. His hand was still steady. As summer became fall and he meshed his target practice with his class lectures, he learned the heft and the alien sweet explosive response of his gun. He took the state's gun safety course and qualified for his deer license.

#

Jody called in November to say she was going to something called Grief Counseling. "You have to let go," she explained. "You have to go on with your life. You just can't go on blaming yourself for something you can't change."

#

On ninety acres of leased forest land off Oak Hollow Road, the Rod and Gun Club had erected four deer blinds, plank platforms like tree houses. Each blind had a rough ladder of slats nailed to the trunk, a couple of milk crates to sit on, and a clear view along a deer path. The blinds were out of gunshot range of one another, but the trail in to Number Two, the best of the four, passed within thirty yards of Number One. When Ben saw that Vinnie Mazzarola had signed up to use Blind Number Two on a Saturday in December, he put his name down for Blind Number One.

The night before, he hardly slept. By four-thirty he was switching off the Jeep's headlights in the parking lay-by beside

Oak Hollow Road. Gun over his shoulder, deer-slug shells in the pocket of his jacket, a thermos of coffee in a little rucksack on his back, he picked his way by flashlight over the stones and roots of the ridge trail and down the incline to the hickory tree that supported Blind Number One. He switched off the flashlight and stuffed it in a pocket. His booted feet found the slats.

On the platform, he unslung the rucksack and laid it at his feet and settled onto a milk crate with his back against the tree, facing not down the deer trail, but back the way he had come, toward the ridge trail. Pulling off his gloves and laying them on top of the rucksack, he eased the gun out of its case by touch, broke open the breech, and loaded it. He laid the gun on the plank floor beside his feet and worked his hands back into the fleece-lined gloves.

Darkness pressed on his eyeballs. Now and then he heard the rustle of a small animal foraging under the dry leaves on the forest floor. After a while his eyes adjusted and he could see the trees looming at the edge of his vision, dissolving into the darkness when he turned his eyes toward them.

Hoo-hoo hoo-hoooough...

His mind named a barred owl, owner of the night in which he trespassed. He thought about how the sound was too native to the night to be startling. A speck of coldness touched his cheek and he thought of the snow that was forecast.

Slowly, then, his thinking grew still.

After a long stillness that was not time, the darkness thinned and he saw the dark forms of the trees, and with his back against the solid unmoving hickory trunk, he thought about the earth's slow wheeling from darkness into light; about how, sitting motionless, he had all along been moving; and for a moment he seemed to feel his body and the forest and the ancient bedrock of the Highlands rushing, all together, through vastness.

He heard old leaves on a near-by oak rattle in the breeze, and he thought about how people spoke of the forest as a cathedral, arching to point to heaven, and about how forests had pointed to the sky for millennia before his race had thrust cathedrals into being; he thought about carved leaves in the groins of cathedrals and the leaves that rattled on the oak; he thought that all the hauling and building and carving, and all pain and rage and grief, were less than a wisp in the millennial rolling of the earth. *Vengeance is mine,* he thought, and he thought of the vindictive white-bearded old man in the sky who tortured a good man to devil the devil. He thought about Frieda, how she laughed, and about Sara's delicate skull and feathery curls under his stroking hand, and about ashes in the wind. A breeze flung cold specks against his face, and now he could see the snowflakes sifting in the grayness between the trees. They danced a little in a breeze, and he thought with wonderment and terror of raging and warring over how many angels could dance on the point of a pin.

He heard a snow-muted scuffle. It could have been deer. Through the screen of falling snow he watched figures appear among the tree trunks on the ridge. There were three of them, men, not deer, gray in the dawn, shotguns under their arms, two of them carrying a beer cooler between them. They passed without looking across at his blind, and he heard the scuffle of their footsteps fade among the trees.

Over his head, a flock of chickadees suddenly scolded; and at last, in the strengthening gray light, the cold awakened pain. He stood and stamped his aching feet on the snowy planks, stirring the chickadees to louder scolding.

He bent and shook snow from the rucksack, uncapped the thermos clumsily with gloved hands and gulped coffee hot down his throat and recapped the thermos and buckled it back into the rucksack. He lifted the naked wet shotgun from under the humped snow at his feet and shook the snow from it, looking at it for a moment with wonder, as if it were an artifact from a lost realm. He pulled off a glove and broke open the breech, conscious with an awareness as acute as joy of the pain of cold steel on the skin of his fingers. He unloaded the shells into his pocket, closed the gun, and slipped it, still wet, back into its case. He pulled his glove back over his wet hand, slung the rucksack and the gun over his shoulders, and climbed down the ladder, sharply aware of his aching toes inside his boots kicking snow from the slats, of his booted feet slipping and stumbling over snow-masked stones and roots on the path, of the cold snowflakes fingering his face.

The red pickup was parked next to his Jeep. He laid the shotgun and the rucksack on the floor of the Jeep's back seat, remembering that he must clean and oil the gun well when he got home, because Earl Beattie would not buy back a corroded firearm. When he slammed the door, a little avalanche whispered off the roof to the ground. He went around the Jeep brushing off the rest of the snow, and when he came to the rear, he looked across through the falling snow at Vinnie Mazzerola's red pickup.

He stepped through the snow to the rear of the truck bed, pulled the glove from his right hand, and ran his fingers over the yellow sticker. The curling edges pricked his cold fingertips.

And then, like a physical rending, the double exposure in his mind slid apart into separate images. For the first time, he looked in conscious memory, not in a dream, through the July downpour at the dwindling rain-streaked tailgate of the pickup.

There was no yellow sticker on that tailgate.

His heart began to hammer.

The pickup in the rain was not this pickup.

He laid his hand flat on the cold metal of the tailgate. It was not this pickup.

"Angels..." he whispered.

It was not Vinnie Mazzarola.

His heart racing in his chest, he whispered from a throat husky with terror and reprieve, *"Angels and ministers of grace defend us!"* running his fingers again across the yellow sticker.

Then he pulled his glove back on, turned from the truck, and made his way with careful strides across the snow. At the edge of the lay-by, he eased down onto his back and stretched out his arms to each side and slowly, with a motion he hadn't used in fifty years, began to fan them in the fallen snow, slowly, then faster, the snow caking his sleeves, the falling snow pelting his face. Astonished, he felt himself smiling and then, tears mingling

with the snow that blessed his face, laughing aloud as he fanned
his arms up and down, up and down, up and down in the fallen
snow.

At last he got to his feet and beat the snow from himself and
tramped back to the Jeep. He had to pull off his boots and rub his
feet for several minutes before he could trust them on the pedals.
Then he started the Jeep and backed around the red pickup and
turned onto the road, not disturbing the snow angel at the edge of
the forest.

*   *   *

Because the organizers know books and the convention is
small enough not to overwhelm individuals.

FINGER IN EVERY LIE

by Denise Swanson

Denise Swanson has been a school psychologist for seventeen years but has been writing stories since she was ten or eleven. A few years ago she was working as a school psychologist in a spooky rural town and thought to herself: someone should write a book about this. At the same time she realized she was in the unique position of having access to information that few others ever knew existed. And although she would never use confidential data, these insights led her to believe that a school psychologist would be the perfect amateur sleuth for a mystery series.

Her first book, *Murder of a Small-town Honey*, began the Scumble River Mystery series which features school psychologist Skye Denison. It was released July 10, 2000 by Penguin Putnam's mass market line, Signet. It was among the top ten on the annual IMBA bestseller list and has won the Reviewers' Choice Awards for Best Debut and Best Amateur Series. A large-print edition of this book is available through Thorndike Publishers.

Murder of a Sweet Old Lady was an April 2001 release. *Murder of a Sleeping Beauty*'s publishing date is January 2002. Ms. Swanson also has two short stories appearing in anthologies. "Finger in Every Lie," featured in this anthology and "Not a Monster of Chance" which will be in Signet's *And the Dying is Easy* Anthology June 2001.

Ms. Swanson is originally from a small town in northeast Illinois called Coal City, but has made her home in Plainfield, Illinois for the past ten years. She lives with her husband, Dave, and her black cat Boomerang.

FINGER IN EVERY LIE

by Denise Swanson

The crowd was starting to get ugly. This wasn't surprising, considering the mood in which the residents of Bellbridge Estates had arrived. Stephanie Danielson listened to the angry babble as she made her way to the empty chair beside her mother, Millicent Spicer.

Millicent grabbed Steph by the arm, silver-tipped fingernails digging into her daughter's flesh, and complained. "Where were you? I was afraid you'd left me here by myself."

"Parking the car." Steph raised an eyebrow. "Where else would I be? I only dropped you at the door five minutes ago, and I'm pretty sure you have all the escape routes barricaded."

A look of confusion swept over Millicent's face and Steph felt ashamed of herself. Since her parents' divorce, her mother had developed an obsessive need for Steph's presence, and a fear of being abandoned. Steph tried to deal with her mother's irrational behavior with humor, but unfortunately Millicent often didn't get the joke.

Steph gently removed her mover's fingers from her biceps and patted her hand. "Looks like the meeting is going to start late."

Millicent frowned. "Geoffrey Randolph probably won't even show up. Now that we've bought his houses, he couldn't care less about us. I heard him say to his assistant the other day that *senior citizens* were the easiest people to sell to, because they died before they could take you to court."

"He sounds like a real pri...ah, prince." Steph smoothed her beige linen slacks and looked around. "He sure has ripped off you guys."

Bellbridge Estates was advertised as the Midwest's first active adult community. It was supposed to be similar to the ones in the South like Sun City, where people over fifty-five could live a country club existence, with no small children to worry about running over with their golf carts.

But the Bellbridge residents had gotten fleeced. Instead of the beautiful clubhouse they had been promised, they were crammed into a wing of the sales center that had been hastily, and cheaply, converted into a theater. Drapery sagged on its rods, the carpet was badly stained, and the makeshift stage creaked whenever anyone stepped on it.

The golf course looked more like the craters of the moon than the smooth green expanse they were expecting. And worst of all, their houses were full of structural problems.

Millicent pouted. "I did not get ripped off, as you so elegantly put it. You were the one that was so anxious for me to buy a house out here."

Steph opened her mouth to refute her mother's delusion, but before she could speak, someone finally stepped up to the head table and started the meeting.

"May I have your attention please?" An elderly man, obviously not used to speaking into a microphone, tried to quiet the crowd, but instead produced a god awful electronic screech.

People moaned and covered their ears.

Finally a blonde woman wearing a designer suit picked up a gavel and rapped it sharply on the table. "Quiet down. We have a lot to discuss."

Another woman, this one wearing a golf outfit, read the minutes, and another man, dressed in plaid Bermuda shorts, polka dot shirt and black socks, gave the treasury report.

After a few minutes of silence, the blonde reluctantly took the mike and spoke. "We're waiting for Mr. Randolph. His office just buzzed us on the intercom and said to start the meeting. He was on his way, so he should be here any second."

As she finished speaking, a scowling man, trailed by a worried-looking woman, strode through the door that connected the theater to the rest of the sales building.

He stepped behind the table, and without a word, snatched the microphone from the blonde's hand. "You have fifteen minutes to ask your questions, then I'm leaving."

His assistant silently folded her tall frame into a nearby chair, and flipped open her memo pad.

Millicent whispered to Steph, "That's Geoffrey Randolph."

"How charming."

"And his assistant, Karen Jennings. Everyone says they're having an affair."

"Why would anyone care?" Steph asked.

Before Millicent could reply, someone in the front said, "Mr. Randolph you've been promising to have my garage door opener fixed for months. When are you going to get to it?"

Randolph exposed small pointy teeth as he smiled. "How about never? Is never good for you?"

A gasp ran through the crowd.

A man in the back stood up and shouted, "How about the clubhouse and the pools? When are you breaking ground for those?"

Other voices joined the man who was standing. "How about my plumbing?"

"We need a new keypad at the gate."

"There are cracks in my basement."

"My floors aren't even."

After a few minutes of this Randolph boomed into the mike. "Shut up! Are you all senile as well as deaf? I'm not fixing anything else. I've had workmen out here every day for the past six months, and you're never satisfied. They'll be around for one more week, and that's it." He walked away from the table, his short grayish-brown hair bristling. The muscles in his arms bulged obscenely under his white shirt as he yanked open the door. He spoke over his shoulder, "I'm out of here after Friday. Bellbridge Estates can rot in hell for all I care."

The woman who had followed him into the room, followed him out. But now a look of surprise replaced the look of worry she had worn earlier.

The crowd was silent. Finally, the remaining man seated at the committee table spoke. The overhead lights deepened his tan, and the black polo shirt he wore outlined his broad shoulders and nicely muscled arms.

Steph put her lips to her mother's ears and whispered, "I thought you said everyone out here had to be at least fifty-five. That guy's not even close."

Millicent's mouth curved into a cat-like smile. "Isn't he handsome? His parents were among the first to buy a home out here. Unfortunately, they died soon afterwards and he inherited. He was going to sell the house, but when he found out how much was wrong with it, and how much money he'd lose if he sold it as is, he decided to move in and make Bellbridge fix it. He was elected to the board at our last meeting."

"Looks like his job just got more difficult."

The man spoke. "Most of you know me. My name is Jack Peterson. How many of you still have major problems with your houses?"

Every hand in the audience went up.

"How many of you have had someone come and supposedly 'fix' the problems?"

The hands remained raised.

"More than once?"

No one put their arm down.

"Are we going to sit here and let Geoffrey Randolph get away with this?"

"What can we do? He said he's leaving," someone in the audience shouted.

"We need a lawyer. Someone to get a court order to look at his books, and see what's going on." Jack shook his head. "I find it hard to believe that Geoffrey Randolph would just abandon a multi-million dollar project. We need to find out what's going on."

A murmur swept the crowd. A voice rose above the babble. "How much is that going to cost us?"

Jack leaned into the microphone. "The real question is how much is it going to cost us if we have to pay for all the repairs ourselves."

Someone else shouted, "That's all right for you to say. You don't live on a fixed income. You got money to waste. Some of us don't."

A grumble of agreement went through the throng.

Jack's handsome face darkened. "Fine, if the rest of you aren't willing to stand up for your rights, I'll do this on my own. No way is that bastard Randolph getting away with this."

The residents' meeting continued for another boring hour, but nothing was decided. Everyone's dissatisfaction was focused on Geoffrey Randolph, except for one woman who had bought a house along the golf course, and couldn't understand why golf balls kept breaking her windows.

Jack listened patiently, then spoke, "Ma'am, thank you for expressing your concern. We're all refreshed and challenged by your unique point of view."

The meeting was adjourned on that note, and most people left frowning.

As Steph drove her mother home, she asked, "Is everyone as mad at Randolph as the people tonight?"

Millicent nodded. "It's the only subject of conversation at exercise class."

***

"Someone should kill Geoffrey Randolph!"

Steph looked up from the mystery she was reading, and met sea-green eyes that matched her own. "I know he's a jerk, but murder seems a little extreme."

Millicent thrust out her lower lip and her voice quavered. "Thirty-one."

"Thirty-one days until Christmas, thirty-one jelly beans in the jar, thirty-one what?" Steph was used to her mother's moods, and usually tried to jolly her out of them.

"Thirty-one things wrong with this house." Millicent sagged dramatically back on the white leather sofa, and dabbed at her eyes with a lace handkerchief. "I'm ruined. After your father divorced me, I used all my cash to buy this house, and it's a worthless dump. How could you let me do this?"

After her divorce, Millicent had taken to blaming Steph for all her woes.

Steph reluctantly marked the place in her book. "I told you I have an appointment with Mr. Randolph later this morning. We'll get things straightened out before he leaves."

"How did you get an appointment?" Millicent seemed surprised. "After what he said last night, I thought he wasn't willing to see anyone."

Steph smiled. "Old reporter's trick. I told his assistant I had a check for him."

"For what?"

"I was vague and flattering."

"You shouldn't lie."

Steph shrugged. "A girl's got to do what a girl's got to do."

Millicent seemed to lose interest, and ran a finger over the glass-topped coffee table. "That new cleaning lady isn't doing a very good job."

Steph's gaze swept the ultra modern décor of her mother's living room. Everything was white and black. Sometimes she felt as if she had been sucked into a noncolorized movie from the forties.

"I told you we had to let the housekeep go, Mother. We can't afford her salary. Besides, this house is so much smaller than the one you and Daddy lived in, so we can easily keep it clean ourselves."

Millicent's sobs trailed over her shoulder, as she ran into her bedroom and slammed the door.

Steph signed. She always forgot how close to the surface her mother's emotions were. Steph kept her own feelings buried so deeply, she almost wondered if she still had any.

***

"Mr. Randolph? I'm Stephanie Danielson." She knocked on the half-opened door, and poked her head into the office.

Geoffrey Randolph barely looked up. "Put the check on my desk."

"Well, it's a little more complicated than that." Steph eased into the room. "May I sit down?"

Randolph's small black eyes appraised her. "Have a seat."

Her skin crawled under this inspection. Suddenly she wished she would have worn something less feminine than her soft pink dress and delicate pearl cross.

He growled, "You sitting down or what?"

Steph straightened her spine. She had gotten this far, and she wasn't about to run away like some scared schoolgirl. She sat on the metal folding chair he indicated and cross her legs.

His gaze shot to the nylon-covered calf she had exposed and she hastily tugged the two flaps of her dress together.

He leaned back and folded his hands over his stomach. "So, where's this check you got for me?"

"Gee, your secretary must have misunderstood me. I said I wanted to see you to check some things out. I'm Millicent Spicer's daughter. She lives on Ivy Court. We really need to schedule her repairs before you leave."

A nasty smile crawled across his lips. "You seem like a reasonable lady, unlike those old biddies I've been trying to deal with. Maybe we can get a few things straightened out for your Mom before I go. What needs fixing?"

"The air conditioner still doesn't work, the shower in the guest bath goes from red hot to ice cold, but seems to have no happy medium, and the garage door is possessed—it opens when no one has pushed the button and refuses to budge when the controller is activated."

That's a lot of repairs. What's in it for me?" Randolph's eyes had fastened on her breasts.

"The satisfaction of doing a job right."

He rose, walked around to her, then sat on the edge of his desk with his knees touching hers. "I was thinking of another kind of satisfaction."

Steph moved her chair back and got up. As she edged her way to the door, she said, "Those are just the major problems. The minor ones include a ceiling fan hung crookedly, a drip in the master bath, a crack in the wall near the cathedral ceiling—shall I go on?"

"We've had repairmen at your mother's house almost every day since she's moved in. Nothing satisfies that woman." Randolph followed her.

Steph's eyebrows rose, but she kept her tone smooth. "Perhaps, but there are certain items I must agree with my mother about."

He backed her into the wall and put a hand on the wall on either side of her. "We can't be spending all our time fixing things. We have houses to build for paying customers. Of course, some homeowners do get special consideration."

Before she could move or speak, the door was flung open. Randolph's assistant, Karen burst into the office waving a letter. She turned on him, "How could you, Geof? You promised me we'd be together for ever."

When Randolph didn't react, the woman turned on Steph. "Are you really willing to sell yourself for some plumbing and a paint job?"

Steph ducked under Randolph's arms. "Hey, don't blame me. I see no evil, hear no evil, and certainly date no evil."

Randolph glowered at her. "Making a fool of a man is no way to get your repairs done."

"Women don't make fools of men—most of them are the do-it-yourself type."

He stammered. "If you don't cooperate, your mother's house can fall to the ground before I'll lift a finger."

Steph hurried to the door. "I'm sorry you feel that way. It sounds like sexual harassment to me. I'll call our attorney and have him make an appointment with you."

Randolph turned his back on her and his outraged assistant. "Fine, don't think you're going to scare me with no lawyer."

Steph closed her eyes, she really hadn't wanted to go down this road, it still hurt too much to talk about her husband. She took a deep breath and forced herself to speak. "Mr. Randolph, did my mother ever mention to you what my late husband did for a living?"

"No, what?" Condescension hung on the man's every word. "I'll bet he was a hit man for the mob."

"No, better." She smiled thinly. "He was an investigative reporter for channel nine."

"So?" Randolph's voice faltered for a second, then recovered its nasty tone. "He's dead. What's your point?"

Steph paused, his cruel words had found their target. She swallowed back a lump that had formed in her throat. She knew this was going to be hard. "When I leave, think about this. Who do you think are reporters' friends? And would you really like Bellbridge Estates put under a microscope? The last I counted you had seven hundred and eighty-eight empty lots, not to mention the condos with empty floors, and the townhouses with empty units." Before he could answer she added. "I expect to see repairmen swarming over my mother's house by noon tomorrow or trust me, you'll be very sorry."

As Steph left, she heard Randolph's assistant screaming at him. "You liar. You told me you were just giving the old people a hard time about leaving on Friday. If that's true, what's this letter from Arizona about? You're planning on sneaking out of town, aren't you?"

Millicent was waiting by the door when Steph got back to the house. "I hope you didn't make Mr. Randolph mad at me."

That was another quirk of her mother's that had grown to unreasonable proportions since the divorce. Millicent could no longer stand for anyone not to like her.

"I'm sure his feelings for you haven't changed." Steph reassured her mother, before going into her bedroom and closing the door.

Steph had known it would be difficult to live with her mom, even just for the summer, but she had no idea how hard it was going to be. At this rate she'd be better off moving into a cardboard box.

***

Steph checked her watch for the tenth time, then looked back out the front window. It seemed that every house on the block, except her mother's, had a repair truck parked in the driveway.

She sighed. Randolph was pushing her into a corner. If she didn't get things fixed for her Mom, she'd end up staying with her for the rest of their lives.

Steph had only agreed to spend the summer with Millicent in order to help them both out financially. Her mother had spent too much on the new house, and wouldn't get any more money until the next alimony payment in September.

And Steph found out she was broke when she started to settle her husband's affairs after he died. He had cleaned out all their bank accounts, except for a couple thousand in the everyday checking, cashed in his insurance, and taken a second mortgage on their condo before his death.

She had been able to locate a teaching job, but both it and its salary didn't begin until the fall. Meanwhile, she'd had to sell everything and move in with her Mom.

Millicent walked into the living room drying her hands on a kitchen towel. "Are you watching those women next door?"

"What?" Steph had no idea what her mother was talking about.

"You know. I told you about them when they moved in. They're very strange."

"I don't remember you telling me about any strange women." Steph looked at her mother.

"Yes, I did. The older one is a retired gym teacher or something athletic. She dresses in those nylon shorts and T-shirts all the time. The other one says she's a social worker, but her job must have really odd hours. She always wears those long pleated skirts and these really weird-looking sandals. And neither one of them shaves their legs."

"So?" Steph couldn't figure out where her mother was going with this conversation. "Your point is?"

Millicent leaned forward and whispered. "I think they're, you know."

"No. I don't know. And why are we whispering?"

"I think they're Lebanese."

Steph buried her face in her hands and tried not to laugh. Finally she got a hold of herself and said, "Could be, Mom. They could even be Legionnaires."

Millicent looked confused and changed the subject. "We need to leave soon, or I'll be late for my two o'clock beauty shop appointment."

Steph looked at her watch. "Time flies when you're being driven crazy." When Millicent didn't react, she spoke over her shoulder as she continued to watch the activity in the street, "I was hoping one of the repairmen would get here before we had to leave."

"They won't show up. They never do." Millicent's voice echoed from down the hall.

Steph turned from the window. "Well, I'll call Maxine if there's no sign of them by the time we get back."

Millicent, returning to the living room with a fresh coat of lipstick and powder, wrinkled her nose. "That nasty woman, why?"

"Because she's the one who assigns the stories to the reporters." Steph grabbed her keys from the table in the foyer. "And she's not nasty. She just uses that language to fit in with the men. When she first started in the business, there were very few women, and they had to be tougher than the guys to survive."

"I wouldn't know about that." Millicent climbed into the passenger seat of Steph's beat-up Neon.

No, you wouldn't Mother, because Daddy always protected you from that sort of thing.

Millicent continued, "And I still don't understand why we don't drive my Lincoln."

Steph put the Dodge into reverse. "Because we're trying to save money, and your car uses twice as much gas as mine." *Plus I feel like the Queen Mother when I drive it.*

A man sitting in a lawn chair across the road caught Steph's attention. He was pointing a hair dryer at the cars as they drove down the street.

She turned to her mother and asked, "What is Mr. Bass doing?"

"Oh, he's trying to get people to slow down. He thinks the drivers will mistake that old blow dryer of his wife's for a speed gun."

Steph smiled. Silly? Yes. But it was sort of ingenious. "I didn't realize we had a problem with speeders on this road. It's only five blocks long."

"It's the repair people. The way they race by here like a bat out of hell, someone's going to get killed some day."

***

It was nearly five o'clock when Steph pulled back into their driveway. After getting her hair and nails done, Millicent had insisted on stopping at Marshal Fields, Carson's, and Ulta3 Cosmetics. Steph totaled her mother's purchases, and winced as she realized that Millicent had spent more than their month's allowance in one day.

Millicent hopped out of the Neon. "I'm going to take a look at that rose bush out back, and see if the flowers are ready to pick. You take the packages inside."

Steph was wondering if she could find some part-time work for the next couple of months, before her real job started at the end of August, when she heard her mother's scream.

Dropping the forest green Fields' bag on the front step Steph sprinted around the house. She skidded to halt a couple of feet from her mother, who was slumped over on the lawn. "Mom, are you all right? What's wrong?"

Millicent pointed a shaky finger and Steph looked beyond the bulk of the air conditioning unit. A man lay sprawled and nearly hidden by its side. Still, she could easily see that his head had been savagely beaten in.

She forced herself to move closer. Blood and something she didn't want to identify was scattered across the blades of grass and metal condenser.

Steph forced back the gorge rising in her throat, and felt for the man's pulse, but there was nothing.

"We need to call 911." Steph reached down and nearly dragged her mother upright. They turned their backs on the body, and made their way inside.

After calling the police, Steph made her mother a cup of tea. Millicent had curled herself into a fetal position on the white leather sofa. She silently sipped the tea Steph handed her.

Steph paced, casting worried looks at her mother.

Finally, the doorbell rang. Two men were on the step. One wore the uniform of the security company that patrolled Bellbridge, the other wore the uniform of the local sheriff's department.

The real police officer stepped forward. "Stephanie Danielson?" When she nodded, he said, "Deputy Hacker. You reported a murder?"

She nodded again. "Yes, officer, the body's around back."

He gave her a quick look and said, "Show me." Turning to the security guard, he ordered, "Stay here."

Steph lead the way. He stopped her at the corner of the house. "That's close enough. Do you know the victim's name?" "Geoffrey Randolph, the owner of Bellbridge Estates." Deputy Hacker walked around the body, spoke into his walkie-talkie, then returned to Steph's side. "Let's go inside." The security guard, who said his name was McNair, trailed them into the living room.

It looked like Millicent hadn't moved. Steph introduced her mother to the men. Millicent barely blinked.

"I'd like to talk to your mother alone," Deputy Hacker said. Turning to McNair, he continued, "Take Ms. Danielson into the kitchen."

Steph watched through the kitchen window as the back yard filled with police. Some were sketching, some taking pictures, some measuring, and a lot seemed to be searching for something.

Nearly a half hour went by before Deputy Hacker walked into the kitchen and said, "McNair, switch places."

Hacker took a seat. "Ms. Danielson, please sit down."

When Steph complied he continued, "Your mother says you had a meeting with this Geoffrey Randolph yesterday."

Steph sat up straighter. This sounded like he was accusing her of something. "I spoke to Mr. Randolph about some repairs we needed."

"I see." Hacker clicked on his pen and made a note. "I understand you had a disagreement with him."

What in the world had her mother said? "Yes, I wanted him to fulfill his obligation, and fix the things that were wrong with my mother's house. He felt he had finished with this project." Steph added, "I understand most people in Bellbridge had similar disagreements with him."

"I see." Hacker cross his legs. "Now tell me what you did today from say noon until you phoned 911."

Steph went through her day.

He had her repeat her story several more times, but finally rose from the table. "You're not planning on any trips or anything, I hope."

She shook her head.

"Good. I'll call you when your statement is ready to sign."

**

Brrrg! Brrrg! Steph reached an arm out from under the sheet and hit the alarm clock beside her bed, but the annoying ringing that had woken her persisted.

Never an early riser, she hadn't been able to sleep the night before and had only dozed off as the sun began to appear. She narrowed her eyes trying to see the time. The red numbers glowed eight o'clock.

She fought her way from under the covers and stumbled out of bed. The noise continued even after she scooped the receiver off the kitchen wall. Where was that sound coming from?

Finally, she realized it was the front doorbell being pressed without pause. Shoving her hair off her face and behind her ears, she ran back to her bedroom for a bathrobe. *Where in the heck is Mom?*

Steph pressed her eye to the peephole and saw Deputy Hacker leaning on the bell. Irritated, she flung open the door, "Yes?"

"Ms. Danielson." He coolly look her up and down. "You need to come into the station with me."

"Now?"

"As soon as you get dressed."

"Why?" Steph was trying to force her mind to function.

"We'll discuss that there. Please go change clothes."

He strode through the door, uninvited, and started to follow her down the hall.

"Where do you think you're going?" Steph was waking up.

"I'll be outside your door while you change."

Alarm bells started to ring in her head. Something was seriously wrong. He was treating her like a suspect. Why? As she dressed, she cursed herself for not having had a phone installed in her room and for having given up her cell phone. Once again, she had been penny wise and pound foolish.

Steph's emotions ranged from anger to fright. How dare he burst in without warning and drag her to the police station? Was he going to put her in jail?

A few minutes later, she emerged dressed in khaki pants and a white short sleeve blouse, her honey blond hair back in its usual chignon. She hadn't worn her hair loose since her husband died six months ago.

On their way out, she peeked in her mother's room. It was its usual mess, but there was no sign of Millicent. She had probably gone to the seven-thirty exercise class.

Steph wrote her mother a note, before Hacker led her outside and into his car. At least he didn't put her in the back seat.

Once they were at the station, Hacker deposited her in an interview room. It contained two metal chairs and a small wooden table. He left her there without comment.

Steph stared at the mirrored wall. She had read enough mysteries to know that she was probably being observed. After fifteen minutes Hacker returned with a tape recorder.

At first she thought he was going to record what they said, instead he pushed the play button and her voice poured out of the tiny speaker. "I expect to see repairmen swarming over this house by noon tomorrow or trust me, you'll be very sorry."

Hacker finally spoke, "Is that you?"

She nodded.

"Did any repairmen show up?"

She shook her head.

"Would you say Geoffrey Randolph is very sorry now?"

Steph opened her mouth to answer, but changed her mind. "I'd like to call my lawyer now."

"Why?" The deputy sat back in his chair. "You're not under arrest."

The word "yet" hung in the air.

"But I can't leave?"

"We're asking for your cooperation." Hacker's smile didn't reach his eyes.

"There's nothing I can help you with."

"Let me ask you a few questions." He crossed his legs. "You can always stop."

She knew she shouldn't, but if she could clear things up without calling her attorney that was one less bill to pay. "Okay, what do you want to know?"

"Tell me about the conversation you had with Mr. Randolph the day before yesterday."

"Why? You obviously have the tape." She sat up straighter. "The tape that was made without my permission or knowledge, I might add."

"Humor me. Give me your side."

Steph outlined the problems with the house, and told Hacker about her encounters with the other residents, who also wanted a pound of flesh from Geoffrey Randolph.

Hacker continued to go over her movements leading up to discovering the body. "So, you dropped your Mom off at the beauty shop and picked her up nearly two hours later. Where did you go?"

"I went to a bookstore and browsed."

"For nearly two hours. Did anyone see you?" His words dripped with disbelief.

She shrugged. "Lots of people saw me. Do I know any of them? No. Would anyone remember me? I doubt it."

"Did you buy anything?"

"No. I usually just jot down titles and then get the books from my library."

"So, you had plenty of time to drive home, bash in Randolph's head, and pick up your Mom." Hacker looked pleased.

"But I didn't. Why would I kill him?"

"Because you and your mother are both broke and he was screwing with the only thing of value she owned."

Steph frowned. "How do you know I'm broke?"

"I spoke to the police in your old neighborhood. They tell me your husband's death was suspicious, although they finally ruled it a suicide after your financial situation was revealed."

Steph felt as if she had been hit in the chest by a wrecking ball. She still had so many questions about her husband's death. She didn't believe for a minute he had committed suicide.

In her heart, she was convinced he had been investigating something or someone, and been killed when he got too close. But she never could figure out an explanation for the missing money. The police had hinted that there was another woman, but couldn't offer any solid evidence.

Hacker was staring at her. Had he asked her a question? She stared back.

The deputy finally blinked. "Do you have anything to add?"

"I didn't kill Geoffrey Randolph." Steph's gaze never wavered. "Did you talk to the neighbors? The area is full of people who spend a lot of time in their yards, on their decks, or staring out their windows."

"We canvassed the area. No one saw anything. The guy across the street from your house says he was in his lawn chair checking for speeders the whole time, and there was no one unusual or suspicious in your yard."

Steph's brows drew together. "Did he see Randolph?"

Hacker hesitated. "Yes. Saw him walk behind your house about three o'clock."

"Alone?"

"Yes. But he never saw him leave."

Steph thought fast. "This neighbor didn't see me in the yard, right?"

Hacker frowned. "No, but you could have gone into the house through the garage, then out to the back through the sliding doors."

"So could anyone else, go through the back yards I mean. So the witness wouldn't have seen him or her going around our house."

He shrugged. "But no one saw any strangers in their back yard either."

She nodded and chewed her lip. "Are you putting me in jail?"

"No, I'll give you a ride home, but don't leave the area."

"You said that yesterday." She got up and picked up her purse.

"I'm saying it again."

***

"I don't know why I can't go with you." Millicent stood by Steph's side, as Steph peered into the refrigerator.

"You have company coming for cards." Steph grabbed an apple.

"You could wait until after my bridge group leaves."

"Besides, I think he'll talk more freely just to me." Steph escaped into the shower. One of the few places her mother didn't follow her.

Steph waited until she heard the women playing cards, then slipped out the front door before her mother could ask her to wait until later to go. Steph felt like she was sixteen again, and sneaking out to meet her first boyfriend.

She had looked up Jack's address and found that he lived in the next block over. His backyard very nearly touched theirs. Standing on his doorstep, waiting for him to answer her ring, Steph rehearsed what she was going to say. She had worked as a reporter before quitting a couple of years ago to write a novel. The novel that still lay in her bottom drawer unpublished.

When the door swung open, Steph lost her train of thought. Jack Peterson was even more handsome face-to-face. She looked up. At five seven she was not used to men towering over her, but he had to be at least six foot four.

Icy blue eyes narrowed, "May I help you?"

She stuttered, her brilliant plan forgotten, "I'm Stephanie Danielson. I just moved in around the corner on Ivy Court."

"Yes, I know. You found Randolph's body yesterday." His bulk filled the doorway.

"Ah, well, yes. I suppose it's that talk of the neighborhood."

"Certainly, plus I had a birds-eye view from my deck."

"Oh." Steph chewed her lip. "Could I come in a minute? I wanted to talk to you about Mr. Randolph."

He ran long elegant fingers through his crisp black hair, revealing glints of silver as the strands were pushed back. "Sure, would you like some coffee or a soft drink?"

"Coffee would be wonderful. I never did get mine this morning." She cursed herself. She was already saying too much.

He led the way into the kitchen. "Have a seat."

Steph sat in a leather and wooden chair at a small round table. "So, do you work at home?"

"Yes. I'm a writer."

"What do you write?"

He shrugged. "You name it, I've written it. But right now I'm working on a suspense-thriller." He put a cup in front of her. "And what do you do?"

She felt her cheeks get red. "I was a reporter."

"But not anymore?"

"I quit a few years ago to write a novel. And no, it's not published."

He pulled up the chair next to hers and sat down. "A couple of years isn't all that long in the writing game."

She didn't meet his eyes. "Anyway, I was wondering if you noticed anything odd going in the back yards yesterday?"

"Depends what you mean." He paused. "Look, I'm guessing you suspect me because I hated the guy, but as I told the police, I have an alibi. I was on the phone with my agent or editor almost continually from two-thirty to five-fifteen yesterday afternoon."

"Oh." Her heart sank. She was never going to clear herself at this rate. On the other hand, maybe he saw something while he was talking.

"Were you looking out back while you talked?"

He grinned. "Better yet, I was on the deck the whole time."

She brightened. "What did you see?"

Suddenly, he seemed to remember something and grew distant. "Why do you want to know?"

"Because I'm the police's chief suspect," Steph blurted out.

"I see. Did you do it?"

"No."

"Well, even if you did, I can't see any harm in telling you what I saw." Jack turned slightly and muttered. "Besides that bastard deserved to die for what he was pulling on old folks like my parents."

Steph made an agreeing sound in her throat.

He refilled their coffee and sat back down.

"My agent called about three while I was reading on the deck. I answered her on my portable. She had an offer for a book I'm writing and two more with the same hero. About the same time, I noticed Randolph poking around your back yard. He stuck out like a corn stalk in a bean field because he was wearing a black suit and digging around your rosebushes. I figured he was up to no good."

He took a drink from his cup and continued. At about three fifteen or a little later, my agent wanted some information that I had to go inside for. I was gone about ten minutes, and when I came back, Randolph was gone."

"Of course now we know he wasn't gone. He was just where you couldn't see him from here." Steph grimaced.

"Yeah, but I was on the deck for the next couple of hours and didn't see anyone else."

Steph sagged back in her chair. Somebody had to have seen something. "Well, somebody had to have been around. They obviously killed him in that ten or fifteen minutes you were in the house."

"True." He looked at her. "I take it you don't have an alibi."

She shook her head. "Nope. I was alone in a bookstore."

"Receipt?"

"None. Didn't buy anything." She sat for a couple more seconds then rose from the chair. "Thanks for talking to me. I'd better get back to my mother."

"Yes, I imagine you better. I've met your mother, and I'll bet it takes a lot to take care of her."

"It's a thankless job, but I've got a lot of bad karma to burn off." Steph shrugged. "But seriously, she's had a rough time since my dad left her."

He smiled and took her hand. The warmth felt good on her icy fingers. "It's nice to have someone near my age out here. Try to stay out of jail."

She reluctantly freed herself. "I'll give it my best shot, believe me."

As she walked back, she noted the repair trucks lining the streets. She wondered who would take over for Randolph, and if that person would hire some repairmen who could actually fix things. These clowns seemed to be out every day and still nothing was ever corrected.

Steph stopped in midstride. Had the police questioned all the repair people? Maybe they saw something? She hurried home, nodded to the ladies still playing bridge in the living room, and snatched up the phone.

Hacker came on the line almost immediately. Steph explained about the workmen and asked if they had been questioned. There was a pause and she could hear paper rustling.

Finally, he spoke, "No one mentioned any repairmen around. Are you sure they were there yesterday?"

"Yes. I was ticked that they seemed to be at everyone's house but ours."

Another pause. "I'll send someone out to question them right now."

"Thank you. I know you think I did it, but I didn't."

The deputy's voice was cool. "Unlike TV and books, we want to catch the real killer, not just someone to clear our board."

***

It was nearly six when the phone rang again. Steph had cleaned up the mess from her mother's bridge party, and been trying to read a book. So far she hadn't made it off page two. "Ah, Deputy Hacker. Did the men see anything?" "No. They all claimed not to have noticed anything." Steph sat down hard on a kitchen chair. "Well, thanks for trying."

After she hung up, she paced. There was no such thing as a perfect crime. What were they missing? Finally, she lay on the couch, and let her mind drift as she half-watched an old movie.

Suddenly she shot off the sofa. How could she have been so stupid? Steph looked at the clock. It was nearly two in the morning. She'd have to wait until business hours to call Hacker.

***

The next morning at eight o'clock exactly she dialed the phone. Once Hacker got on the line she explained her theory. "Hi, Stephanie Danielson again. I think I figured out how Mr. Randolph was killed without witnesses seeing anyone. The killer dressed like a repairman."

There was silence on the other end of the line. So she hurriedly explained. "Yesterday, when you told me no one had mentioned the repairmen as being in the neighborhood, even when the street was crawling with them, something stuck in my mind. Last night it came to me. Repairmen are all but invisible. So, as long as he's careful not to be seen during the few minutes he's actually killing Randolph, no one will remember him."

"I'll check it out." Hacker hung up.

***

Jack Peterson dropped by a couple of days later. After he had settled on the white leather couch he said, "Did you hear? They caught Randolph's killer."

"No, who did it turn out to be?" Steph leaned forward in the side chair.

"You know the police questioned the neighbors and repairmen again?" When she nodded he went on. "Well, people finally remembered seeing one workman who didn't seem to have a truck or anything to do. Anyway the more they talked to the witnesses, the more they remembered. It seems this repairman was tall and really thin. And Mr. Bass, from across the street, said he was sort of a weakling."

"Good old Mr. Bass." Steph smiled fondly.

Jack went on as if she hadn't said anything. "So, the police did a little more checking and decided to search Randolph's offices. They found a blood-spattered workman's uniform stuffed in his assistant, Karen Jennings's, desk. They confronted her and she confessed."

"But why did she kill him?"

"The usual reasons." Jack shrugged. "She'd put up with his womanizing ways for years, but when she found out he planned to sneak out of town and leave her holding the bag for this mess of a housing development, she went crazy. She borrowed a suit of gray work clothes from one of the guys' lockers, followed Randolph until he was alone, and smashed his head in with a wrench."

"I knew she was upset with him when I heard her yelling the other day, but I would have never guessed she'd do something like that." Steph looked at Jack's smirk. "And don't trot out that old chestnut about a woman scorned."

Jack raised a brow and quoted, "When lovely woman stoops to folly, and finds too late that men betray, what charm can soothe her melancholy? What art can wash her guilt away?"

*   *   *

Mayhem is a wonderfully warm and intimate conference. There are no barriers between authors and readers. It is well organized with lots of interesting panels.

HICKORY DICKORY DOC

by Mary V. Welk

Mary V. Welk is the author of the Caroline Rhodes Mystery Series including *A Deadly Little Christmas*, winner of the Readers' Choice Award for Best First Mystery, Love is Murder 2000; *Something Wicked in the Air* and *To Kill a King*.

For more info on these books, or to read selected chapters, please visit Mary's web page at www.mysterykleworks.com.

HICKORY DICKORY DOC

by Mary V. Welk

"Good lord, Ben. Jack Fielding a murderer? Impossible. Simply impossible."

Lawrence Wainsworth III latched the half door on King Tut's stall and turned to me with an impatient shake of his head.

"I can't believe you'd fall for such a cock-and-bull story. I'll agree Jack was annoyed when Monty called him a skinflint in front of everyone at the ball. But Jack *is* a skinflint. People have been saying that to his face for years, and he knows it's true. Why would he fly off the handle and kill his neighbor on the greatest night of his life? My God, man. He'd just won the Hunt Club Trophy!"

I shrugged and muttered something inane about a camel and a straw. Fortunately, Larry chose to misunderstand me.

"We're talking horses, Ben, not camels," he snapped, his bushy white eyebrows beetled into a frown clearly meant to put me in my place. "Jack was on top of the world last night. As I said before, he was obviously aggravated with Monty for bringing up that business of the wood shavings. Still, he kept his temper in check."

Knowing Jack Fielding, I found that a little hard to believe. But who was I to doubt Larry's story? He'd been a ringside witness to the main event, while I, Dr. Ben Benjamin, youthful veterinarian to some of the most pampered horses in the state of Maryland, hadn't even been invited to the Hunt Club Ball. I tagged along behind the older man as he strode out of the barn still expounding on Jack's innocence.

"Monty was behaving badly because for the first time in years he hadn't won the trophy. He baited Jack, but Fielding had the good grace to treat the entire matter as a joke. He looked that obnoxious old coot right in the eye and told him that Squire Dan had the ability to overcome any obstacle, including the mistakes of his owner. I'll tell you something, Ben. Jack came out on top in that exchange, and everyone at the party noticed it. Yessiree, Bob. Everyone noticed it."

Larry tends to forget his breeding and revert to colloquialisms like 'yessiree, Bob' whenever he gets worked up. I decided to take my leave before the plight of his dearest friend raised Larry's blood pressure another dangerous notch.

"I have to get over to the Blakely place, Larry. Pat's mare is wheezing again."

Wainsworth nodded distractedly.

"Keep your ears open, will you, Ben? As local veterinarian, you're privy to more of the neighborhood gossip than I am. Let me know if you hear anything that'll help Jack beat this rap."

I hesitated only a second. Much as I disliked Fielding, Lawrence Wainsworth III was a good guy. He was also a very wealthy man. Visions of unpaid student loans danced in my head as I screwed on a smile and replied, "Sure, Larry. If you're that convinced of his innocence..."

"I am, Ben. Jack Fielding and I went to school together at Mansfield Prep. I can guarantee you no graduate of that institution would ever stoop to something as plebeian as stabbing a man with a steak knife."

Having uttered that truism with sublime self-assurance, Larry dismissed me with a solder-like two-finger salute.

I felt a bit like Alice wandering through Wonderland as I threw my medical bag in the back of my pickup, climbed into the cab, and switched on the ignition. I did a good job of keeping a straight face until I passed the big stone pillars guarding the entrance to the Wainsworth property. Then I let out a hoot that could have been heard clear back to town. My best client had just waved the old school tie in my face, and while I had no doubt of his sincerity, Larry's defense of his former classmate tickled my funny bone. Apparently graduates of Mansfield Prep were not above killing off their enemies as long as it was done in a dignified manner. It was too bad dueling had been outlawed ages ago. Harry Montgomery might have stood a sporting chance if he and Fielding had lived in an earlier time.

I was driving down Stone Road, happily immersed in a fantasy featuring the two protagonists battling it out on a field of honor, when my pager beeped me back to reality. I glanced at my watch before pulling over to the side of the road. It was high noon, which meant the page was probably from my wife. Tory knew my schedule better than I did. When her lunch break coincided with mine, she rang me up for a quick chat and exchange of news. If I was out of the office at lunchtime, she'd page me and punch in 4-5683-968. Translated, those eight little numbers read 'I love you'.

I thumbed the button on the side of my pager, read the message, and reached for my cellular phone. As I'd guessed, the call was from my bride. Instead of our usual code, though, she'd left the number of the police station in town where she worked as a dispatcher. I wondered what was up.

"The Chief wants to talk to you about Harry Montgomery's death," Tory said when I identified myself. "He wants to know how soon you can get here."

I told her about Patricia Blakely's mare and promised to show up at the station after I'd seen to the horse. Tory said that was fine and hung up before I could ask her to elucidate on the request. My curiosity piqued, I continued on to the Blakely farm completely in the dark as to why I'd been summoned by the police.

As far as I knew, the case against Jack Fielding was wrapped up tighter than a boxer's fist. Montgomery had been found stabbed to death in the parking lot of the Barrington Country Club only minutes after the conclusion of the annual Hunt Club

Ball. Buried in his chest was a steak knife from the club's dining room, its handle covered with Jack Fielding's fingerprints. Several people had seen Jack wandering around the grounds shortly before the Ball ended, and although he claimed he'd stepped out to enjoy a cigar, he'd been alone at the time and therefore had no real alibi.

Despite Larry's assertion that Jack had brushed off Montgomery's jibes, Chief of Police Patrick Brody painted an uglier picture of the encounter when we sat talking in his office later that day.

"Oh, he was angry all right," the Chief said with a nod. "We have plenty of witnesses who will testify to that. Montgomery's wife sat next to Fielding at dinner, and she told us that after a curt 'hello', he refused to say one word to her during the entire meal. She claims to have overheard Jack threatening her husband when she was leaving the club."

"Anyone else hear these threats?"

Brody shook his head. "People saw them talking together in the hallway, but no one seemed inclined to join the discussion. It appears neither man was well liked."

The Chief leaned over the desk and handed me a clear plastic envelope with two withered leaves inside.

"Ever see this kind of leaf before?" he asked.

I barely glanced at the envelope before answering, "I'm a veterinarian, Chief Brody, not a horticulturist. What's so important about a couple of leaves?"

Brody leaned back in his chair and extended his long legs under the desk. Lacing his fingers over his ample stomach, he smiled at me.

"We found those in the pocket of Harry's dinner jacket. Several more leaves were discovered in Harry's office along with a receipt for a load of stable bedding he'd purchased. He paid for the bedding in cash, and he specified it was to be delivered to Jack Fielding's farm."

I was beginning to see where all this was leading to, and I wasn't liking it one bit.

You're telling me Harry Montgomery purposely sabotaged his next-door neighbor."

Brody nodded again. "That's why I wanted to talk to you. You treated Squire Dan when he took ill last month, didn't you?"

It was my turn to nod. "Jack called me at home and said Squire Dan was behaving oddly. The horse was listless and unwilling to move out of his stall. He also seemed to be breathing more rapidly than usual."

"Did you go over to Fielding's place?"

"Of course I did. The symptoms sounded too much like colic."

"That's a dangerous disorder in animals, isn't it?"

"Horses can die of colic," I told him. "When I got to Jack's farm, he was in quite a state. He'd pinned all his hopes for winning the Hunt Club trophy on a healthy Squire Dan, and now the horse was sick."

"Pretty devastating circumstances then."

"You could say so. I examined Dan from head to toe. He was exactly as Jack had described him, and worse. When I checked his legs, I detected clinical signs of laminitis, an inflammation of a bone formation in the hoof. On a hunch, I inspected the bedding in Dan's stall."

"And?"

"I found dark wood shavings mixed in with the straw. I guessed they were from a black walnut, a tree containing a toxin which affects horses. I told Jack he had to remove the bedding immediately, and while he and his foreman did that, I led Dan outside and hosed down his legs. Cooling can sometimes relieve a horse's discomfort, and Dan did seem more alert when I finished with him."

"Obviously, the horse recovered."

"Within a matter of days he was his old self again. I sent some of the shavings to a friend who works at a university, and he confirmed my suspicions."

"Did Fielding mention how that particular load of straw came to be in his stable?"

I shook my head.

"It's common knowledge Jack is a tightwad. I suspected he'd gotten the stuff for next to nothing, and I explained to him in great detail the importance of purchasing bedding material from a reputable dealer. He denied buying the wood shavings. He swore up and down he'd never skimp on his horses. He was pretty angry with me for even suggesting he was a cheapskate."

"Well, now we know Fielding was telling the truth. The way I figure it, Harry Montgomery knew Squire Dan was a better horse than his own nag. He was bound and determined to win that damned trophy, and he decided the only way to do it was by putting Jack's horse out of commission."

"You think Jack found out about it."

"He admits that he suspected Harry was the one who sabotaged his horse. He claims Montgomery made a joke about it at the Ball, so he waylaid him in the hallway and warned him not to try anything funny in the future."

"Was that the discussion Mrs. Montgomery overheard?"

"Yeah. She developed a migraine headache and left the party early. Harry stayed behind, but he did see his wife to the door. That's when Jack accused him of tampering with the bedding."

"It looks like Fielding had a pretty good motive for murder."

The Chief smiled broadly.

"I agree with you, doctor. And since we found walnut leaves on Harry's body and in his office, I suspect the man was planning another attack on Squire Dan. He may have waved those leaves under Jack's nose at the party, and Fielding just went berserk."

"Hold on a minute, Chief."

I picked up the plastic envelope and examined the dead leaves more closely. When I looked up at Brody, the expression on my face must have given me away. The big policeman just sighed and shook his head.

"You're not going to mess with my theory, are you, Doc?" he growled.

I felt like a kid caught cheating at school who knows he's disappointed his favorite teacher. Chief Brody was staring at me sadly, just waiting for me to open my mouth and tear apart his neatly woven case.

"I'm afraid these didn't come from a black walnut," I murmured. "I did a little research on the trees after the incident with Squire Dan. Black walnuts have long leaves consisting of twelve to twenty-four separate leaflets, and they're mainly green in color." I pointed to the envelope. "These leaves have only seven leaflets each. The leaflet tops are greenish, but the undersides have a bronze hue to them. I'd say these came from a tree related to the black walnut..."

"But they're not *from* a black walnut." Brody swiveled his chair until he faced the window. I could tell by the set of his shoulders that he was upset.

"I may be wrong, but I'm guessing someone wanted you to find these leaves."

"You think they were planted on the body."

I nodded at the Chief's back. "The killer tried to frame Jack Fielding."

"Have you forgotten the fingerprints on the knife?"

I'll admit I had. The tiny lightbulb in my head dimmed considerably, and I was left wondering if my theory wasn't based more on my earlier conversation with Larry Wainsworth than on reality.

"Are you a friend of Jack Fielding?" Brody suddenly asked.

"Me? A friend?" I almost laughed out loud. "Jack calls on me when he needs a vet, but that's where our relationship ends. He hasn't paid one bill I've sent him, and he hangs up on me when I call him about it. The man has a lousy temperament and a very tight wallet."

"How about Montgomery? You did work for him, didn't you?"

"Sure. Harry doted on his horses. He was the exact opposite of Jack when it came to spending money on them. Nothing was too good for his stable."

"What do you know about his wife?"

I shrugged.

"Tory could tell you more about her than I. I know she's a lot younger than her husband, and she's a fairly good rider. She's not from around here, is she?"

"No." Brody answered abruptly. He spun around and pushed a pad of paper and a pen across the desk. "Give me the name of your friend at the university. Looks like I'll have to pay him a visit."

I dutifully noted the information on the pad and handed it back to the Chief.

"Anything else I can do to help?"

"You've done enough already," the Chief said as he motioned for me to leave.

Tory was busy on the phone when I passed through the main area of the police station. She waggled her fingers in the air when I kissed her on the back of the neck, and I took that as a sign she'd call me later at the office. I was sure she'd be interested in hearing about my conversation with her boss.

I had no appointments that afternoon, so I decided to take a ride out to the Barrington Country Club. I wasn't sufficiently high on the social ladder to qualify for membership there, but I doubted anyone would chase me out of the parking lot if I just sat quietly in my pickup looking around.

I'll admit I was curious to see the scene of the crime. We hadn't had a murder in town since I was a kid, and even then it had been unintentional. A Saturday night party had gone awry when two young drunks started throwing punches. One of the men ended up dead; the other landed in prison.

I wondered how Jack Fielding would adjust to jail life if convicted of Harry's murder. Jack had to be at least sixty, and Harry had been his elder by a good ten years. There'd been bad blood between the two ever since Harry's marriage five years ago. Before that, they'd competed against each other, but always in a friendly manner.

Apparently I wasn't the only curious soul in town. A policeman had been stationed outside the Country Club to discourage sightseers. He was busily waving off cars as I approached the gated entrance. I rolled down my window and waved.

"Hi, Joe. I'll bet this murder is keeping you hopping."

Joe Richards was new on the force, but he recognized me as Tory's husband and walked over to my truck.

"You can say that again, Doc. What are you doing here?"

I sidestepped the question rather adroitly by replying, "I've just come from the station. Chief Brody asked me to assist with the investigation."

Joe's eyes narrowed as he contemplated the idea of a veterinarian sticking his noise into police business. I attempted to assuage his suspicions with a hurried explanation.

"I know a little something about black walnut trees. Apparently some leaves were found on Montgomery's body."

"Oh." Joe blinked, then brightened considerably. "Oh! I get it. You're here to check out the trees. Well, drive right through, Doc. If you need any help..."

"Thanks, but I think I can manage."

I threw the pickup into gear and headed up the driveway at a speed totally unexpected of BCC guests. There was a distinct possibility Officer Richards might experience second thoughts re my presence at the club, so I wanted to fade into the background as quickly as possible. If Joe decided to contact Brody, I wouldn't have a leg to stand on.

Niggling doubts about Jack Fielding's part in the murder continued to plague me. I was pretty sure those leaves were the product of some kind of hickory tree, but they definitely weren't from the toxic variety of the family. Why had they been in Harry Montgomery's pocket? As far as I knew, no other hickory could wreak havoc with a horse's system. If Harry meant to harm Squire Dan again, he'd certainly have known that fact. Had he carried those leaves simply to wave them in Jack's face and enrage him as Chief Brody believed? Or had he mistakenly thought they were from a black walnut?

"Harry wasn't dumb enough to try the same trick a second time," I muttered to myself as I parked the pickup in an inconspicuous section of the lot. I got out and strolled up the walk to the club entrance. Through the floor-to-ceiling windows bracketing one corner of the building I could see an unusual number of members gathered in the bar. Prepared to give up my snooping rather than face the inquisitional stares of a dozen or more of my clients, I turned on my heel and was almost to the truck when I remembered Mike O'Malley, the club's head groundskeeper.

Mike's office was in a separate brick structure set well behind the main building and hidden by a dozen nicely trimmed bushes. One reached it via a gravel path that jutted off the main walk. I took the path and was almost to the office when the burly groundskeeper emerged from a side entrance. Dressed in khaki slacks and a burgundy polo with the club's insignia embroidered on the pocket, Mike stopped in his tracks when he saw me, a scowl distorting his normally pleasant Irish features.

"Sorry, sir. No visitors beyond...Oh, Doctor Benjamin! I didn't recognize you with the sun shining in my eyes. Sure is a bright day, isn't it?"

"It's a beaut all right." I grasped Mike O'Malley's outstretched hand and was rewarded with a bone crushing welcome. I tried not to wince as I extricated my fingers from the groundskeeper's grip.

"I've come to ask a favor of you," I said with a forced smile.

"Anything you want, Doc. Say, you really worked a miracle on Duke. That dog is friskier than ever now."

Mike's mutt had suffered a broken leg after an encounter with a Nissan on the highway. The fracture was easily fixed, but the animal was so overweight that the prognosis for total recovery was limited. Fortunately, Mike loved his dog enough to take my advice and place him on a diet. Now, six months later, Duke was a lean, mean, running machine, and Mike was advertising my skills all over the county. I was properly pleased with both results.

"Glad to hear it, Mike." Intent on my mission, I forestalled further discussion of Duke with a question. "Could you tell me if you have any hickory trees on this property?"

"Hickories? Why are you interested in them?"

I repeated the line I'd used on Officer Richards, and Mike accepted it without batting an eyelash.

"There's a stand of shagbarks up at the north end of the golf course. They're the only hickories we have here, and they're pretty old. Do you want to take a look at them?"

I said yes, and minutes later we were scooting over the manicured greens in a motorized golf cart. Thrilled to be included in a murder investigation, Mike rambled on about the case until we reached a small forest of trees far out of sight of the clubhouse.

"Here they are," he said as he brought the golf cart to a halt in the dense shade cast by a dozen seventy-foot giants. I hopped out and stared up at the canopy of green blotting out the sun above us.

"Magnificent, aren't they?"

I nodded as I took in the sight before me. The vertical gray strips of bark encircling each tree curved away from the trunks like layered crinoline skirts on leggy ballerinas. The leaves were green in color and consisted of five finely toothed leaflets, the terminal leaflets being anywhere from five to eight inches long.

The shagbarks were indeed magnificent, but they didn't hold the answer I was seeking. Not one leaf bore the bronze underbelly of those found in Harry's pocket.

Mike drove back to the office at a slower pace. He seemed preoccupied, slowing down to look at certain areas of the course and frowning now and again. When I asked what the problem was, he told me a horse had gotten loose on the property the night before. One of his men had reported finding several shredded bushes and a trampled bed of flowers near the putting green. He'd been about to inspect the damage when I'd arrived with my strange request.

"Are you sure it was a horse?" I asked in surprise. "People around here are pretty careful to lock their stable doors at night. Now, deer on the other hand..."

"Deer don't wear shoes," Mike quipped. "At least, none of them that I've seen."

"Oh," I replied a bit shamefacedly.

We rode the rest of the way in silence, each of us absorbed in his own thoughts. Back at the office, I thanked the groundskeeper for his time and was about to leave when Jean, Mike's wife, came trotting up the gravel path. Jean was an old friend of Tory's, and she gave me a big hug before bursting into a commentary on the murder.

"Isn't it terrible what happened to Harry Montgomery? I can't believe Jack Fielding would do such a thing!"

I murmured something about waiting for all the facts to be known, but Jean brushed off my politically correct statement with an abrupt wave of her hand.

"Everyone knows Jack killed him," she insisted. "Poor Doris is just a wreck over the whole thing."

"I didn't know you and Mrs. Montgomery were on a first name basis," Mike remarked wickedly. He winked at me and said, "Jean keeps house for the Montgomerys. She's privy to all the gossip surrounding that pair."

"What gossip?" I asked curiously. "I haven't heard anything about them."

"That's because you don't listen, Doctor. You're so wrapped up in your animals you forget they have human owners." Ignoring a scowl from her husband, Jean plunged on. "The word was that when Doris took off to visit her cousin in South Carolina last month, she was really going there to consult a divorce lawyer. But then she returned a few days ago looking like a new woman. She was bright and cheerful, and even Harry's comments about all the new clothes she'd brought back didn't seem to bother her."

"She bought a lot of stuff, huh?" Mike shook his head. "I'm sure glad you don't overdo it with our credit cards."

"Harry could afford it," Jean said dismissively. "Look at all the money that man spent on his horses. He was only tight when it came to the household budget. You'd think he'd have known when he married her that keeping Doris happy would prove expensive. She's a woman who adores parties and pretty clothes."

"Fielding and Montgomery were friends at one time, weren't they?"

Jean took my change of subject in stride and prattled on.

"Two peas in a pod, I always said. Then Doris came along and the rivalry started. Both of them dated her, you know. She chose Harry over Jack."

"I wonder why," I mused. "She's so much younger than either man."

Jean shrugged. "Security, I suppose. Some women are willing to trade love for money."

My beeper went off, and I glanced over at Mike.

"Come on in the office," he said. "You can use my phone."

It was Tory again, and just like before, she'd left the number for the police station.

"What's up?" I asked when she answered on the first ring.

"Brody just returned from the university. He said to tell you that your friend confirmed what you said about those leaves. They're definitely not from a black walnut."

"But they are from some kind of hickory tree, right?"

I could almost see Tory's face as she sat there nodding into the receiver.

"A nutmeg hickory. Funny thing about it, Ben. Nutmegs don't grow around here. They're kind of rare, and they're only found in the south."

"What part of the south?" I asked suspiciously.

"Some of the coastal states. Texas, Louisiana, Alabama, South Carolina."

Bingo! Now if I could only figure out the rest of the story.

"We also got the results of the autopsy. There's no doubt that the steak knife we found was the weapon used to kill Harry. There were two external stab wounds in the chest, but listen to this, Ben. The pathologist said there were three internal wounds. The killer stabbed Harry once in the lower chest and twice in the same place just left of the sternum. Weird, isn't it?"

"Where's the Chief now, Tory?"

"He's interrogating Fielding again, this time with his lawyer present. Jack still denies murdering Montgomery."

"Hmm. I need to check something first, but I'm going to call you back in a few minutes. Stay put, Tory, and make sure Brody doesn't leave the office."

"Sure, Ben. Anything you say."

I could hear the puzzlement in Tory's voice, but I didn't have time to explain. I hung up the phone and turned to Mike.

"Go down to the gate and get Joe Richards. Take him to that spot where the horse chewed up your shrubbery last night. The two of you rope it off, and make sure nobody disturbs those hoof prints."

Mike trusted me enough to do what I said without asking unnecessary questions. His wife was a horse of a different color.

"Why do you want to talk to the kitchen staff? They don't know anything about the murder."

"Please, Jean. Just introduce me to whoever's in charge over there, and you'll soon understand why this is so important."

I could tell Jean thought I was crazy, but a few minutes later we were sitting in a small clubhouse office speaking to Mabel Morris, the matronly boss of the catering staff and an old buddy of Mrs. O'Malley.

"The police have already inquired about the knife, Dr. Benjamin," she replied after I'd stated my business. "I'm not sure I understand your interest in the matter."

"Come on, Mabel," said Jean. "You know you're as curious about this murder as the rest of us. Just humor the doc, OK?"

Mrs. Morris glanced in annoyance at her friend. Exasperation tightened her pencil-thin lips into little more than a bright slash above her ample chin, and her entire body quivered with irritation. I sensed the poor woman was about to explode.

"Why couldn't he have died somewhere else?" she growled at us. "The staff is walking around like zombies today, and my entire schedule is thrown out of whack."

"I can certainly sympathize with you, Mrs. Morris," I said in the same tone of voice I used on my more temperamental patients. "But you must realize, Jack Fielding's problem is much greater than yours. He's facing a murder charge. It would be a terrible thing if the police arrested the wrong person in this case."

The woman threw me a withering look, but relented with a drawn out sigh.

"What do you want to know?"

"Do your people count the silverware after a dinner party like the one last night?"

"Of course they do. You wouldn't believe how many folks walk away from this place with forks and spoons. I have to pay for replacements from the staff budget."

"Were there two knives missing after the Hunt Club Ball?"

Mrs. Morris shook her head.

"Only the one the police now have."

"Are you sure about that?"

"Doctor Benjamin..."

Jean broke in before Mabel lost her patience entirely.

"Dear, would it hurt if we talked to the wait staff on duty yesterday? I know how reluctant you are to disturb them, but perhaps one or two will remember something they failed to recall last night."

Mrs. Morris hemmed and hawed, but in the end she threw up her hands in surrender.

"God knows none of them are good for anything today but talking about this damned murder. You might as well shake them up a bit more."

With that said, she rose from her chair and led us back to the kitchen area where a half dozen or so people were gathered around a radio listening to the latest news on Montgomery's death. One look at Morris's face and the group quickly scattered.

"Attention, everyone. Dr. Benjamin is here at the request of the police. He wants to ask you something."

I tried to ease the tension with a broad smile.

"Chief Brody was told there were two knives missing from the table after the banquet last night," I lied. "Can anyone here confirm this information?"

The group stood there like stone clones of Lot's wife. Not one face registered understanding of my question.

"I told you what to expect," hissed Mrs. Morris. "They're all out of it today."

I was about to agree when a young woman in the back of the room spoke up.

"If you count the one Mr. Fielding dropped, there might be two knives missing."

I showered the girl with a beatific grin and asked her to repeat what she'd said.

"Mr. Fielding dropped his steak knife on the floor, and I had to get him a replacement. I don't know if anyone picked it up after the dinner."

She looked at her companions, but all of them shook their head.

"I was on the clean-up crew," offered a middle-aged man with a balding head. "I can guarantee you, we didn't find no knife. I saw a purse on the floor between two of the chairs, but a lady came and claimed it as we were clearing the dishes from the table."

The noose was getting tighter and tighter.

"Do you know who she was?" I asked.

The man shook his head, and no one else spoke up. I turned my attention back to the girl.

"You say you saw Mr. Fielding drop his knife."

The waitress nodded. "He bumped elbows with the woman sitting next to him, and the knife just slipped from his hand."

"Thank you very much," I said. "Chief Brody will be here soon, and I'm going to ask that none of you leave until you've talked to him."

I needn't have spoken because at that very moment the kitchen door opened and Patrick Brody strode into the room with one of his sergeants. After hearing what the wait staff had to say, he left the other policeman in charge of taking statements, and the two of us headed for his car.

It took only five minutes to reach the Montgomery spread, and only another five for Doris Montgomery to realize we were on to her. She clammed up tighter than a shell when Brody asked if she'd cooperate.

"I want my lawyer," she said sullenly as the Chief led her out of the house.

"You'll need a good one," Brody grunted in reply.

It was only after the second knife was found buried behind the stable along with her bloody clothes that Doris broke down and confessed. I wasn't present at the interrogation, but Brody told me about it the next day in his office.

"She married Harry for money, choosing him over Jack because she'd heard of Fielding's reputation as a penny-pincher. Unfortunately, Harry was equally tight when it came to anything other than his horses. After five years of hearing Harry gripe every time she bought something new, Doris decided to divorce him.

"She left for South Carolina shortly after Harry pulled that bit with the black walnut shavings. She'd seen the receipt for the bedding, so she knew what her husband had done. She mentioned the story to her cousin who then pointed out a couple of nutmeg hickories growing near her house. The cousin told Doris that the two trees were related to each other."

"And that's how the whole thing started."

Brody nodded. "Doris knew she wouldn't get much of a divorce settlement out of Harry Montgomery. She'd be much better off if he was dead. Since everyone in town knew Jack Fielding blamed Harry for the incident with Squire Dan, Jack seemed the perfect fall guy for the crime."

"And the Hunt Club Ball seemed the perfect occasion for murder."

"Doris made sure she was seated next to Jack at dinner. She waited until he reached for his knife, then she purposely bumped his elbow. When he dropped the knife, she simply placed her purse over it on the floor. She pretended to forget the purse when she and the others left the table. A few minutes later, however, she returned to the dining room. She slipped Jack's knife into her purse, having already secreted her own in it. Then she feigned a headache."

"That little scene between Jack and Harry in the hallway fit right into her plan."

Brody smiled. "Doris couldn't believe her good luck when the two of them started arguing in front of all those witnesses. She took off in her car, and when she got home, she changed clothes and saddled up her mare. She rode the mare back to the club and left it tethered to a tree near the putting green. We took molds of the mare's feet and casts of the hoof prints found in the flowerbed. They match perfectly. The district attorney thinks he can use that fact to his advantage when prosecuting the case."

"Doris knew Harry enjoyed his cigars."

"Yeah. That's the one thing he and Jack had in common. Doris lightened Harry's cigar case by three stogies before they left home. She knew Harry would eventually go out to his car to get the extras he kept in the glove box. She waited in the parking lot, and when he arrived she simply walked up to him and stabbed him twice with her own steak knife. Then when he'd fallen, she took Jack's knife and pushed it into the wound next to the sternum. Doris thought she had it all figured out, but she didn't realize it was practically impossible to guide the second knife exactly along the path of the first weapon. The autopsy clearly showed a third internal wound."

"She planned for Harry to be found dead with Jack's fingerprints all over the weapon. Pretty clever, when you think about it."

"Yeah, Doc, but Doris didn't count on you recognizing the difference in the hickory leaves."

I shook my head. "Placing those leaves in Harry's pocket was like gilding the lily. It was totally unnecessary given all the other evidence against Jack."

"You're right. It was a dumb mistake, but one I'm glad Doris made. Without those leaves, we might never have caught on. Jack Fielding would be facing a lifetime in jail."

I pictured Jack in prison blues, the glint in his eyes dimming over time as he grieved the loss not only of his freedom but also of his precious Squire Dan.

"How true," I replied. I stood up to leave, and as I did, I caught sigh of Jack Fielding through the office window. He was leaving the police station after signing his final statement. Larry Wainsworth III was at his side, his arm draped over Jack's should and a big smile plastered across his face.

All I could think was, thank God for stupid criminals.

*   *   *

Why should someone attend a Mayhem in the Midlands convention? Mayhem in the Midlands is one of the friendliest and best-organized conventions I've ever attended. The organizers provide great opportunities for fans and writers to mingle in an intimate atmosphere. Site choice is excellent, the hotel's lovely patio being a huge drawing point for those who enjoy chatting with others in a beautiful outdoor setting. Everyone who attended was treated with equal courtesy, whether they be a best selling author, a new author, or a fan.

THE CASE OF THE BOOGERED BOOKS

by Lance Zarimba

I'm an occupational therapist in Sioux Falls, South Dakota, currently working on a mystery series. Taking the advice to write what you know, my protagonist Taylor is an occupational therapist, and with the help of Molly from the Boogered Books short story, they continue their adventures in: "Shock Therapy," "Family Therapy," "Missing Therapy," and "Vacation Therapy." Another of my stories, "Reservations for Home," won the VLP Short Story Contest and will appear in the 2001 issue of the Vermillion Literary Project.

THE CASE OF THE BOOGERED BOOKS

by Lance Zarimba

Fridays were wild enough, but to be greeted by your first customer before the bookstore even opened warned Molly what kind
of day was ahead. She pulled into the parking lot of **Look Book**
at ten to nine. She glanced over at the station wagon idling next
to the door. February had been cold and frosty in the mornings,
but little snow covered the ground. The afternoon sun had melted most of it.

Molly stopped her car and sat staring straight ahead for a few
seconds, mentally preparing herself for the day. When she saw a
customer waiting to get into the store before it opened, especially in this cold, Molly knew she should have called in sick. The
morning had started off on the wrong foot. She couldn't find her
car keys, she ripped her new nylons, and her two-year-old son
baptized her with oatmeal as she walked out the door.

Molly pulled her coat around her neck tightly, stepped out of
the car and hurried to the glass door. As she turned the key to
unlock the business for the day, she noticed a clump of oatmeal,
which still clung to her sleeve. She flicked it off and watched it
spiral down to the sidewalk. She entered the store and flipped the
light switches up. The store's lights and the red neon open sign
welcomed the public.

Used books were in high demand, but Molly was in even
higher demand. Her knowledge of the literary business amazed
her customers and other bookstores in the area. She had many
offers for more money at the "major" bookstores in Sioux Falls,

277

but South Dakota was not Minneapolis by any means, so Molly's aspiration for "Big Business" was simply to do what she was doing, and she enjoyed every minute of it.

She had a faithful following of customers who loved her. She had heard many complaints about her bosses, but since she didn't own the business, there was little that she could do. If this had been her store, she would have run it differently. So much for pipe dreams, but she did the best she could.

Ann pushed the door open with her back and pulled in two K-Mart bags full of books to trade. Molly glanced at the bulging bags. All small romances. Great, Molly thought. She hated all the thousands of numbered volumes that she organized each month, and now more were coming in.

Ann stepped up to the counter and slammed her bags down. "Is the manager in?" She tilted her head forward to peer over the fogged lenses of her glasses.

"You know I'm the manager around here, Ann." Molly chuckled to herself with that thought. Sure, she was the manager of the store, but the store's owner and his wife were the only other employees of the business.

"Well, I have a problem that I hope you'll be able to fix for me." Ann rifled in one of her bags and pulled out a few books and handed them to Molly. "What do you have to say about these?" she demanded.

Molly took the three Janet Dailey romances and turned them over in their hands. The covers and bindings looked as if they had been read, slightly abused, but they seemed to be tight copies that hadn't been warped by water. "What's wrong with them?" She opened the cover to see the red **Look Book**'s logo stamped inside.

"Turn to page 36 and 37 in that one." Ann pointed to the top book.

Molly opened the book and flipped to the stated pages. They were stuck together. Carefully, she tried to pull the paper apart, so they wouldn't rip. The pages released and opened to her inspection. Dark green-and-black blobs were flattened out across the paper. "Are they bugs?" She looked hard trying to figure out what they were.

"Look closer," Ann demanded.

Then it dawned on Molly what they were. She slammed the book closed and dropped it down onto the counter. She wiped her hands together to rid herself the image in her mind. "What did you put them in there for? Don't you have facial tissue at home?"

Ann saw no humor in Molly's comment. "I didn't put them there. So. What are you going to do about them?"

Molly picked up the three books and threw them into the garbage can. "There. Happy?"

"Is that all?"

"I'm not picking out what was in there. If that's what you're expecting, you got another thing coming. You can go find replacement books for those three, the same titles or different ones, whatever you prefer."

Ann stood there for a few seconds, pondering a solution. She waited.

"You want more?" Molly leaned forward. "There were only a few little boogers in them, after all."

Ann continued to stare at Molly.

"All right, I'll give you six books for your trouble, but that's all. Take it or leave it. And if you pick up another 'loaded' book, that's just your tough luck."

"That'll be fine with me." Ann nodded her head and hurried off into the rows of books.

"And if you find any more of those boogered books, bring them up here. I'll take care of them." Molly put her handbag under the counter and turned on the cash register. She looked over at the books in the garbage can and shook her head. She could have kicked herself for not calling in sick today, dreading what her next task of the day would be.

A few minutes later the door opened. Molly looked up. "Good morning, Taylor. How nice to see you so early in the morning. Are you looking for a new job?" Molly asked.

Taylor's face flushed a deep red and he looked around nervously. "How did you know...? Why do you ask that?"

"Chill out, I was wondering if you wanted to help me out today. You obviously have the day off. So are you really looking for a new job?"

"Maybe, but it's too early to say anything about that right now." He paused. Taylor changed the subject. "I worked last weekend so I have today off. What are you up to now? You look a little stressed."

"I'm on booger patrol."

"What?"

"You don't want to know."

"Try me."

"If you laugh, I'll have to hurt you. My first customer of the day brought it to my attention that I was selling books with boogers in them."

"And that's not legal in this state?" Taylor smirked.

A book flew over his head.

"I see my humor is wasted on you today. So I think I should leave before encyclopedias start flying."

"I'll give you ten free books if you help me today." Molly waited for his response. Nothing came. She rubbed her chin and spread a black smudge across it. A glimmer of an idea danced in her eyes.

Taylor shivered at this look.

"You're the best mystery expert in this town. I think you could...no, that's silly. You'll never go for it. I'll see you later." Molly kicked at the floor and looked down, trying to play coy, but her scheming mind was working overtime.

"I can see right through you. What do you want? Just tell me. You know you don't have to flatter me or try to pique my curiosity to get me to help."

"Okay," she said with excitement, "You and I are the mystery experts in this town. Right?"

"Yes, but I..."

"So we should be able to figure this out in no time."

"Figure what out?"

"Who put the boogers in my books."

"Why was I afraid of that?"

"Here, take a look at this." She handed a book to Taylor, who held his hands in refusal.

"I'm not touching that," he said, backing up from her.

"Oh come on, you work in a hospital. You're used to working with all those gross body fluids. Like you've never had to wipe somebody's nose while working as an occupational therapist at the hospital. You can't deny that, can you? So you should be perfect for this job." Molly's excitement wasn't contagious.

"But it's snot," Taylor protested.

"Like I'm enjoying myself here?" she sneered.

"I might as well help you. I'll never hear the end of this if I don't. And it's not as if I have something better to do today, that's the sad part. So what do you want me to do?"

"Oh, good." Molly clapped her hands together with excitement. "I knew you'd help me. This is going to be so much fun."

"For who?" Taylor asked.

"Okay, let's go over this again. We've only found the boogers in the small romances by Janet Dailey, all of them under two hundred pages. We haven't found any in the other books, mysteries or the large romances. So we know that whoever is doing this doesn't have good taste in fiction. At least, she knows who to thumb her nose at, or is it blow her nose in?" Taylor laughed at his summation.

"That's kind of sexist coming from you, you know," Molly scolded.

"I know, and I'll admit to having read the occasional romance, but only from the big name authors: Jayne Ann Krentz, Barbara Delinsky, and Tami Hoag."

"Well, they all got their start in the small romances. Look at some of your favorite authors: Carolyn Hart, Joan Hess, and Janet Evanovich. They all started writing small romances, and I know you have signed first editions of their books," Molly teased.

Her smug smile dared Taylor to respond.

"If you don't want those books in your collection, I'd gladly find room for them on my bookshelves."

"I take it back. I forgot I was talking to the book expert of Sioux Falls."

"That's Miss Expert to you. Romance is just another genre of fiction, and it has its place."

"I'll remember that. So far as I can see, whoever has brought in Janet Dailey's books over the last few months could be the guilty party. Can you think of anyone?"

"Well, I've been racking my mind..." Molly began.

"That shouldn't take long."

"And I've come up with four ladies: Mary, Helen, Ann, and Phyllis." Molly held up a list and crossed off Ann's name, "I know that Ann didn't do it, so now we have three suspects. Each should be coming in later today. My customers are creatures of habit."

"I think they're just creatures."

"Remember, you're one of them."

"I know." Taylor smiled. "I'm probably the worst one. So now we wait."

Taylor ran to pick up lunch, and while he was gone, Mary brought in two of Janet's books that were clean. Molly crossed her name off the list before Taylor returned.

The front door opened. "I hope Long John Silver's is okay," Taylor said lifting up a bag.

"That's fine. I just have to go wash my hands in bleach, and I'll be right back. Watch the store for me." Molly ran to the back of the store to the restroom.

"Attention, shoppers. All books are on sale for a dime. A buck for a bag of books," Taylor said, in his best carnie voice.

"Cute, Taylor," Molly yelled from between the shelves.

A middle aged lady walked into the store and set a bag of books down on the counter. "Molly sick today?" she asked.

"They picked her up and committed her to the pysch ward yesterday, so I'll be helping you today," Taylor said from behind the cash register.

"REALLY! Oh, poor Molly. I love her so—she's my favorite. It can't be true." The woman's worried expression panicked Taylor.

"Oh, I'm sorry, I..." Taylor stuttered, as Molly walked around the corner of the book racks.

"Oh, hi, Ma. How's it going today?"

"Fine dear, I'm glad you're out of the loony bin."

"I am, too. Taylor, this is my mom," she turned to Taylor.

"We've met," Taylor and Molly's mother said in unison.

"What are we waiting for? Let's eat," Molly said digging into the bag.

Just as they finished lunch, Helen entered the store.

"Suspect number two," Molly whispered. "Hi, Helen, how are you today?"

"I'm all plugged up. My allergies have been acting up again. I keep having to blow my nose. It's so disgusting."

"Tell me about it," Molly said evenly.

"Did you bring back any of those Janet Dailey books today?"

"Oh, I think there's one in there. Why, do you need more?"

"One of my customers had a few problems with some of her books, so I was just asking."

"No, my books were fine." She reached into the bag and dug one out, "See?" She handed the book to Molly.

Molly flipped through it quickly and saw the book was in good condition.

"Looking for money in there?" Helen asked.

"Something better." Taylor smirked.

"What? By the look on your face, young man, I can see that it has to be good."

"Oh, don't listen to him. He doesn't know what he's saying." Molly bumped her hip into Taylor and pushed him out from behind the counter.

"I'll go look for some new ones. You can add up my credits and holler how much I have." Helen strolled off in search of her new books.

Molly was typing in Helen's credit, when she heard Helen blow her nose. Molly jumped out from behind the counter and spied on her. Taylor's head poked out from around the other side of the bookrack.

Helen wiped her nose with a pink handkerchief and folded it tightly and placed it into her purse.

Taylor returned to the front. His eyes met Molly's.

"Phyllis is the one—she has to be," Molly hissed.

"We can't jump to conclusions. Remember, innocent until proven guilty."

"She's the only other suspect we have." As if on cue, the door chimed a customer's arrival. "Phyllis, you're here early today."

A short chubby woman waddled up to the cash register and set her books down. "I'm going out of town for the weekend so I needed some reading material." She waddled off into the rows of books for her search.

Molly and Taylor raced over to the pile of books and scrambled for the Janet Dailey. Molly ripped it out of Taylor's hand and turned her back to him. She flipped frantically through it, then turned to face Taylor with a blank look.

"Nothing," she said.

"Nothing?"

"Nothing."

"So now what?" Taylor asked.

"I was sure that one of those women would be the guilty one. They are the only Janet Dailey readers I could think of who have bought a book from me in the last three months."

"I guess that leads us to anyone who traded in a Janet Dailey book over three months ago."

"Like I would be able to remember that. I'm good, but not that good."

Taylor picked up another book on the pile and stamped it with the **Look Book** logo. "Is your boss ever going to change the name of this store to what it was supposed to be?"

"I've tried to get him to do it, but he has too many things with the logo on it now. He was going to change it last year, but all of his customers threw a fit and he backed down, so I guess we're stuck with **Look Book** and those big googely eyes staring at us."

Taylor stared off into space for a second. "Maybe Ann did it. She could have brought it to your attention, just to throw the suspicion off of her and onto someone else. You know how the killer sometimes finds the body, just to throw the police off the trail."

"I thought about that already, but I just can't see Ann doing that. I can't see any of my customers doing that." Molly frowned, deep in thought.

"Didn't you tell me that Janet Dailey stole her ideas from another romance writer? Maybe one of the other author's diehard fans would do a thing like that to Janet's books."

"You mean Nora Roberts. Do you know how many women read Nora Roberts? All my customers would be suspects if that was the case. I'll never be able to follow up on that idea," Molly moaned.

"Well, what else can we do? Is there another way to pinpoint who checked out those books? Maybe I can bring in a booger and get the DNA analyzed and then we would be able to find out who did it," Taylor suggested.

"Could you really do that?" Molly asked hopefully.

Taylor shook his head. "I was just kidding—this isn't a federal offense.

"To me it is. This is my livelihood. My customers count on me to sell them good books, not books filled with boogers. Too bad our store isn't computerized, and we don't save receipts with customer's names on them. There's no way to track who bought what from us, just my memory. And we all know how good that is." Taylor laughed until Molly hit him with another book. "You won't be able to sell that one now."

"Why not?" Molly demanded.

"It's damaged merchandise, with all of my muscles and all..."

"That hot air is more like it."

Molly and Taylor checked more of the shelves and the rest of the Janet Dailey books. They pulled all the copies with the offending material and carried them to the garbage. Molly looked at one of the covers. She thought, *Janet Dailey had a few choice prizes in her books.* Molly happily threw those directly into the garbage can. *Steal from other authors, umpf.* She turned her nose up. She mused under her breath, "At least I only stick my nose up in the air and didn't blow anything into her books."

"What's that?" Taylor asked.

"Nothing." Just as Molly spoke, a familiar noise was heard.

From the small romance aisle came the honk of a blowing nose. Molly and Taylor's eyes meet and smiled. Bingo!

They raced around the counter and looked down the aisle. Had they just found their new suspect? Both sets of eyes searched down the aisle, just in time to see a slender hand reshelf a book.

"Hold it right there!" Molly demanded as she rounded the shelf.

A startled man in his late forties looked surprised.

"What?" he asked, as Molly approached.

"Did you just blow your nose in that book?" Molly asked as her index finger stabbed him in the chest.

The man looked as if he were going to run, but as soon as he saw Taylor, he stopped. He quickly grabbed the book back from the shelf and held on to it tightly. He then thrust it behind his back, trying to hide the evidence.

"Give me that book. Now!" Molly stepped forward, hand outstretched.

The man cringed away from her. His eyes dashed around the store looking for an escape. When he found none, sheepishly, he gave her the book.

Molly opened it to a gooey, slime-coated page, which was still warm. She slammed the book shut. "This is so disgusting," she said, shaking the book at him.

He took it back, afraid she would hit him with it. "I'll buy it."

"You're darn right you're going to buy this book and all the other ones we've found. I should call the police. What do you say to that?"

Taylor made a motion to go use the phone, when the man said, "Wait."

"So why did you do it? A few of my customers were pretty upset with what they found in their books. What do you have to say for yourself?"

"I'm sorry. My ex-wife always had her nose in a Janet Dailey book, so I always wished that I had put boogers in her books so she wouldn't read so much. So I guess I subconsciously wanted her to get these books, since I didn't do that to her books at home. I guess I haven't gotten out of the habit yet."

"Oh, yes you have! I'll give you a box of facial tissue to use, but leave the books alone!" Molly's face blazed with anger.

"So, how much do I owe you for the books I've ruined?"

They walked up to the cash register, and Molly pointed to the garbage can.

She bent over and retrieved the stack of discarded books. She counted them and rang up the total. "$38.50 should cover the damage. Wait, I forgot the one you have in your hands. That should make it an even $40.00 plus tax. The state has to get its share, but don't think that with this check all is forgiven."

The man quickly wrote out a check, very self-conscious. He looked as if he wished the floor would swallow him. After he handed Molly the check, he stood looking at her and waited. "Well, aren't you going to put them in a bag for me?" he asked finally.

"What do you plan to do with them? You're not going to be trading them back in here for credit. You can forget that idea right now, and I'm calling the other stores in town to beware of all the Janet Dailey books that come in. Even if you pick all those boogers out, I'm not taking them back. No way." Molly nodded her head sharply to further punctuate her words. She tossed the books into a brown grocery bag.

"No, I'm not gonna try to trade them in for credit." He gave a weak smile. "I just got an idea of what to do with them."

"And what is that?" Molly demanded.

"I'm going to send them to my ex-wife as a gift. I'm sure she'll love them. I wish I would have thought of that before." He smiled an evil smile and walked out of the store with his boogered books in tow.

"Another happy customer," Taylor said. "You sure can work miracles with your personality, Molly. But then, we sure do have some strange characters living in South Dakota."

"Where else would they live?" Molly laughed. "Look at you and I, we live here. Don't we?"

*   *   *

Mayhem in the Midlands is the perfect size. The attending authors are able to be on multiple panels and are able to speak on a variety of topics. At last year's Mayhem, I had the chance to spend quality time with my own favorite authors and tell them how much their stories and characters mean to me. Writing is such a solitary task. I was able to pick up energy and excitement needed to recharge my own writing efforts. I've recommended Mayhem to my mystery book and writing groups.

COPYRIGHT PAGE

Printed in the United States
54761LVS00001B/125

9 781587 360916